These days are passing over me at the speed of light,

And standing here in their shadow I'm silenced at the sight,

Like water on the wind I sense the change to come,

All that I've held in like teardrops run.

I am clay and I am water falling forward in this order

While the world spins 'round so fast,

Slowly I'm becoming

Who I am

Nothing ever stays the same, the wheel will always turn,

I feel the fire in the change but somehow it doesn't burn,

Like a beggar blessed I stumble in the Grace,

Reaching out my hand for what awaits…[1]

Also by Susan McGeown:

Rosamund's Bower

A Garden Walled Around Trilogy:
Call Me Bear
Call Me Elle
Call Me Survivor

Rules for Survival
Recipe for Disaster

The Butler Did It

A

Well Behaved

Woman's

Life

By Susan Lee McGeown

Faith Inspired Books

Published by Faith Inspired Books

3 Kathleen Place, Bridgewater, New Jersey 08807

www.FaithInspiredBooks.com

Magnificent Cover Art courtesy of Laury Vaden

magentaswan@patmedia.net

<u>Just in case you're wondering:</u>

All characters in this book have no real existence outside the imagination of
the author and have no relation whatsoever to anyone bearing the same
name or names.

I will admit that some parts of this story are distantly inspired by some wise
and wonderful individuals this author has had the privilege to know and
love.

In addition, all incidents within this story are pure invention.**

**Well, at least you'll never get me to admit that they're true!

To all those Godly Women I have had the privilege to learn from:

Those Biblical Ones that have gone before me-
The Widow With Two Mites, Rahab, Leah,
The Wise Woman of Abel, and Deborah,

~ And ~

Those Present Day Ones that I am blessed to be able to call friends-
Marylynn, Wendy, Laury, Patti, Maria, Judy,
Lisa, Melony, Jenn, Jen, Beth, Kim, and Kate

~ Truly ~

We know that in all things God works
for the good of those who love Him,
who have been called according to His purpose.[2]

Table of Contents

Do not be afraid or discouraged, for the Lord is the one who goes before you. [3]

The Widow's Might

The transformation was instantaneous it seemed. It was the final insult over the course of two years of hell. She stepped into the shower a woman and stepped out an old lady. Standing nude, dripping water all over the carpet she stared in stunned horror at a vision that would define the rest of her life: *she had a gray pubic hair.* She finally sat down on the edge of the tub, her body already feeling the effects of age. Her hip ached. Arthritis. Her neck and shoulders cramped. Scoliosis.

She desperately searched through the file of her mind looking for reassurance that she *wasn't* old, she wasn't nearing the end of her life. Words crashed around in her head that did nothing to soothe her: widow, grown children, Nice 'N Easy # 37… She glared at the shower in a fury of accusation; it was like an evil time machine. *Things would truly never be the same.* But what was she thinking? Things were *never* as they seemed. She already knew that. Life was just one big lie.

In those early moments as she shuffled around her bedroom she considered just going to bed, pulling the covers up and waiting for the inevitable – death. It could only be a few weeks away ... But she had obligations at church that morning. She may be old, but she was still responsible. *Until Alzheimer's took over ...*

Church attendance had been a part of more than half of the 52 years of her life. A legacy her mother had left in her that she had not been able to shake. *Can't teach an old dog new tricks*, her head said. She'd done her share of active involvement over the course of the years: Sunday school, youth group, and Vacation Bible School when the kids were little, attendance at adult Bible studies once the kids were older. She had friends there. When Jonathan died, the church family had rallied around her with a solid show of love and support that had helped her through those dark first days and weeks and months while she gradually adjusted to the new club of Widowhood.

At first the concern and outreach had been much appreciated. The phone calls, the notes, the meals, and the visits had kept her from drowning in the ocean of sorrow and loneliness and strangeness that in the blink of an eye had become her life. But she could not be shielded from the harsh realities of life – Widowhood *and* The Truth - forever. Eventually, she had to face the facts of what her life and her marriage had been: a lie. That's when she began to withdraw. Recede from the real world into an imaginary, dulling fog of numbness. Inquiries of how she was feeling, how she was coping, how she was *making it now* were answered with vague, automatic responses that had no basis in fact or reality. They just kept everyone at bay so she could continue to try to cope. It was an act of survival. As she quietly, slowly began to withdraw from life, she became just a mere shadow of what she once was. No one knew The Truth but her. She kept it bottled up inside her partly because of pride and partly because she saw no reason to tell it. What good would it do to tell anyone that her great grief initially rooted in her husband's death was overshadowed with rage when she discovered that he had been unfaithful to her? She grieved not the death of her husband in the end, she grieved the loss of her entire adult life. All thirty plus years.

Driving to church she realized that The Shower Incident (as her mind now referred to it) was the first emotional jolt she'd felt in months.

Hell, years. She was approaching the second full year of Widowhood and for the life of her this second year was nothing but a dull, gray blur. She had gotten quite good at not feeling, not reacting, not noticing anything really, all under the guise of being a functional, sane woman. She'd stopped going out almost entirely. She'd even found a local food store that delivered groceries to her once a week. The days went by one after another in a fog of blissful nothingness, growing into weeks and then months ... People who knew her well finally accepted that the woman she was now was the woman she was going to be. Flat. Unemotional. Withdrawn. Solitary. And now, she'd add a new one to the list. *Old.*

She was doing the scripture reading today at church. It was the only church duty that she was still performing after all her years of service. Not that she hadn't tried to get out of it. Requests to be left off the rotating list of volunteers had been met with various excuses. "Oh, I forgot you'd asked." "Please, we're short handed in that area, can't you do it for one more rotation?" "Really? You're still on the list? I thought we'd taken care of that ..." When she'd gotten the call this past week to remind her she was up this weekend she'd been rather forceful and abrupt. She'd been assured that she would be removed from the list this time. So, this was well and truly the last time.

The smiles of welcome (and pity) were acknowledged by her with polite yet distant responses. One tall, scholarly looking gentlemen hovered at the doorway to the sanctuary and as she brushed by him he asked if he could speak with her briefly after the service? He needed to ask her something but didn't want to make her late ... She mumbled an answer that could have been interpreted any way he saw fit and hurried to find a seat. Good grief, he probably wanted her to sit on another committee or volunteer for some "just" cause. Old widow women did those sort of things.

The scripture passage was read without her brain comprehending the words that came out of her mouth. The hymns were sung without her appreciating the verses. Her mind wandered as the announcements were being given. Still, church was the only place that she still could not always escape into numbness. The lies and the deceit somehow seemed bigger, worse. How could Jonathan have sat in a House of God and pretended to be the devoted husband when he was doing what he was doing? Flashes of memories poked through the gray cloud to cause a pain so intense that she almost doubled over with it. It was in this place that the memories of Jonathan and even the children as they grew stole into her carefully guarded emotions and brought her agony to life. Lies, all of it lies. In a blinding flash of the obvious she determined then and there that this would probably be her last time to attend church. With the acknowledgement of old age would come a final change in behavior. She'd become a heathen as well.

A word jarred her out of her thoughts. She could have sworn that she had heard the minister say, "Widow." She looked up at him, standing high in his podium, his robes perfectly arranged, his hair carefully combed, his glasses slightly askew. He was a sincere sort. She couldn't find fault with him really. He was new, only here a little over three years. Young, too, with a sweet, energetic wife and three children that were pure hellions on earth. She couldn't even remember his name. Talk about numbness. Curiosity made her pick up the bulletin and had it not been so utterly inappropriate she would have laughed out loud. His sermon topic was "The Widow's Mite or The Widow's *Might*." She remembered that the minister always tried to come up with catchy titles for his sermons to drag the unsuspecting in.

She remembered this story. The old woman gives just two pennies – or mites – and yet Jesus makes a big fuss because it wasn't the amount she gave that was important but more importantly that she'd given *everything she had and had trusted that God would care for her*. She reflected just briefly that perhaps her situation was moderately better than this poor Biblical widow . . .

Financially, she was well off. Hell, thanks to Jonathan's death she was close to being a millionaire. Life insurance policies taken out when the children were small and the mortgage was big to cover the unthinkable had succeeded in providing for her in comfort for the rest of her days. At a time in her life when the children were finished with school, the mortgage was paid off, and the necessities of survival cost her minimally she had more money than she knew how to deal with.

"The measure of the gift was not how much was given, but how much there was to give," the young minister intoned. She had a brief, unchristianlike thought that perhaps it was his way of saying the giving was down and they needed a few more dollars in the plate. When was the last time she'd written a check to the church? She had no idea. She used to give so faithfully. Most of her bills were automated now with direct withdrawal out of her checking account. Another area she no longer had to deal with or think about. She fumbled through her purse and wrote a magnanimous check and tossed it into the plate as it passed her by.

She left before the final hymn was finished being sung. She was half way home before she realized she'd escaped speaking with that gentleman who'd wanted to ask her a question. Good. Her conscience was technically clear because she hadn't *intentionally* avoided him. He'd have to find another willing widow to volunteer some of her vapid, empty expanse of a life. What bitter thoughts she had. Old. Withdrawn. Widow. Heathen. Flat. Unemotional. Solitary. And now bitter. Wow, she was coming up with quite a list.

She didn't go home. She drove aimlessly. It was a new way to pass the time of numbness. She briefly considered stopping in with one of the kids but she couldn't deal with their sorrow any more than she could deal with her own. To hear them speak fondly, with love and longing for a man that had been nothing but a false illusion made her throat ache from the want of screaming the truth. After two years, Jonathan's presence was still everywhere. Even in this car she drove she realized. She was stopped at a light at a huge intersection, lost in thought. The minister's words rolled around in her head. *The Widow's Mite. The Widow's Might.* Across the intersection colorful flags snapped in the breeze, helium balloons danced on the ends of their strings, and someone dressed as a little old lady (cane, gray haired wig, spectacles, and big orthopedic shoes) danced a jig on the corner. She blinked her eyes twice, disbelieving what her brain acknowledged and processed. The sign, with bright red letters at least four feet high proclaimed, "Escape the Old! Buy A New Car Today!"

She'd use her widow's might spending her widow's mite. She'd buy herself a new sports car.

She'd bought a new car once, in her early twenties. *Almost thirty years ago*, her mind told her glibly. She'd been terrified back then of negotiating and getting taken advantage of. She'd read up on all of the information about the car of her choice, written her best offer down on a piece of paper so she wouldn't have to negotiate and had been pleased at the results. Standing in the air-conditioned showroom looking at all the shiny cars she was overwhelmed at how young all the salesmen looked. They all seemed younger than her youngest son! Any nerves she had about dealing with them evaporated. She knew how to handle over-confident children. She'd lived with three of them.

She wandered over to the stacks of brochures. Colorful and inviting. Promising laughter, love, fun, blue skies, and any other positive hopes and dreams you could imagine.

"Can I help you, ma'am?" a voice said behind her.

He was *no more* than twenty-two she decided. Dark hair, blue eyes, reeking of cologne, and oozing false sincerity. *Piece of cake*, she thought. *This might even be fun.*

"Yes," she heard herself say. "I want a car. Small, sporty, bright color, zippy engine. If you play your cards right and offer me an excellent deal I'll pay you *cash* right this moment. Talk fast but don't give me any crap. I'm not in the mood." Then she smiled at him. *The Widow's Might*, her head thought.

An hour later she drove out of the dealership in a shiny red convertible with a five speed manual transmission and an engine that tended to sound like a large cat purring. By the time she was home she was in the depths of despair again, however. Pulling into the garage, parking the new car next to Jonathan's, she was overwhelmed with her folly. She was now an Old Woman with a sports car attempting to recapture her youth. And everyone knew that her youth was gone. As well as her future.

The pastor called her on Monday morning. She was still in bed lost in the numbing grayness of her life. "Mrs. Lawson?"

"Yes," she said, straining to make her voice not sound like it was the first time it had been used that morning.

"It's Pastor Duncan. I was calling to see if everything was all right with you."

Oh, right. That was his name. Another conciliatory call. She sighed and said in a somewhat exasperated voice, "Yes, I'm fine, Pastor. Why would you think otherwise?"

He hesitated, sensitive to her tone and perhaps fearful of her emotional state. Who knew? "Well, you seemed so preoccupied yesterday and left before the service was over. I just wanted to let you know that if you ever need to talk …"

"How old are you, Pastor Duncan?" she asked him abruptly.

He seemed surprised by her question. "I'm thirty-four."

"How much experience do you have with fifty-two year old widows, Pastor?"

She could almost hear him smile. "Well, believe it or not, more than you'd expect. My mother's a fifty-five year old one and my father's been dead for ten years. And my mother-in-law is a forty nine year old one. She's been widowed for the past three years. In addition, at church -"

She cut him off. "Okay, you've made your point. Since you're so vastly experienced, why don't you tell me what you think I'd like to talk with you about?" If she was determined to become this heathen thing so late in life, she'd better nip this caring, God fearing man out of her life but quick.

"Oh, I don't know. Life. Your Future. Opportunities. Anything you'd like." She had a momentary but brilliant flash of her dripping wet, gray pubic hair. *Opportunities? Future?*

"I've got my life and any future I've still got left all arranged nicely, thank you. No concern there. As for opportunities, I think I'm just going to sit back and float along and see what life drifts by my way. But I've got your number and I appreciate your concern. I'll call if I need any advice. Thank - you. Good - bye." With that, she hung up.

The phone rang again, almost immediately. She looked at it like it really had a nerve, hesitated, and then picked it up. "Hello?" she said in an annoyed, how-dare-you-call-me-back voice.

"Mother?" It was her daughter, Grace.

"Oh, it's you."

"Who were you expecting?!"

"No one. What's up, dear?"

"I was wondering if you'd like to come to lunch today. I've got prep before lunch so we could actually have more than my usual forty minutes." Grace was a 3rd grade teacher three towns over. She remembered when she had been a teacher at one time, though briefly. A quite good one, too. The kid's had liked her. The parents had liked her. The administration hadn't been too thrilled with her all the time, though. What had Jonathan called her? Oh yes, a maverick. She'd loved flouting the rules, being successful, and then having them let her get away with it in the end because of her successes. That was a million years ago.

"Mother? Are you there? Can you come to lunch?"

"Well," she started to come up with an excuse like she was really busy but didn't have the energy. It was easier to just say yes. "Well, okay."

"Don't sound so enthusiastic," she heard her daughter say.

"I'm sorry, I'm just tired. I haven't been sleeping well," she lied.

"You should make an appointment and have a complete check-up," Grace said. "When was the last time you did that?"

God knows, she thought. She really couldn't even remember the last time she cut her toenails. She threw back the covers and looked at her neglected feet. Yuck. "I don't know," she heard herself say. "What time do you want me to come by?"

"My prep starts at 11:30. We could go to the little deli down the street if you'd like."

"That sounds fine. I'll see you at 11:30." The call ended and she continued to lay in bed for another minute or two. The bedside clock said 10:15. She padded into the bathroom and ran the shower. On impulse, as she was toweling herself dry, she rummaged through a drawer, found a pair of tweezers and ripped the offending pubic hair out. It hurt like hell. She searched for others but there were none. She wondered if at some point she would use Nice 'N Easy #37 in places other than her hair. No way, she decided.

She was never one for make - up or high fashion. Shower, comb, dress, moisturize, a bit of blush and a quick flick of the mascara. She was ready to go in thirty minutes. Standing, looking at herself in the reflection of the bathroom mirror, she felt like she was looking at a solemn stranger. Who was this woman, she thought with all sincerity. Where had she come from? Where had she been? Where was she going? What was she doing? She didn't have an answer for any one of those questions. It was almost as if with Jonathan's death and the discovery of his duplicity, her life had disappeared. There were no memories to sustain her because none of them had been true. She was just a void. She had a flash of an idea and rummaged through the linen closet and found a basket. It was filled with nail polishes of every color. She and Grace used to paint their toenails different colors in the summer. She selected a pale pink and gave it a good shake. It was hard as a rock. So was the purple, the black, the green, the orange, the yellow, the clear with blue sparkle glitter. Thunk, thunk, thunk. In they each went into the garbage can, one after another. Finally, in disgust, she threw the whole basket in. As she went to shut the closet door, sitting on the shelf pushed to the far back was a bottle of red polish. As she reached for it to throw it in the garbage she heard the distinctive click of the small metal beads that they put in the bottle to aid in mixing. This one wasn't dried up. She spent five minutes painting her toes. Another five letting them dry. Then she left.

She stood in the garage for the longest time staring in horror at the sports car. *What had possessed her?* She had no desire to drive it. None. And yet driving Jonathan's car was out of the question. She had not set foot in it in over two years. She was not even sure how it got back to the house from the train station where Jonathan had left it. It was covered with a fine film of dust. It probably wouldn't even start.

She sighed. What would Grace say when she saw the sports car? Hopefully, she could park it and get into the school before she noticed. They could drive in Grace's car to the deli.

She'd misjudged the traffic and arrived late. Grace was standing outside of the school with her purse watching the road impatiently. She pulled up in front of her and Grace never even glanced at her. "Grace."

It could have been funny, but it wasn't. Slowly, Grace bent down to look into the passenger window. *"Mother?!"*

She sighed. "Hop in," she said in a voice she forced to sound bright and airy.

Grace opened the door and folded herself into the passenger seat. "Congratulations," she said to her daughter, "you're my first passenger! Which way to the deli?" Grace, at a loss for words, pointed to the right. Off they roared.

"When did you decide to get a new car?" Grace managed to ask once she found her voice.

"Exactly 61 minutes before I bought this," she volunteered. At the stop sign, she looked at her daughter for direction. Grace was staring at her with a look of stunned incredulity. She arched her eyebrow at her. "Which way?"

She ordered tuna salad and Grace had a turkey club. They both drank water. She caught Grace looking down at her toenails at one point and instinctively tried to curl them under to hide them. It didn't work.

"How are you, Mother?" Grace asked between bites.

"Fine," she lied. She lied a lot lately she realized.

"No really …" Grace persisted.

"Why does everyone keep asking me this?" she countered impatiently.

"Who's everyone?"

"Oh, the pastor called this morning just before you did."

"Ohhh," Grace said in a knowing sort of way.

For some reason that irritated her. "What's that supposed to mean?" she asked.

"I didn't understand why you were so ornery when I called this morning. Now I get it, that's all," Grace said with a shrug.

"How are Neil and the kids?" she asked solicitously in an attempt to swing the subject away from her and how she felt.

"Fine. Neil said we need to get wills written. I don't know what the big rush is. The baby cut a new tooth. Zoe's driving the sitter nuts. She crayoned all over the dining room wall *again*. How is it they know where to find stuff you think you've hidden?"

"Neil's right. You need wills. Especially now that you've got the two kids. Buy Zoe a bucket of chalk. Let her color all over the walls outside. The rain will wash it away."

Grace looked at her for a minute. "That's a good idea. You always seem so capable to me, Mother. You seem to just take a moment, think, process, and react. I've always wished I had that ability ..." Grace smiled at her. "I've got some colored chalk in the classroom."

She was startled by the perception her daughter seemed to have of her. She found herself frowning to herself struggling to find concrete examples of the woman her daughter had just described. She mentally shook her head. If she *had* existed (and that was doubtful) then she most certainly was gone now.

Grace cleared her throat and looked uncomfortable for a moment. *Oh,* she thought. *There was an ulterior motive to this luncheon date.*

"How are you *really* doing, Mom? We're worried about you."

"Who's 'we'?" she asked to stall for time.

"The boys and I," Grace said in a hurt, you-should-know-that tone. "What are you doing with yourself? How are you filling your days? What are you doing for fun and excitement?"

"I'm having a wonderful time, living life to the fullest," she said a little too brightly.

"Such as?"

"Driving around in my new sports car and painting my toes and the town red."

"Mother ..."

"What?"

"John, Todd, and I think you should go get some counseling. Some sort of grief therapy or something. You're slowly shutting yourself off from everyone and everything and we're worried about you."

"I don't need to see a therapist," she said in a firm voice. "I'm old, decrepit, lonely, marginally bitter, and unemotional. I am even considering becoming a heathen. But I am certainly *not* crazy and in need of therapy."

Grace looked at her with a stunned, open-mouth kind of expression. "*Heathen?*" she finally managed to say. "Did you say *heathen?*"

"Yes, I'm considering no longer attending church," she said. "I'm tired of all the pitying glances and the solicitous inquiries into my well being. So, I've decided to give up church for a while. It's a *widow's right,*" she finished with a brief smile at her play on words.

"A widow's right? What does that have to do with anything? Mother, you are not making any sense. If you think you're putting me at ease, you're not!" She looked at her watch and took another bite of her sandwich. "And you're *not* old. God! You're only fifty-two! Why would you think such a thing?"

She looked at her daughter and sighed and then looked down at her sandwich. How could she explain things to her? The hands holding her sandwich looked old to her now even. They had wrinkles and – oh *no* – there were even a few age spots. *Tweezers aren't going to take care of them*, the voice in her head said with great finality. Gazing back into her daughter's eyes, she saw real concern. "What would you have me do, Grace? I'm doing the best I can. I'm adjusting to the death of Jonathan, as I know all of you are." She paused, working on the mixture of emotions that worked up and clutched at her throat. *I'm adjusting to the discovery that I've never had a life even though I'm over fifty.* "I find myself ... rather aimless. I just can't seem to find a passion for anything anymore. I'm just kind of floating."

"Mother, I'm asking you this in all seriousness. You're not thinking of doing yourself any *harm* or anything are you? I know the process of grief is different for everyone and some people take longer to go through it than others, but, well ..."

She snorted then. A great, loud, unladylike snort. She saw a construction worker at one of the other tables turn and look in their direction. She ignored him. "Grace, look at me. If I was thinking of *harming* myself, I would have done it already. It would have been much easier than dealing with all this pain and adjustment. But I've seriously not even considered it. I'm lost. I'm unhappy. But I'm not suicidal."

Grace looked at her for long moments weighing the truth of her words and then looked at her watch again. "I've got to get back," and began to crumple up her sandwich papers and gather together her other garbage. She followed her daughter's lead and stood ready to go.

In the car, on the way back, Grace said suddenly, "Wait until Todd sees this car, Mom. He'll go nuts." She hadn't thought of that. It made her smile a little bit.

As Grace got out of the car, she leaned over and said, "Oh yeah, I forgot. Zoe's choir is singing this Sunday at our church. Would you come and see?"

So much for becoming a heathen, she thought. "Yes, of course I will," she said.

"Good, the service is at 11:00. We'll save you a seat." She blew a kiss, gave a brief wave and rushed back into the school. The red car engine purred waiting for direction.

Over the next few days the car attracted far more attention than she wanted or anticipated. It was rapidly becoming another of the great mistakes of her life. In an effort to gain some privacy she searched around the house and uncovered a battered old baseball cap that had belonged to John or Todd. She added dark sunglasses to the look. Now when she went out, whether the top was up or down she hoped sincerely that no one would recognize her. On Wednesday, she stopped at a traffic light. While waiting for the green she turned and looked to her right. A young man, seated in his own sports car, looked directly at her, smiled, nodded, *and winked at her,* then roared off. At first, she looked to her left to see who he'd been looking at. There was no one there. She was so completely stunned by the realization that *he had meant her* that she sat there for a full course of the light changing. It was only an impatient horn sounding that made her finally move on.

Todd was waiting for her in the driveway when she came home, leaning against his car, arms crossed. He was the spitting image of his father. Only he was twenty-three and to the best of her knowledge he wasn't a cheating bastard. John had been named after his father but Todd had gotten the likeness. Tall, thin, sandy hair, brown eyes, easy smile. *Her baby*. She could barely stand the sight of him. Not only did he look like his father, he had all the same mannerisms, too. Down to the slow lazy smile and the way he cocked his head to the right when he was listening to you talk to him. She couldn't look at him without thinking of Jonathan. And thoughts of Jonathan made her spiral down into the agony of suppressed emotions. To express the fury and hate and sorrow she had inside her would make her insane …

"Hey, Mom," Todd said as she pulled into the driveway. He squatted down by the driver's side and smiled at her. "Grace said I had to come over and see what you bought. Said I'd go nuts when I saw it. You bought a *Porsche?*"

"Is that what it is?" she responded. "I bought it because it was red and had a zippy look to it."

He shook his head at her ineptness. "Can I drive it?"

"I suppose so."

"Scoot over. I'll take you for an ice cream."

She got out because it was impossible to "scoot over" in the car's small interior. He watched her walk around the car and then grinned at her. "Nice hat."

She'd forgotten she was wearing it. "I found it in the basement. When the top's down my hair blows all over. Was it yours?"

He grinned at her again. "No, it was John's. He never wore it though …"

"Why?"

"You don't know, do you?"

"Know what?"

"Mom, it says *Hooters* across the front. That's a tittie bar. Someone gave it to John as a joke."

She snatched the hat off her head, horrified that she'd been driving around wearing it out in public. She looked at him and mumbled, "I thought it was a baseball team …" That made him laugh out loud.

They went for ice cream a little ways up the local highway. They stood outside in the sunshine, leaning against the car, licking their cones and watching the world whiz by. "How are you doing, Mom?"

She sighed. "I know, I know, you're all worried about me. Afraid I'm going to do myself in or something. I'm *fine*."

"I'm not worried about you."

"You're not?" she asked, turning to look at him in surprise. That was a first.

"Nope. You've always been tough and sure of yourself. You've always done things just the way it suited you whether it was the way things normally were done or not. I figure you're going to grieve in your own unique way and everyone should just leave you the hell alone." He shrugged his shoulders and bit off the bottom of the cone to suck out the ice cream. He looked at her with the face of his father and smiled at her with that familiar grin. "Why change now?"

"Can I ask you a favor?"

"Yeah, sure."

"Would you get rid of Jonathan's car for me? I don't want it in the garage anymore."

"You want me to sell it?"

"I don't care if you drive it off a cliff. I just don't want it anymore."

He studied her for a minute and then slowly nodded his head. "I have a friend that's looking for a car. I'll ask him if he wants to buy it."

"Fine."

Twenty minutes later she was standing in her driveway waving goodbye to him as he backed his car out. At the base of the driveway, he turned into the street and then rolled his window down and shouted something to her.

"What?" she yelled back. "I didn't hear you!"

"*I said,*" he shouted at her, "*nice toenails, Ma!*" Then he roared off down the street away from her.

She thought a lot about what he'd said to her that night. The numbness didn't settle in right away. She made herself an omelet and let the voice in her head keep repeating the words Todd had said to her. They were kind words. *You've always been tough and sure of yourself. You've always done things just the way it suited you whether it was the way things normally were done or not.* She had a flash of her and the three kids eating chocolate cookies and grapes for dinner by candlelight because the power had failed. The three kids were terrified of the thunderstorm and the darkness and so she'd served them the ridiculous dinner to make them relax a bit. She smiled remembering one of the early baseball games she'd gone to for John and in her great pride she'd screamed, *"I gave birth to him!"* when he'd hit a home run. Both the boys had had a long talk with her that night discussing exactly what she could say and what she couldn't say. She'd driven a hard bargain. They never were able to get her to stop yelling, *"That's my son!!!"*

She liked the opinion Todd had of her. For a brief flash it warmed her and made her feel strong again. *The Widow's Might* she thought. From now on, when Todd reminded her too much of Jonathan and the sight of him made her want to go insane, she'd close her eyes and remember him shouting, "Nice toenails, Ma!" Jonathan always hated it when she painted her toenails.

They are not the same anymore, for the old life is gone. A new life has begun!

The Heathen's Heart

Sunday morning as she headed for the door dressed and ready to go to Grace's church despite her decision to turn heathen, the phone rang.

"Hello?"

"Mother?" Grace's voice sounded somewhat strident. "Thank goodness I caught you. Zoe's just thrown up all over *everything*. There's no way we're going to make it to church and I wanted to call and let you know."

"Oh, okay. You just caught me. I was heading out the door."

"Sorry, Mom. I'll let you know next time- *NO ZOE! NOT ON THE COUCH -*" The line went dead. She stood there holding the receiver for a few moments and then slowly hung up the phone. Now what? *All dressed up and no place to go*, the voice in her head glibly sung out.

Without a specific plan, she wandered out, got in the car, and drove. She heard the bells to her church before she really registered where she had driven. Sitting in the parking lot, she knew she was late, she knew she had decided she wasn't going to attend anymore, she knew some of her greatest sorrow could still be felt just inside that building. But she got out anyway and slowly wandered in and found a seat in a far back pew. She'd missed the first hymn, the announcements, and even the Bible reading. Boy, she really was late.

She opened up the bulletin, intent on reading it to pass the time. Rarely had she ever followed a sermon from start to end. In the early years, when the kids were little, she was too preoccupied with keeping them quiet and not disturbing others around them. Later on, her life was so busy, she often used the time to plan out her week. Regularly, the church bulletins were covered with "to do" notes by the time they left to go home.

Pastor Duncan stood up, offered a prayer of understanding for the sermon, and then began to talk. He strolled out to the center of the pulpit and for a moment looked out across the sanctuary.

"Whore." He said loud and clear out into the sanctuary.

"Clever."

"Traitor."

"Heathen."

"Wise."

"Courageous."

"Faithful to God."

"Hero."

"Missionary."

"Ancestress of Christ."

He paused, for a moment then. Letting the words sink in a bit and then smiled at the congregation. "Those words don't all fit together, do they?" She saw some people shaking their heads "no". "But, believe it or not, they are all true – in their own moment of time – about one particular woman of the Bible. Rahab."

At the word "heathen" her head had snapped up, stunned to once again hear a private thought from her head so publicly spoken out loud for all to hear. She was less familiar with the Rahab story, probably because the widow with the two mites story was much easier to present in children's Sunday school. And teaching children's Sunday school was where most of her Bible knowledge came from.

Pastor Duncan took just a few moments to put all the words in order and paint a brief story of her life. Rahab had been a heathen (meaning she wasn't Jewish) prostitute in the city of Jericho in the ancient Biblical land of Canaan. When the famous Joshua sent spies in to scope out the city before his attack, she became a traitor to her own people by protecting them and helping them escape safely. She embraced the God of the Hebrews, turning her back on her own heathen upbringing. She secured the safety of her entire family when the famous battle of Jericho occurred by tying a scarlet thread in the window of her home that was literally built right into the walls of the city. When the walls fell, Rahab and her family remained safe and were eventually rescued by the Israelite army. They were the only ones to escape from the city alive. She went on to marry one of the spies who was from the Israelite tribe of Judah. In the book of Matthew in the Bible, she's listed as one of the ancestors of Christ.

Pastor Duncan walked out from behind the podium and stood again at the front of the altar where he had originally begun. "If you remember only *one thing* from this sermon, let it be this: With God, it isn't who you *were* that matters; it's who you *are becoming*. *Our past does not determine our future.* It didn't with Rahab and it certainly shouldn't with you. Let us pray."

She wasn't sure what she was more stunned about. The fact that she *listened* and *followed* an entire sermon or the actual message that he had just imparted. She had a flash then that made her sit bolt upright with burning embarrassment. *Grace had called him after their lunch on Wednesday.* Grace had told him about her bizarre ramblings about becoming a heathen. She felt her face flush with such a rush of embarrassment that even after the prayer ended she kept her head down to hide her shame. She would *never, ever, ever* enter this church again. Never.

The closing hymn began and her embarrassment was still monumental enough that she chose to stay in her seat rather then leave early and draw more attention to her already humiliated self. Then came the painful process of filing out of church, past well meaning friends. *Goodbye to all of you*, the voice in her head sang over and over again. *Take a good look at this old, ridiculous fool for it's the last look you're all gonna get.*

She caught a brief glimpse of the tall gentleman that tried to speak with her last week. God in heaven, if he attempted to speak to her she'd scream the roof off. Abruptly it seemed she was standing in front of the smiling face of Pastor Duncan. He extended his hand and said, "It's so good to see you Mrs. Lawson. I hope you had a good week."

She couldn't help herself. "Did my daughter call you this week?" she blurted out in a harsh whisper. She studied his face determined to read the truth, not necessarily believing he would speak it but certain she could see it in his expression if he was lying or trying to cover something up.

He looked absolutely perplexed. "Your daughter? No, she didn't call this week. Is she ill? Should I contact her myself? I'm not sure I have her number or even her married name. Could you give it to me?" He began to hastily hunt inside his jacket pocket for a pen and paper.

She turned without a word and stalked out. *Goodbye to all of you*, the voice sang one more time.

Monday morning the doorbell rang as she was sitting in the front room, still in her pajamas, drinking a cup of tea. She'd never been much of a morning person. Now that the kids were grown and her life was her own she made the most of it. There were some days when she never even got dressed. She walked cautiously to the front door and looked through the peephole. She groaned and rested her forehead against the cool painted wood. God help her, it was Pastor Duncan, clutching what appeared to be two coffees and a bag from Dunkin' Donuts.

Go away, her mind willed him. *Go away, go away, go away.* The doorbell rang again and then she heard the screen door open and the knocker get clunked against the door. "Mrs. Lawson? It's me, Pastor Duncan."

She tied her robe tighter around her waist and ran her fingers through her hair. She began opening the door when the doorbell rang a third time.

"Most people would get the hint by the second doorbell ring, Pastor Duncan," she said as she opened the door.

He smiled at her. "Ahh, but you forget Mrs. Lawson. *I'm a Pastor.* I'm used to being unwelcome so we have to push harder to get ourselves in the door. Besides, if you didn't answer the door, I'd be forced to eat both of these donuts." He held up the bag, grinned, and waggled it at her. "Cream filled."

She sighed. "Why are you here?" and for the first time in months and months she felt the pressure of tears behind her eyes.

"Could I come in and tell you?"

She didn't invite him in but just turned and walked into the house. By the time he'd managed the door - with the donuts and coffee it was a bit awkward - she was sitting in one of the two wing chairs in her living room. He settled in the other one. He went through the ritual of unpacking what he'd brought. A coffee for her, (black, he explained so she could doctor it up any way she wanted), and one cream donut for each of them. She was determined that she would not talk. He came here, he could carry the conversation. She looked out her front window and concentrated on the clouds. And being numb.

"I love donuts. It's one of the perks of being a pastor. I figure, it's always a welcome treat to bring when you're going to go visiting and in the process I get to enjoy a sweet myself." He paused and looked a bit thoughtful. Almost to himself he mumbled, "I guess that's a bit selfish if you think of it ..."

She remained absolutely silent. Searching for the blessed numbness to come and steal her away. "Your daughter didn't call me. I really felt I needed to impress that upon you because you seemed so upset yesterday. I decided to stop by because last week's phone call hadn't been the greatest of my successes."

In the face of her silence, Pastor Duncan continued. "I have heard many wonderful things about you and your family, Mrs. Lawson. You have been a blessing to this church for many years and yet I feel that I have been remiss in my duties to comfort you and give you the support you needed since your husband's death. I know the church family has been absolutely wonderful trying to stay connected and helpful to you, and up until this point I felt, as they had a greater connection and familiarity with you and your family that perhaps that was the best route. However, lately, I've begun to get the distinct impression that perhaps I should have been more proactive in ministering to you and your family. I hope, if that is the case, that you would accept my sincere apologies and be assured that from this moment on I am at your disposal in any way you need me to be."

She turned to him then and said in a dull, dead voice, "What wonderful things have you heard about me and my family, Pastor?"

He seemed startled by the question at first. "There's quite a list actually. On the service side, you have been a faithful servant in many capacities: Sunday School teacher, Vacation Bible School helper, nursery caregiver, and youth group leader. Your husband was a valuable participant on numerous church committees and was even an ordained elder. On the personal side, you've been a wonderful model of a Christian family, devoted to each other and your children. Your grief over Mr. Lawson's death is a powerful testimony to the devotion the two of you shared and the level of sorrow you're enduring."

"He died on a business trip to California."

"Yes, I know."

"He did a lot of business in California."

"Yes, I know."

"He was out there about two weeks out of every month, for years and years."

"Yes, I know." Pastor Duncan sounded puzzled.

She looked at him then so that, *perhaps*, he would in some small way view the magnitude of the emotions that she had contained within her self. Her throat ached from the effort to keep the screams inside. "He left another wife and two children in California. I believe the boy is ten and the girl is twelve. He died at his *other* home with his *other* family. I believe he was a fine Christian role model on the west coast, too." And then she sat there drawing her gray numbness around herself and watched Pastor Duncan process what she told him.

He was speechless. Of course. What else would he be? She had a moment of smug satisfaction with the knowledge that she'd made a pastor speechless. Even if he was young he'd have to have heard quite a few hair raising stories. He looked at his hands, dusted with powdered sugar, holding his cream donut and sighed a great, world weary sigh and closed his eyes for a brief moment. Then he looked up at her.

"So you are not grieving for him, but for yourself. That's why it is so much ..."

She saw no reason to answer him, just continued to stare at him in silence.

"Do the children know?"

She hesitated, and then shook her head "no" and looked away.

"You are a good woman. You've allowed the children to retain their memories. You've spared them a multitude of additional sorrow."

She looked at Pastor Duncan. *Good woman?* "Sir, I am old, bitter, angry, filled with hate, stupid and foolish, but I am *not good*. I did not tell my children to spare *them* but rather to spare my own pride. Bad enough that *I* know what a gullible, pitiful, idiot I have been all these years. I don't need my children to know as well."

He shook his head. "No. Sorry. Don't agree with you. It would have been far easier to rage it out to the world and let everyone know what a ... farce your husband has been to all of you.

"How soon after his death did you find out?"

"He requested to have a closed reading of his will with just me present. His lawyer knew. He'd made provisions in his will to provide for both ... families. I found out sitting in the lawyer's office about six weeks after the funeral."

"And so you've been living with this all by yourself for almost two years? Have you confided in anyone?"

"Feel privileged," she said after a few moments.

Pastor Duncan set his donut down and used a paper napkin to dust off the powdered sugar. She'd spoiled his appetite with her story. Carefully, he asked her, "What was it about my sermon that upset you so much yesterday?"

She sighed. "I thought my daughter had called and spoken with you about a conversation we had earlier in the week."

"And what? You thought I'd preached to you personally from the pulpit?" He actually sounded quite stunned.

Turning to Pastor Duncan again, she hesitated then nodded. "You see, I've decided to stop attending church. To become a heathen. I can just about escape the pain and fury by making myself numb over the course of the week, but Sundays ..." She looked out the windows and squinted but it wasn't because of the sun, but because of the pressure of tears again. "Sundays, sitting in church, I just can't seem to keep the pain and the memories at bay. They seem strongest then and I just can't bear the pain of it." She didn't look at him and swallowed hard.

Pastor Duncan stood up and walked over to the picture window and was quiet for a long time. The grandfather clock in the corner ticked by the moments. "I'm doing a series on women of the Bible. They're a neglected lot in my opinion. The Bible is full of these courageous, strong, exemplary women and so often only the guys get credit; Moses, Daniel; Joseph, Paul, Peter ... I was thinking last fall about what I would be doing this year for sermon ideas. I decided I'd focus on a few Biblical woman that were my particular favorites in the hopes that others would eventually share my same opinion. The women are already chosen. The sermons are already planned out. You mustn't think that I've chosen this series or a particular woman just to make a point from the pulpit that I don't have enough guts to make face to face." Pastor Duncan turned to look at her. "Would you at least promise me that?"

After a moment, she nodded her head and then shrugged. "It doesn't matter, I'm not going to attend church anymore."

He absolutely stunned her by laughing out loud. She looked at Pastor Duncan and he grinned at her. "Oh yes you will. I may not have planned this sermon series with you in mind, but *God* perhaps did. You may *think* that you're done with church and God and choosing to become a heathen, but you must remember you are not in control of any of this. You're very fortunate you know."

"Have you lost your mind?"

He kept grinning and shook his head "no" while he began to gather up the donuts and cold coffee. "No, I haven't lost my mind. But I've been privileged to watch God work in mysterious ways more than once and there isn't a doubt in my mind that this is going to be *very enjoyable* to witness."

Pastor Duncan looked like he was considering saying something else and then pressed on. "The Lord is sorrowing right along with you, Mrs. Lawson. But He has given you *many wonderful things* to help you cope with this very moment in your life. You have your children, your church family, your own strong, vital personality, and – I hope you will not think me too pompous – you have me. You *do not* have the heart of a heathen. I know that. God knows that. And I think, you know that, too. You came to church last Sunday, didn't you? Even though you had told your daughter you were going to do the very opposite thing just a few days prior." He smiled again, a kind understanding smile. "I even understand your desire to not want to come to church. Really I do. But you have to look at your time at church not as your time remembering the past, but your time preparing for the future. *With God, it isn't who you were that matters; it's who you are becoming. Our past does not determine our future.*"

When he'd gotten the garbage all carefully collected and no evidence of his visit was obvious except him standing in her living room he said, "I like you Mrs. Lawson. A lot. I like that you're frank and outspoken. I like that you tell me I'm an idiot when I'm an idiot and I look forward to the time when you'll tell me I've done a good job. And whether you believe me or not, God's got great plans for you. Just wait and see."

"You're an idiot, Pastor Duncan."

He folded his arm across his waist with the bag of donuts in his hand and the coffee tray and cups in the other and did a formal bow. "Thanks. I appreciate your honesty and so does God." And with that, he let himself out the door.

Thursday, Alita came to clean the house. Alita had been faithfully cleaning her house for twenty years. It had started out as a business arrangement and moved into a friendship over the years. Alita had watched the children grow up, been with her through the death of her two parents and watched Bee carefully as she'd turned into a bitter, nasty, old lady. While Bee had been able to distance herself from all of her other friends with various stories and excuses, Alita had remained. Out of necessity and persistence. And a whole pile of stubbornness.

"Good morning, Mrs. Bee," Alita said as she came into the kitchen. Alita had had her own key for years and Bee couldn't recall a time when she hadn't arrived as scheduled. There had been mornings when Bee had not been out of bed, behind closed doors, and had simply said, "Skip my room, Alita," and never shown her face. For those visits, they're only interaction had been Bee listening to Alita's beautiful singing voice as she worked her way through the house. Alita knew that to find Bee in the kitchen, even if she wasn't dressed was better than it could have been.

"Good morning, Alita, is it that time again already?"

"Yes, and what have you done these two weeks, may I ask, Mrs. Bee? Have you been in that bed all of this time or have you gotten yourself out and about?"

Alita never minced words. That was one of the things that Bee had always enjoyed about her. Why, if the truth be told, part of *her* outspokenness had been learned from the directness of her friend, Alita. Bee poured them both a cup of tea and handed a steaming mug to Alita. "I bought a car."

"That is good. Cars are always good to have conversations with and fill empty hours."

Bee ignored her. Sometimes that was the easiest tactic. Alita had been after her for this past year to get moving, to get over things, to start living again. That was some of the reason it was easier to avoid her and stay in her room on certain days.

Bee asked the question before she had time to really think it through. "Are you happily married Alita?" She knew Alita had two teenage sons that she adored and often referred to her husband.

"Yes," Alita said after a moment's pause, "but I am still working on it."

"What's that mean?"

Alita went over to the linen closet and began taking out all of her cleaning things. "When we first married, I was so in love with Rafael. Oh how I loved him." She smiled a small smile at the memory. "I did everything to please him and lost myself in the doing." Getting out some rags, she sprayed one with Endust and started dusting the furniture as she spoke. "And then Rafael broke my heart and I thought I would die. The boys were tiny …"

"How did he break your heart?"

"He took another woman. He did it twice. After the second time, I thought I would just leave him so that it would not destroy me. But for me, marriage and the vows that go with it are important. I thought I would make some effort before I just up and left. So I talked to Rafael and helped him see things my way. And things were better after that."

The story missed pieces that Bee all of a sudden desired fiercely to know about. "What did you talk to him about?"

Alita looked at her and gave her a sweet smile and then continued dusting. Her dark hair was pulled back in a no nonsense pony tail, but even so you can see it was thick and rich. She had eyes that danced with mischief or delight and the most gloriously smooth skin. "I told him. 'Rafael, I will not look for you. I will not run or chase you. I will not beg or plead. I will just say to you this: look around and see what you have. You have a good woman. You have two beautiful children. You have a lovely home. If you cannot be happy with this then you can leave. But you will leave with nothing but the pants you are wearing. Or, maybe not your pants either.'" Alita looked at her then and shrugged. "Rafael saw my way of thinking in the end. He is a good provider. He is a good father. I am not so crazy with my love for him any more. We are both happy now." She hesitated a moment and then added. "My faith is what keeps me happy, really. Neither of us are perfect, but with faith in God I can overlook his flaws and work on my own at the same time."

Alita looked at her and said, "Did you have a happy marriage, Mrs. Bee?"

"I thought I did, but -"

Alita interrupted her. "Do not say that word 'but'. Why did you think you had a happy marriage?"

Bee mind whirred out a colorful display of memories: the children growing up, laughter, times together, dinners, school functions … "We raised three beautiful, healthy, strong children. We had a lot of laughter and fun."

"You do not mention yourself. Were you happy?"

Bee thought. Thought hard. It was difficult to separate the current numbness that hid all the hate and sorrow and fury from the other part of her life. "Yes," she finally said quietly, "yes, I was happy."

"Why were you happy?" Alita persisted.

Why was she happy? "I got to do what I always wanted to do. I became a mother. And a capable woman. Because Jonathan traveled so much, I learned to depend on myself and I did a good job at it, too. Some of our most difficult times were adjusting in those first few days when he got back and the shift of power that would happen in the house with him returning."

"Did you mind Mr. Jonathan traveling and being away so much?"

Bee opened her mouth to say "of course", which was the lip service she had paid to everyone – family, friends, and kids – and then stopped herself. She shut her mouth to think again. The truth sparkled there like a shiny penny you find in the dirt on the side of the road. "No, I didn't mind Jonathan traveling and being away so much. I had a routine and things were peaceful and smooth when he was away. Life was good. Sometimes he'd walk in after being away for more than two weeks and he'd start blustering around with the kids - being 'king of the castle' was what we'd call it - and I actually hated him and couldn't wait for him to leave again." He'd show up with his suitcases filled with dirty laundry, start ordering the kids around and making observations about things he knew nothing about and the peaceful existence would be shattered into a million pieces. "I never dreaded the days he was leaving, but I often dreaded the day he was coming home."

"Do you have any good words to say about Mr. Jonathan?"

Bee looked at Alita, guilty. Then got angry with herself for the guilt. "I don't know what you are asking."

"I am not asking about what you have to say about Mr. Jonathan *now*. I am asking what good things you had to say about him *then*. Were there *any*?"

"He was a good provider. There was no doubt he loved the children, although he struggled with how to show it. He encouraged me to do things I didn't always think I could do. He called me "Busy Bee" and I always thought he said it with pride."

"You speak nothing of love between the two of you."

Bee's tea was cold and she poured it down the drain. She rinsed the cup and put it in the dishwasher and busied herself cleaning up the few dishes from her breakfast. "I married him because I loved him." She had a flash of Jonathan sweating and proposing to her and his hand trembling as he held the ring. She had teased him about that in the early years. "But somewhere, over the course of life, I think I stopped. I think I was more appreciative than in love. And somehow I lost the ability to tell or even care about the difference."

Alita nodded her head sagely and began to clear the kitchen counters so she could clean them. "Love cannot be neglected. Love must be encouraged. For Rafael and I, our love needed to find a balance. For you and Mr. Jonathan, I think maybe you let the business of life take over in places you maybe should not have." She looked at Bee. "You two never fought. I always thought that strange. At first, I worried, because Rafael and I ... well, we have our moments." She shrugged her shoulders and went back to cleaning the counters. "But you two, were always quiet and polite. Love has fury. It has anger. It even has a little bit of hate now and then. At least that's my idea."

Bee decided she would tell Alita. The horrible Truth of their marriage. "I found out that when we were married-"

Alita interrupted her again. "Mrs. Bee, my mother had a saying that she used to say to me all the time." She struggled, translating it in her head. "'*Don't let the tail wag the dog.*' You are going to tell me things that you found out once Mr. Jonathan died. I know from what I see with you that they are horrible things. But they were *his things*, that *he chose*. You have just told me about a good life. One that maybe was not a great love story, but one that was a *good life*." Alita looked Bee right in the eye. "Don't let the tail wag the dog." Bee heard Pastor Duncan saying, '*With God, it isn't who you were that matters; it's who you are becoming. Our past does not determine our future.'*

Alita resumed her cleaning and shrugged. "You've got plenty of time to still find your great love story. But I would tell you something I am absolutely sure about."

Alita stopped talking and she turned and looked at Bee, waiting and expecting. "What?" Bee finally said a little too impatiently. *"What."*

"You are *for certain* not going to find any great love story with a *new car."* Alita rolled her eyes and headed to the linen closet to get out the vacuum. *"Anyone* knows that."

On Saturday evening the phone rang. It was Pastor Duncan. "Mrs. Lawson, I'm worried about my sermon tomorrow and I decided to call you."

"You're calling to ask me advice?"

"No," Bee heard a smile in his voice. "I'm concerned you'll think I'm preaching to you from the pulpit again."

"You forgot, I told you I'm not coming anymore."

"You forgot. I told you I didn't necessarily think that was true."

"What's the topic?"

"It's about Leah."

She thought for a moment. "I'm not familiar with her."

"Well, maybe I should just tell you the sermon topic then."

"I'm waiting."

"I called it, 'Leah, The Unloved Wife'."

She was silent for a long time. He was patient, letting her think. "Good thing you prepared me."

"I thought so."

"Does it have a happy ending?"

"Yes," Pastor Duncan said without hesitation. "It does."

"It better."

"Will I see you tomorrow?"

"I'm not making any promises."

"I live for the unexpected and the unknown."

"Good night, Pastor Duncan."

He chuckled. "I'll pray you into church tomorrow. Just you wait and see."

It's just enough to be strong, in the broken places, in the broken places
It's just enough to be strong, should the world rely on faith tonight[5]

The Unloved Wife's Discovery

"I want you to close your eyes and imagine your wedding day," Pastor Duncan began Sunday morning, "and your wedding night. Go ahead, take a moment." She was sitting in what was rapidly becoming "her" pew, in the very back corner of the sanctuary. Close to the door, easy access for quick escapes and avoidance of all unwanted contact. She saw some in the congregation following his instructions and closing their eyes. Others were simply sitting, quiet and thoughtful.

"Now, I want you to imagine *this* as the wedding morning: as the groom awakens and looks at his bride, he has a moment of foggy confusion, followed by moments of panicked bewilderment, followed by moments of shock and outrage. He begins to scream, "Liar! Cheat! Deceiver!" and as he pulls his clothes on he runs howling from the bridal suite in search of the father of the bride.

"By the end of the first week of that marriage the groom would have not one but *two* wives. The bride, although forever to be assigned the esteemed position of "first" wife, would also bear the unenviable position as the unloved wife. For you see, the groom had always wanted the bride's younger, more beautiful sister. *She* was the one he had always loved. The one he had always wanted to marry. The one he had worked for seven years to have the privilege of marrying. The one he *thought* he had married on the wedding day. And the one he pledges to work for another seven years for in order to marry." Pastor Duncan paused and let the congregation digest what he'd just described.

"This was the story of Leah, The Unloved Wife. She married Jacob. But Jacob loved Rachel. On that first morning after the wedding, he found himself married to Leah. How could that happen you might ask?" Pastor Duncan shrugged his shoulders. "The Bible doesn't specifically say, but perhaps wedding veils and a little too much celebrating on Jacob's part? Who knows." There was some chuckling in the sanctuary.

"I cannot imagine what it must have been like for Leah. Always the unloved and the unwanted wife. The Bible doesn't tell us that she *ever* was able to achieve the love she must have surely craved. And if you think it couldn't get much worse, Jacob went on to marry two more women; Leah's maid and Rachel's maid. Some makings for a dysfunctional family, eh?" More chuckles.

"But as you read the story of Leah in the Bible, if you really take the time to study the nuances, read between the lines so to speak, you discover that this *was* a story with a happy ending. And Leah gives us a tremendous spiritual lesson to embrace and apply to our own lives."

"You know, the Bible doesn't always give us as many details as we'd like. Often, there seems to be a frustrating lack of them. But I've discovered, as many professional and amateur scholars of the Bible have, that if you *take the time to research a bit* sometimes more details are evident than you originally thought. And that's the case in Leah's story.

"We know some things, simply by reading the Biblical account. Most importantly, although Leah was unloved by her husband, the Lord blessed her with children. Back then, the birth of children was a woman's claim to status within society. Healthy children meant you were favored by God; blessed. The lack of children meant you were not in God's favor. And so while Leah had to deal with the fact that she was the unloved wife,

God blessed her with the glory of children while her beautiful sister, loved and treasured though she was by her husband, failed to have any children for a major part of her marriage.

"It was in the children that we can peer more closely into the personal anguish and spiritual growth of Leah. And it was all contained in the way she named her children. Watch." The screen overhead behind Pastor Duncan lit up.

"Leah eventually had six sons and one daughter. In addition, because Jacob married *her* maid, she had the authority to name the two sons that her maid gave birth to as well. So, all in all, Leah had the responsibility of naming nine children. Her first son she named *Rueben*." On the screen behind him, in big bold letters it said, 'Reuben: *Behold a son.*'

"The name Rueben means literally 'behold a son'. In Genesis, it tells that upon naming her first child, she said, "The Lord has noticed my misery and now my husband will love me." Pastor Duncan walked out from behind the pulpit and looked at the congregation. "Doesn't that just about break your heart?" He shook his head. "The Bible doesn't really give us much information about their relationship aside from the first impressions we get. Personally, I don't think that she ever felt truly loved or wanted by her husband. I think Jacob only had room in his heart for Rachel.

"Her second son," Pastor Duncan nodded at the person changing the slides, "she named Simeon which means 'Hearing', and Leah said at his birth, "The Lord has heard that I am unloved and has given me another son." Even at the birth of her third son, Levi, she said, "Surely now my husband will feel affection for me, since I have given him three sons." The slide changed a third time. "The name Levi meant 'joined'. I wonder, what was she thinking? Joined to what? Her husband? Her children? Or, perhaps it was God ..."

He looked a little sheepish at the congregation. "Again, I'll give you my opinion. I think that after the third child, she realized what the course of her life would be. I think she looked around at her beautiful children and her life – they *were* wealthy and prosperous – and realized what God had blessed her with. She saw her sister, Rachel, favored by being the 'loved' wife, making everyone miserable – including the husband – for the *lack* of children. I think Leah looked at herself and determined that she would rejoice in what she *had* rather than what she *had not*." Pastor Duncan looked pointedly at the congregation. "When you can accomplish that in your life, you become very powerful. It is freeing. Watch what she named her consecutive children."

"Child number four was named Judah. His name meant 'Now I will praise the Lord.' The fifth child she named is by her maid, Zilpah. Remember, she has the privilege of naming him, as the customs dictated. Leah called him Gad which meant 'How fortunate I am.' The sixth child Leah named is also by her maid, Zilpah and she named him Asher. That meant," he pauses and smiled a slow smile, "*happy.*" Leah gave birth to her fifth child and it was the seventh child she named. She called him Issachar which meant 'There is reward'. She said at his birth, "God has rewarded me."

Pastor Duncan looked at the congregation. "Are you seeing a pattern here? A progression? Do you see her spiritual growth?" Many in the congregation nodded their heads. *"How can you not?"*

"We are almost to the end of Leah's story. Her sixth child, her last son, and the eighth child she has had the privilege of naming, she called Zebulun, which meant 'Honor'." Pastor Duncan had spent almost the entire sermon standing in the center of the altar, rattling off the names of the children while the slides flashed in support behind him.

"There is one more child for Leah to name, because remember I told you that she named nine in all." He walked over to the pulpit and stood behind it. "I think she saved the best for last. The final child she gave birth to was her first and only girl. One girl in amidst all those boys! She named her Dinah, which meant," he paused and grinned, "justice."

Pastor Duncan paused to gaze out at the congregation. "Were all of us to be given the opportunity to choose our path in life I do not think that there is even one of us who would be able to anticipate accurately what God had planned for us. Let me tell you quite plainly, *it is not our place to do so.* Our place is to take what the Lord has given us and *make the most of it.* Not all of us have experienced the rejection that Leah felt, and yet each and every one of us has experienced profound disappointment and sorrow in our life. Those times are *not* times that God has forsaken us. More correctly, those times are for us to look around us and search to find *what God has given us* to see us through *and beyond* those difficult times."

Silently, Pastor Duncan walked out from behind the pulpit and stepped down the steps from the altar to stand in front of the congregation and folded his hands in front of him. "God does this for each and every one of us so that at the end of *your* story you can feel *honored, happy, and justified* just like Leah. Isn't that what happy endings are all about?"

Bee heard what Pastor Duncan had said. All of it. Wasn't quite sure what to make of it, but she'd heard it all right. She felt a little like when you try some new food for the first time and the taste is so different, so new, that you're not sure if you like it or not, so you savor it trying to decide. One thing was certain. Her experience at church today had been different. There were no powerful memories that wrenched her painfully from past to present. There was no brain boredom while she waited for the minutes to tick by to the end. She'd sat and listened. Good God, was it possible she'd actually gotten something out of the sermon?! After all these years.

Bee went through the closing motions of the service and filed out with the rest of the people. Preoccupied, thoughtful, not even bothering to answer or deflect comments sent her way. At last she was standing in front of Pastor Duncan.

"*We* are glad to see you here today, Mrs. Lawson." The plural pronoun was not lost on Bee and Pastor Duncan knew it.

"I won't need a phone call or a visit this week, Pastor Duncan," she said to him. But it wasn't said abruptly.

"Not even to discuss the sermon? I'd love to hear your thoughts ..." He smiled at her, relieved probably that she wasn't making some sort of scene *again*.

"Have a good week, Pastor," she said as she headed toward the bright sunshine outside.

For a moment, her eyes had to adjust from the dim church interior to the blazing outdoor sun. She stood and collected her bearings lost in thought.

"It's taken me three weeks, but I *think* I might actually get to have a word with you today," she heard a male voice next to her say. She knew before she even turned around that it was the tall gentlemen from a few weeks ago. Sigh. Just when things had maybe started to look up a bit.

She turned to look at him, squinting in the bright sunlight. When he noticed her difficulty gazing into the brightness he turned a little and motioned towards the parking lot. "Can I walk you to your car?"

She nodded. No sense giving him any encouragement, though. In fact, why not save him the embarrassment of her inevitable rejection? "Look, I'm sure your committee is very worthwhile, but I'm not at all interested in becoming involved with anything right now."

The man looked startled and quickly looked right or left as if searching for someone. "Are you talking to me? What committee? I'm not sure what you're talking about … Perhaps you have me confused with someone else? My name is Peter Gannon. And you are …?"

She was stunned. "You're not on a committee? And you don't even know my name?"

He started to chuckle. "This is *not* going well, at all. Here I've been trying to introduce myself, get your name and invite you to go out for coffee for three solid weeks and it seems you've been avoiding me thinking I'm someone who's trying to catch you up onto some God-awful church committee …"

She stopped walking, stood in the crunchy gravel of the parking lot and looked at him like he'd lost his mind. "You've been trying to *ask me out for coffee?*"

He stopped walking too, turned, smiled and nodded. "It took me a good couple of weeks just to get up the nerve. Add in the three weeks that you've been avoiding me. This seems like a disaster before it even has a chance to start."

He sighed, seemed to mentally shake himself and then extended his hand. "Hi, my name is Peter Gannon. What's yours?"

She looked at his extended hand. When was the last time she'd touched anyone? She could not remember. She hesitantly put her hand in his warm one and looked up at him, still stunned. "My name is Bee. Bee Lawson."

"Bea. I knew your last name was Lawson, because I had heard Pastor Duncan call you 'Mrs. Lawson', but I didn't know your first name." Peter Gannon smiled, "And now I do. Is that short for 'Beatrice'?"

"No, it's just Bee."

"Oh." He looked around the parking lot. "Where's your car?"

Bee pointed vaguely off to the left of the parking lot and they resumed walking. Why was he talking to her? Her brain made every effort to get fired up enough to make some sense of all this. What could he want? For the life of her she could not come up with a valid reason. The need to converse, finding polite words that showed that she was capable of speech, was a daunting task. When was the last time she had to do that with anyone? She had lived an insular life for so long that the skills required for living and existing with others were either dead or so rusty they were not worth consideration. They reached her car and she stopped and looked at it.

"Quite a car, huh?" Peter said with clear admiration in his voice. "Have wanted one of these probably my whole entire life." He chuckled to himself and looked a bit embarrassed. "Used to build models of them when I was a kid. In my twenties I went so far as to get a *Porsche* key ring so that women would think I owned one." He rolled his eyes and smiled at her. "Those were my *early desperate* years."

"And these years are...?" she couldn't help but ask.

"These are my '*just float along and see where life takes you*' years. Which one's your car?"

Bee fished her keys out of her purse. "The one you're drooling over."

"You're kidding me."

"I don't have a reputation for being much of a tease, I'm afraid."

"What kind of reputation do you have?"

Bee looked at Peter Gannon and decided to let him have it. "Outspoken, harsh, bitter, abrupt, and lately rude and nasty."

Her honesty seemed to delight him. He was not fazed a bit. "I can handle it." Peter looked at her seriously for a moment. "I meant it when I said I'd like to take you for a cup of coffee. There's a coffee shop that's just opened down near the county college. It even has outside tables. Are you interested?"

The desire to go and hide and be numb was so all consuming that for a moment she allowed it to envelope her. It felt like a wet, woolen blanket. She shrugged it off. "Okay. But I don't have much experience with this kind of thing."

"What kind of thing? I just intended to talk."

Bee rolled her eyes at him. "That's exactly what I mean."

They took her car because he just couldn't believe that she owned a *Porsche*. The conversation on the way to the coffee shop was filled with his questions about the car. He was incredulous that she knew absolutely nothing about it and bought it simply because it was 'red and zippy'. He laughed out loud when she told him she didn't even realize it was a Porsche until her youngest son, Todd, called it by name.

They got to the coffee shop and she ordered a hot tea. Peter bought them two crumb buns without consulting her. They sat outside in the sunshine, shaded by a big blue and white striped umbrella.

"So, you have how many children?" Peter asked her.

"Three. My youngest son, Todd, is single and lives nearby. So does my daughter, Grace. She is married with two little ones. My oldest, John, lives out in California. I don't see him much unless he's traveling out here on business."

Bee couldn't overcome the surreal situation she was in: behaving like a casual, happy, woman chit-chatting with a nice looking man in a picturesque café on a sunny afternoon in early June. Waves of panic periodically overwhelmed the unrealistic. "Why did you want to ask me for coffee?" she finally blurted out. Bee suddenly, desperately needed to know the reason. Did he know Grace? Had the Pastor talked to him? Was there some kind of bizarre church conspiracy to take pity on her and 'get her out and about' and had Peter lost the coin toss? *Why?* She had a powerful urge to scream the question but suppressed it with all her other screams.

Peter smiled at her again. Did he find her funny? Idiotic? Was that why he was compelled to smile at her all the time? Were his smiles a clever way to cover-up the complete boredom and misery he was suffering in her company? "Hasn't anyone ever asked you out for coffee before?"

"No."

He sighed. "Obviously, I'm not very good at this."

Bee was stunned to think that *he* thought that *he* was inept. "Have *you* ever asked anyone out for coffee before?"

Peter nodded. "Yes, a few times. *Why* hasn't anyone ever asked you out for coffee before?"

What an odd question. "Because prior to being married, I was too young to drink coffee. Then, over the course of thirty years of marriage there was no need for anyone to ask me out. Now, recently, I've just not … been available," she finished lamely.

Peter nodded seemingly satisfied with her answer. "Are you divorced?"

Good grief, he really knew nothing about her. Bee looked him right in the eye. "No, I'm an embittered widow."

"Is there any other kind?" He grinned at her.

Good Lord, he thought she was kidding. She sighed a world-weary sigh. This was too hard. She wanted to go home. Peter seemed to sense her mood and reached across the table to cover one of her hands with his. His hand was warm and she knew hers was cold. Like a corpse. He looked at her with a serious expression. *He wears glasses* her head registered. "Look, I'm relatively new to the area. Been attending church here for about six months now. You're hard not to notice. I -"

"Why am I hard not to notice?" She managed to disengage her hand to pick up her cup of tea. Did her misery radiate in a visible aura? Did her suppressed fury give off warning sounds?

"Why you are -, I mean, you have -," Peter stuttered and stumbled over his words.

"Just spit it out. I can take it," Bee said bracing herself for the truth.

Peter looked at her and in complete seriousness said, "You're quite lovely to look at. You have a regal presence about you. You exude confidence. I've watched you come and go at church. I've noticed how you deal politely with people. Others seem to think well of you and seek you out." He looked a bit sheepish. "You have a beautiful reading voice. I enjoy hearing you when you read the scripture."

Had he stripped nude before her and done a hula dance on the table she would have been far better prepared. Bee stared at him, absolutely and completely speechless. There was no pity. There was no false concern. Hell, the guy had just about told her she was *hot*. Bee's emotions swung from hysterical laughter to hysterical tears.

"Has no one ever told you these things before?" Peter finally asked her.

She looked away from him then and gazed off into the distant horizon. She squinted her eyes to keep the tears in check and stopped herself from getting up and running away because she realized she must drive him back to his car. Bee groaned inwardly when she discovered that. "I can't remember. If someone has, it was a long time ago." She took a deep breath but did not look at him. "I have spent the last two years of my life regretting the last thirty years of my life. I find the impression you have of me inconceivable." Bee looked at him then. "So inconceivable that I am rapidly beginning to think that this is either a very vivid dream or I have at last lost my mind."

Peter smiled at her again. "I would like to take you out to dinner sometime." He put up his hand to stop her from saying 'no' and Bee waited for him to finish. "I will give you my home phone number. You go home, determine whether you are awake or asleep, and then decide if you'd like to go out for a bite to eat."

"Have you heard anything I've said to you?" Her voice sounded strident.

"Yes, I've heard every word. And did you hear what *I* said to *you*? I'll repeat it in case you forgot: *I can handle it.*"

Bee left Peter standing by his car in the church parking lot. Sitting on the seat he'd just occupied was a white business card. Within five minutes, had the card not been there she would never have believed the brief interlude had happened. When she pulled into the garage, she left the card sitting on the seat.

On Tuesday morning, the phone rang and it was her son John. It had been quite a while since they last spoke and a good few months since he had been out on the east coast for business. "Mom? It's John. How are you doing?"

"I'm doing okay. How are you doing, John?"

"All right. Look, I've just found out that I've got to fly out to New York for an impromptu meeting tomorrow. Can we get together?"

"Let me check my social calendar. Hmmm, yes, I seem to be free."

John was quiet for a moment, trying to figure out her mood she guessed. "The meeting's during the day, so I thought maybe we could go out to dinner tomorrow night. I'd love to have some of Max's pasta if we could manage it."

Max's. The favorite family restaurant. A hell-hole of memories. "Okay, I'll see if I can get reservations. Do you have a time?"

"About seven?"

"Sounds good. Will you stay the night?"

"If it isn't too much bother."

"See you around seven then. Have a safe flight."

"Bye, Mom."

My, my, two dinner invitations in less than three days. Things were really picking up for her. Seemed like she should add sarcastic to her list of sterling qualities. Or was that already on the list?

She sat down at the desk where the phone was and got out a piece of paper. She couldn't shake Pastor Duncan's words out of her head. Despite her best effort to surround herself in her numbness, his words kept creeping through. *Our place is to take what the Lord has given us and make the most of it. Search to find what God has given you to see you through and beyond those difficult times. So that at the end of your story you can feel honored, happy, and justified.* Of all the things he'd said on Sunday, that last line — *so you can feel honored, happy, and justified* – was the one that was most powerful for her. She didn't know which feeling she craved more, but she was starving *for all of them.*

It was a novel concept for her to think that God, anticipating what was ahead for her had *given her things* to help her through the tough times. She looked at the piece of paper, determined to prove to Pastor Duncan that he was an idiot once again. She divided the paper in half and wrote 'Why my life has been difficult' on one side. She scratched it out and wrote, 'Why my life sucks' and felt better. On the other side she wrote, 'What God has given me'. She was so prepared for the length of the 'sucks' column that she readied another piece of paper.

She started with the 'sucks' column first and wrote '1. My husband was a lying, cheating bastard,' and again felt much better for it. She prepared to write the second thing and hesitated. Her brain scrambled around and around for a second thing to write. There wasn't one. That was impossible. Surely there were other things that she needed to write down. It was just the numbness, robbing her of her intellectual faculties.

She thought again.

There were none.

Okay, okay maybe if she wrote something in the 'What God has given me' column she'd come up with some more nasty things. Without any hesitation she wrote the first three things: John, Grace, and Todd. Then she added Alita. And her health. And her financial status. The voice in her head said, *Pastor Duncan* which she eventually did write down but only after she swore that she'd never admit she'd put him on that side of the list because she knew she'd never hear the end of it from him. She added her church, and all the well-meaning people that still sought her out and inquired about her. She chewed on the end of the pen. She should add her friends outside the church that had grown distant in the last few years but only at her harsh insistence. She thought about herself personally and remembered talking with Alita and thinking that she was a capable woman. She wrote that down. She thought about Todd saying that she was always so tough and sure of herself and she wrote that down too.

She'd gotten to the end of the column. She needed another sheet of paper. She looked at what she'd written and was overwhelmed. *Look what God had given her.* It was not a small list. It was not an inconsequential list. It was a powerful, monumental pile of people and things that most of them *individually* should have been able to see her through and yet she had ... she counted ... *twelve.* TWELVE. She all of a sudden felt foolish and childish. Look what she'd had all along and she'd ignored it and just kept on whining and complaining. How had God put up with her all this time? The list made her feel new. Like the time she'd gone and been fitted for glasses and realized just how bad her eyesight had become. All of a sudden she felt that she could see things clearly and rationally. She couldn't remember when she had last felt that way. Even before the funeral and The Truth. It had been years, maybe decades. She read the list again and felt even better, stronger. She would read the list every morning to start her day off. Hell, she'd read the list every time the fury and the screams built up in her instead of letting the numbness take over. This list was the start of the end of her life. *So that at the end of her story she could feel honored, happy, and justified.*

She got up and went to the junk drawer and got out the hammer. She dug around and sure enough she found a nail. She went over to the fireplace and took down the God-awful picture that Jonathan had brought home one time from one of his trips overseas. She took the piece of paper, stuck the nail in the top and hammered it into the wall. Not much for decorative sense but she felt a thousand times better.

That night as she got in bed she laid in the darkness remembering her list. It was the first time in two years that she fell asleep with positive things rolling around in her head rather than fury and hate. As she drifted off, her last thoughts were, "*Please, God, let me not loose this feeling ... Please ...*"

She woke in the middle of the night, heart pounding, drenched in sweat. She tried but couldn't remember the dream/nightmare. The nightmares had become less frequent, but were still something she dealt with fairly regularly. All of a sudden, a wave of panic washed over her. *Where was Peter Gannon's business card? What did she do with it?* She switched on the bedside light and padded down the steps. At the kitchen sink she poured herself a cold drink of water trying to retrace the steps from when he gave her the card. *The car.* Out in the garage, sure enough, she saw it there on the passenger seat. *Peter Gannon* it read, *CTW* with a business number and a mobile number. She didn't think she'd ever call either number, but she carefully carried it inside and pinned it on the bulletin board. She stared at it for long moments before she finally went back to bed.

She picked John up at the local train station at 6:48 p.m. He favored her in coloring with dark brown hair and green eyes. Slightly shorter than Todd, he was still at least six feet tall. He was fuller and more muscular. Even if she was his mother, she had to admit he was handsome. He looked a little bit tired and jet lagged and she said so.

"I hate the flight from the west coast to the east coast. It just seems to take so much longer and you loose sleep." John hesitated. "Dad always said the same thing."

As they walked from the train station out to the parking lot, Bee kept her silence. She had no desire to reminisce with John about his father's return from *his other life.*

"How's Janet?"

It was John's turn to be silent and she finally looked at him. He shrugged. "We're through. It just didn't work out."

"Are you okay?" It felt good to be asking the question rather than answering it, Bee realized.

"Yeah, it was hard. We'd been dating for a year and a half, you know."

Bee was genuinely surprised and frowned in confusion. "Really? I hadn't realized it had been that long."

"We just … well we wanted … I thought …" John sighed in frustration. "I just never seemed to get it right with her. I tried, but it just never seemed to make her happy. Then she started talking about marriage and stuff and I said to her, 'How can we talk about getting married when we can't even agree on what restaurant and movie to go to without arguing?'" He looked at Bee and rolled his eyes. "*That* didn't go over very well."

"Do you mind if we don't go to Max's?" Bee asked him suddenly.

John looked surprised. "No, not at all. Got another place in mind?"

She shrugged. "No, not really. I just thought we'd drive for a bit and see what showed up."

"Okay. Where's your car?"

Here it comes, her head said as they neared the bright red monstrosity. Bee stopped and looked up at him. "Here it is," and waved her hand out like she'd seen the models do on some of those game shows.

John looked at the car and then at her, then back at the car again. He grinned a big wide grin. "Todd wasn't kidding me."

"Nope."

"Can I drive it?"

"Yup," and she tossed him the keys.

They ended up eating at a little hole in the wall restaurant in a nowhere strip mall on the outskirts of a small town she was not sure she'd ever been to. It was a wonderful meal and the conversation flowed relatively smoothly. John didn't try to have any serious heart to heart talks with her about what she should or shouldn't be doing. They talked about weather and politics and his job and little tidbits about Grace and Todd. When they'd finished dessert she drove home because he'd had two beers with dinner. Walking in the front door, she switched on the lights and immediately saw the list she'd written and nailed over the fireplace.

Crap.

John noticed it too. "What's that, Mom?" he asked and in complete innocence walked over to examine her new decorating attempt. Bee stood, frozen in the hallway keys dangling in her hand. She could have said something to stop him from reading it but at the last minute she decided to keep her mouth shut. She watched him read through the list. John spent so much time reading it, she was certain he'd read it through at least twice. When he turned and looked at her, she saw not a speck of surprise in his beautiful green eyes, but instead sorrow, defeat, and ... yes, guilt.

"You knew," she said quietly. "YOU KNEW," she said louder fighting to keep the screaming at bay.

"Yeah," John said after a moment and his voice was heavy and tired and filled with loathing. "*I knew.*"

"Do Grace and Todd know?"

John looked at her directly. "Not from me they don't. It was bad enough I had to keep it in my head, let alone share it with others."

Bee knew exactly how he felt. At a loss for words she walked forward into the kitchen and began the motions of making herself a cup of tea. She heard him behind her. "Do you want anything?"

"Yeah." John went over to the cupboard and she heard him pour himself a scotch. *Clink, clink.* With two ice cubes.

"How long have you known?"

He sighed a big heavy sigh. "Probably close to four years, Mom."

"*Four years?!*" She couldn't help herself and her voice was loud and strident even to her own ears. The screams boiled up in her, and the rage. *Breathe,* she told herself. *Take a deep breath and think of The List.*

"It's not like it was this big buddy-buddy secret thing, Mom." John went over and dropped onto the couch, propping his long legs up on the coffee table. She stood there in the kitchen staring at him, waiting for him to tell her. Either he'd tell her or she'd start screaming until the windows shattered and her voice quit. He looked at her and sighed again. "He was never particularly welcoming of me once I started living and working in California. I thought it was kind of strange but I was busy with work and stuff, trying to get settled and established. And his California office was a good three-hour drive from me. It wasn't like we could get together for dinner every night ...

"I had a long weekend. Must have been Memorial Weekend or something and I decided to drive down and surprise him. I knew I had the office address and his cell phone number." He took a long drink from his scotch. "I drove down on a Saturday morning and figured I'd go to the office, see if Dad was there and surprise him. Otherwise I'd call him on his cell phone. He was always easy to get a hold of, wasn't he?"

Bee didn't need to nod because he wasn't even looking at her. Yes, he was always easy to get in touch with on his cell phone. That was part of his gift of deception. John was lost in the remembrance. "There was an office picnic going on when I arrived. Balloons and a deejay. Loads of people walking around and laughing. Kids running around and screaming and yelling. I parked my car and went wandering around looking for him. When I finally spotted him, Dad was standing there, relaxed and casual with his arm around a woman. He saw me walking toward him and it was the way he slowly took his arm off of the woman's shoulder and looked at me that made me realize that something was very, *very* wrong. I stopped finally and looked at the both of them trying to process in my head what I was seeing, what it *looked like*, what I didn't want to understand.

"I just stood there looking at him like an idiot. He finally said, 'John,' and nodded his head to me. The woman looked puzzled, not understanding why these two men were just standing there staring at each other. She finally extended her hand and said, 'Hello, my name is Sarah Lawson. I don't think we've met.' That's when I realized that it was worse than I ever could have imagined." John stopped talking to take another sip of his drink. His glass was empty.

Bee found her voice and said quietly. "And it was worse than even that ..."

John looked at her and his eyes filled with tears. "As we stood there, still silent with each other, a boy came running over. 'Dad,' he said, 'are you going to come play catch *now?*'" Bee watched John impatiently brush a tear off his face. His motions are angry.

"What did you do?" she asked in a voice that was a strained whisper.

John took his big, long legs off the coffee table and put his empty glass down. He leaned forward on his legs and stared down at his feet. "I just turned and walked away. What could I do? My head felt like it was going to explode. I got in my car and drove the three hours back to my apartment." He looked at her then. "Dad never said a word to me that day except, 'John'.

"Dad called me a few days later. I hung up on him. I did my best to avoid him as best as I could after that. I'd find out what holidays he was going to make it home for and manage to miss those and come to the alternate ones. We saw each other only once after that day, at Grandma's funeral. And we never spoke." John sighed a great sigh and scrubbed his face with his hands and rested his head on the back of the couch with his eyes closed.

She searched her memory for her mother's funeral. It had been such a hard time for her that everything was just a vague memory on the periphery of her mind. It was a precursor to the numbness, she realized. She had no clear recollection of the time except to know that everyone, including Jonathan and the three kids, had come to the house after the service and that her mother's church had done a wonderful job of catering it all. She'd done absolutely nothing significant – that she could recall, anyway – but just stand there and try not to get hysterical.

Bee started. "That's why you didn't want to say anything at his funeral."

John looked at her. "Just what could I have said? It was better to say nothing. Grace wanted to say something. Todd wanted to say something. I said I'd sit with you and keep you company and no one thought twice about it. It was easier that way.

"Should I have told you, Mom?" The sorrow and the uncertainty in his voice just about did her in. "Would it have been better or worse?" John looked at her and his eyes told her he needed to know the truth.

The tears started for her then. Just quiet trickles down her cheeks that eventually dripped off her chin. It was like she'd sprung a leak and couldn't find where to stop the flow. Would she have rather known sooner? Would it have been better to have known a full two years before Jonathan died and rather than being oblivious been given the opportunity to be righteously indignant? Would the chance to tell Jonathan to his face of her fury and her hatred helped her any more or less? Would the motions of a divorce and the messiness of dragging John and Grace and Todd into the middle, forcing them to choose sides made her pain and misery any more tolerable? The answer was a resounding *no*. It just would have started the sorrow that much sooner and dragged it out that much longer.

Bee walked over to John and sat next to him on the couch. She leaned against him and put her head on his shoulder. "I'm sorry you have had to carry this secret with you all of this time, John." Still the tears trickled down her face but they had a healing effect for they were not out of anger, just a quiet sorrow. John's breath caught and his shoulders shook and she knew he was crying now, too. Wrapping her arms around him, Bee kissed his neck and smoothed the tears away from his cheeks. "Your decision protected me and kept all of the burden on you. Thank you, for you spared me two more years of additional sorrow and pain."

He put his big head on her shoulder and they sat like that for a long time. Finally he let out a shaky breath and said, "Thanks for saying that."

It was a monumental moment for her. She'd comforted *someone.* Another wave of feeling *good* washed over her from head to toe. Wow, twice in two days. That made her think of her list nailed to the wall in the living room. "So, do you like my list?" she finally asked him.

John snorted a quick laugh. "Remember how Dad used to hate to make marks on the walls? We'd always catch such hell if we so much as put one tack in the wall to hang up a poster. He'd go berserk. It's highly ironic that not only have you *nailed the list to the wall with a three inch nail,* but that it says 'my husband was a lying, cheating bastard'." He laughed out loud then. "*Nice touch, Mom.*" He reached his big hand up and patted her gently on the cheek. Then spontaneously he pulled her to him and kissed her in the same spot with a big, loud smack.

Bee smiled and all of a sudden could hear Todd saying, '*Nice toenails, Ma.*' She plunked her feet, absent of her shoes, on the coffee table and wiggled her toes. "What do you think of my pedicure?"

Well-behaved women rarely make history.[6]

The Wise Woman's Actions

Her life was different after John went back home. She couldn't explain exactly why or exactly how, but it was different. She felt lighter, freer. Not perfect, just better. Like being tied up for a very long time and finally finding out that one of the ropes was *loose* and you knew that with patience and a lot of effort you'd be completely untied *soon*.

Saturday evening, she sat with Peter Gannon's business card in her hand by the phone but she couldn't do it. Hell, she had *never* done it, how could she possibly start now? She put the card carefully by the phone almost as if to prove that *at least she'd gotten that far*.

"My great-aunt Patti's favorite Bible story is the one I'm about to tell you about," Pastor Duncan began on Sunday morning. Bee had arrived just a few minutes early and settled herself in 'her' pew. She saw no sign of Peter Gannon and she was relieved. "I called today's sermon 'The Wise Woman's Actions' and, once again, by the end of this time together, I hope that you, too, will be able to put her lesson into use in your own life." He looked pointedly at everyone. "Whether you're a man *or* a woman."

He looked up at the congregation. "How many of you have heard of the Wise Woman of Abel?" No one raised a hand. "Thought so," he said almost to himself. Then he grinned. "Good! Then you'll be a captive, *interested* audience.

"We're back in King David's time, during the later part of his rule. He'd already slain Goliath, made his *big* mistake with Bathsheba, and dealt with the treachery and betrayal of his son, Absalom. Our story revolves around a man named Sheba, from the tribe of Benjamin who had incited the men of Israel to revolt against David. David had sent his most powerful and brutal military commander, Joab, along with an elite force of men to capture this trouble maker.

"Sheba had traveled across Israel to the city of Abel, where he was actively mobilizing his own clan against David. Joab and his men surrounded the city walls and began to make plans to destroy the entire city." Pastor Duncan looked at the congregation and said in a firm, decisive voice. "It was only a matter of time before the city walls were demolished and the entire city would be annihilated. All because of *one man*."

He did what he liked to do when he preached. He walked out from behind the pulpit out to the center of the altar. "What would you do if you were a citizen of the city of Abel? What would you be thinking? Planning?

"Women at this time in history were *not* in positions of leadership. That was not their role in society. They were wives and mothers and their duties extended only within the sphere that surrounded both of those positions. And yet, there *were* a very few exceptions to this rule recorded in the Bible. And the city of Abel had one of those exceptions."

Pastor Duncan picked up his Bible and read, "When Joab's forces arrived, they attacked Abel and built a ramp against the city wall and began battering it down. *But a wise woman in the city called out to Joab,* 'Listen to me, Joab. Come over here so I can talk to you.'"

Pastor Duncan looked up at the congregation and frowned. "*Where were the men?* Were they hiding? Were they busy? Why was this woman allowed to approach this infamous, powerful, military general? And here's an even better question: *Why did Joab listen to her?*

"Because he *does* listen to her. Joab approached this woman and they talked. She was quite direct with him, which I think was one of the things my Great-Aunt Patti liked so much about her. She said to him, 'Listen carefully to me. Why are you destroying this peace loving, faithful, loyal city? This is a city that *belongs to the Lord*.'

"Joab was a man who had acted in his own best interest his entire career. He was *directly responsible* for at least *three* brutal murders specifically to advance his own purposes. He was no push-over. He was one of those types of people that operated with his own agenda to suit his own purposes. And yet the Bible records a stunning conversation between him and this wise woman. They *conversed*. He *explained* himself to her. This man, who in one battle alone was responsible for the killing of *twelve thousand Edomites*, carried on a civil conversation as if they were sitting at a sidewalk café trying to settle a scheduling problem."

Pastor Duncan chuckled, almost to himself and walked back behind the pulpit. "I tell you these things about Joab so that you can truly appreciate this magnificent woman. Do you know that the Bible doesn't even bother to give us her name ..." He shrugged his shoulders. "The Bible also doesn't tell us where the men were or why she was apparently in charge of this fortified, well-thought-of city.

"Joab said, 'Hand over Sheba and we'll leave the city in peace.' Talk about decisive. Talk about in control. Talk about knowing what was best for herself and all that was precious to her." Pastor Duncan grinned at the congregation. "She said to Joab, 'Okay, we'll throw his head over the wall.'" Pastor Duncan read again from his Bible, "Then the woman went to the people with her wise advice, and they cut off Sheba's head and threw it out to Joab." Looking up at the congregation, Pastor Duncan smiled and said, "And Joab picked up the head and the army left.

"Now, there may be some of you sitting out there all quiet like in your pew thinking that there are a few people that you'd like to ..." He hesitated, smiled and waggled his eyebrows while he made a cutting motion across his throat. The congregation laughed. "That's *not* the lesson I want you to take away today. *Can* you see the lesson in this for you?" He walked out in front of the altar. Pastor Duncan stood with his arms crossed in front of him. "Take a minute and think."

After a few moments he said, "I'll ask you a question to help you, in case you are struggling. Is there something within your life *right now* that is keeping you from being the happy, productive, willing Christian man or woman that God wants you to be? Because that was this wise woman's powerful argument with Joab. Remember, she said to him, '*Why are you destroying this peace loving, faithful, loyal city? This is a city that belongs to the Lord.*' Her argument, her fury was that this military man dared to try to destroy a city *that belonged to the Lord.*"

He stepped down off the altar, onto the floor of the congregation. "Do you belong to the Lord? Have you given Him your life? Is it your desire to be loving, faithful, and loyal? If your answer is yes, then here is the story's lesson for you: what do you have within the walls of your own life that you are allowing to remain that is slowly destroying you? What is preventing you from being all the man or woman that God would wish you to be? There are many things: consuming worries, passionate hates, righteous angers, greedy desires." Pastor Duncan shook his head sadly. "Oh yes, there are *so many*.

"How wise are you? Do you have the courage and decisiveness to identify the problem and take control? Can you hurl this destructive force over the walls of your life so that you can go peacefully back to your home and continue in the path that the Lord would have you go? *Can you?* That's the lesson. It's a huge one that applies to every man and woman in this room. *Everyone.*" He walked back up the steps and stood behind the pulpit once again.

"My Great Aunt Patti loved the whole head being hurled over the wall thing." He smiled. "She was a decisive, take charge kind of lady. I have to tell you that I honestly haven't spoken with her about my interpretation of the lesson in this story." He shrugged his shoulders. "I don't know if she'd agree or disagree, but I do know that she loved the Lord with all her heart. I'd call her a loyal, faithful woman of God. She had some mighty hard times in her life, some that came close to destroying her but she survived. I'd go far enough to even call her victorious. Great

Aunt Pattie took that head and hurled it over the wall of her life rather than let it destroy her and continued on."

He dropped his voice down to a conspiratorial whisper and Bee felt almost as if he was speaking quietly just to her. "I'm going to let you in on a secret. This week, I'm going to pray that God will do one of two things for you. He will either help you see what thing in your life is keeping you from going in the direction in which He wants you to go *or* that He will give you the courage and the strength to face this thing and hurl it far away from the walls of your life. I want you to be free, peaceful, loyal, and faithful to God. For if you can achieve that, then the most glorious freedom awaits you. *And you will become unstoppable.*"

At the receiving line, Pastor Duncan gave her a tentative smile. "Good to see you, Mrs. Lawson."

"If I didn't know better, I'd be *positive* that you preached that sermon just for me," Bee said to him in a voice purposely firm and edged with hostility.

His expression faltered. "As I told you -"

Bee interrupted him by gifting him with a smile that stunned him to silence. "But I know better. I know better than to think you'd preach just specifically to me *and* to tell you I thought so because otherwise you'd be at my doorstep again tomorrow morning."

Bee saw him relax and quickly process that she apparently had been teasing him. While Pastor Duncan still worked to collect his thoughts and composure she thrust out her hand, smiled once more and said, "Good job." Then she breezed out the door.

She stopped at the food store on the way home and bought some things. It was the first time she'd been there in probably a year. The online service had met her basic needs and she really could have cared less if there were certain things that she had to do without because they weren't available. She wandered around the aisles, not looking for anything in particular but feeling good to be with people and yet safe that there was little conversation or interaction involved. She bought a bouquet of flowers, a package of scones and two chocolate frosted donuts. She drove home with the top down eating one of the two donuts and enjoyed feeling good again.

She read the list nailed over the fireplace eating the second donut. She heard John's voice filled with wry humor, *Nice touch, Mom.*

Bee's eyes read her handwriting, *My husband was a lying, cheating bastard.*

She saw Todd yelling through the window of his car, *Nice toenails, Ma.*

She said out loud, "My husband was a lying, cheating bastard."

She heard Alita saying, *Mrs. Bee, don't let the tail wag the dog.*

She screamed as loud as she could, "MY HUSBAND WAS A LYING, CHEATING BASTARD."

She heard her own voice saying to Alita, *He encouraged me to do things I didn't always think I could do. He called me "Busy Bee" and I always thought he said it with pride.*

She saw Grace's face looking at her filled with concern and love, *You always seem so capable to me, Mother. You seem to just take a moment, think, process, and react. I've always wished I had that ability …*

She read her list again. Twelve things. The realization hit her that she could probably double the list if she put just a little bit of effort into it. She walked over to the picture window and looked out the front window and sighed. "Time to hurl my anger over the wall," Bee said out loud to the view.

The picture that had been over the fireplace was still propped behind the couch where she'd left it. It really was an ugly picture. She'd hurl that over the wall with her anger. *Oh yeah, that would feel great.* She looked around the room and saw it for the first time in a long time – if ever. She walked over to the shelf of knickknacks and realized that she had no idea what most of the things were. She picked up one shell, mounted on a piece of driftwood. When she looked underneath it said 'Carlsbad, California, 1998'. She'd never been to Carlsbad, California. Neither had the kids. But Jonathan had. She dropped it like it had burned her and the shell broke into a million bits. She went stomping into the kitchen, found a garbage bag and went back into the living room. She cleared off the shelf in two seconds flat. Then took the shelf off the wall, too. Down came all the pictures that were hanging on the rest of the walls, too. They were all pictures of places that she had never been to and never wanted to go to.

By then, Bee was on a roll. She went around the house with garbage bag after garbage bag filling them with things she no longer wanted in her house. *Her* house. She would make sure it was her house and no one else's. With each bag that 'thunked' down the stairs she felt a little bit better. Well, it seemed that she'd be hurling a heck of a lot of stuff over her wall. Just watch and see. One bag for each good thing on her list. Okay, *two* bags for each good thing on her list. Heck, she'd have to call for an additional garbage pick up.

When Bee fell into bed that night in the early morning hours she felt more alive than she had in almost two years. She felt peaceful. Quiet. Not happy. Not wonderful. Just so much better. Not numb. Just okay. As she drifted off to sleep, she whispered a small prayer. "Thank you for my list. Please, help me to not loose this good feeling ... Amen."

Monday morning Bee sat by the phone with Peter's card in her hand, *again*. She had purposely waited until she was sure he'd have left for work so she would just be talking to his answering machine. She practiced aloud some casual, what she hoped to be light, clever things to say into the machine. They all sounded ridiculous when she spoke them. She decided she'd just leave her name and phone number and tell him if he was interested she'd like him to call her. No fuss. No frills.

On the second ring Peter picked up his phone. She was stunned into silence thinking, *how dare he answer his own phone in the middle of the day.*

"What are you doing home answering the phone in the middle of the day?" Bee blurted out and then covered her face with her free hand, mortified with herself.

He chuckled. "Sorry, I'll hang up."

That made her smile. She sighed. "Hi Peter, it's Bee."

"Guessed that. I'm sharp."

There was a moment of awkward silence. *Come on, girl.* The voice in her head urged her. *You can do this.* "I didn't see you in church yesterday."

"No, I had to work. It doesn't happen often thank goodness." Bee sensed that he took a little pity on her and decided to help her with the casual conversation. "How's the car?" She could hear the laughter in his voice.

"Good, good. I actually drove around yesterday with the top down. I have to admit it was glorious."

"I didn't think you were going to call me."

"I didn't think I was either. If it makes you feel any better, your card's been by my phone for a while. It did make it that far."

"I was trying to decide what my next plan of attack would be."

That brought her up short. "You mean you would have still tried to see me?"

"Oh sure. I'm rather tenacious when I set my mind to something."

"And I'm rather stubborn and hard headed."

"I love a challenge."

"Do you think that you could keep this casual conversation going over the course of an entire meal? I'm not certain I could, so I need to let you know what you're getting yourself into."

Peter's laughter filled her ear and she smiled again all by herself in the quiet of her own house. She propped her feet up on the mountain of garbage bags littering her living room. She liked this banter back and forth and waited to hear his flip answer. "Yes, I think I could manage that. But you must promise me that you'll at least make the effort to help, no matter how painful and difficult it may be for you."

"Okay."

"Shall I pick you up?"

She looked around the room; twenty-seven garbage bags and a list that said 'My husband was a lying, cheating bastard' nailed to the wall with a three inch nail ... "NO," she said a little too hastily. "You love my car. I'll come pick you up and impress your neighbors. Or I could meet you."

"You can pick me up. Do you have a restaurant in mind?"

Bee was silent. "My mind is stunned into blankness."

Peter laughed again. "You're the one calling *me*. *You're* supposed to plan the night. I think that's how it works."

"I wouldn't know. I've never done this before in my entire life."

She could hear the smile in his voice again. "Okay, you do the driving, I'll do the planning this time."

This time. It caused her to panic. *This time* implied there would be other times. She felt the good feelings and slight bit of confidence slip like water through her fingers. Her victory had been in emerging from her numbness and remaining there long enough to have made the phone call and carry it through to the end. Not in forming some relationship that would only lead to disaster and pain and *God knows what else.*

"Bee? Are you there?"

"Yes, yes, I'm here."

"I asked what night was good for you this week."

What a joke. *Let me check my calendar.* "What night is good for you?"

"Wednesday and Friday are best, but I could manage Tuesday."

"Let's do Friday."

"Friday it is." Peter proceeded to give her directions to his place and they agreed on a time.

"See you Friday, Bee. Have a good week."

"You too, Peter."

She hung up the phone and buried her face in her hands. *What had she done?* What had possessed her to make that call? The good feelings and the confidences were gone. One simple phrase, *this time*, had opened all the flood gates of insecurity and disaster that she had thought she had managed to contain. She calmed herself with the thought that perhaps she'd get sick, or he'd get sick or the world would end ... Why there were multiple possibilities.

Thursday the garbage men took away her twenty-seven bags of garbage and brought Alita. She wandered around the living room noting the absence of knick-knacks, book shelves and pictures and then carefully read the list hammered over the fireplace. "I like what you've done with the place, Mrs. Bee," she said finally.

The numbness had kept her company all week. Plus the insecurities and nervousness about Friday night. It had not been a good week. She just stood there staring at Alita wearing the same nightgown that she had been in for the past three days and nights. She could smell herself. She hadn't showered in three days – at least – either.

Alita walked over to Bee and touched her cheek with one cool finger. "It has been a bad week, Mrs. Bee?" she asked carefully searching Bee's eyes for any sign of life she supposed.

"I have a date tomorrow," Bee finally said and watched carefully for Alita's reaction to the news.

Alita never missed a beat. "Well it's about time."

"I can't do it."

Alita waved her hand impatiently. "Don't speak nonsense. What is a date? It is a few moments spent eating some food or watching a movie. It passes the time." Alita looked around her and then back at Bee. "It is nothing that you don't do every day. On your date you just do it at the same time as someone else you choose to be with." Alita began her preparations to clean, humming under her breath and walked into the kitchen and got things out of the broom closet. Bee followed her. Alita looked at her. "I will give you one big tip that would be sure to help the evening go better."

Bee had a flash of hope. Of course, Alita would have wonderful instructions to help her make it through the night. "What?" she asked eagerly when Alita seemed not inclined to continue.

Looking Bee up and down, Alita said, "If you don't plan on showering or changing your nightgown by tomorrow night, go to a dark bar that allows cigar smoking." Alita looked at her pointedly, rolled her eyes and began to dust.

Bee couldn't help it, she smiled. Just a bit. "You liked my decorating attempts. Why not my look?"

"The decorating is *new*. The look is *old*."

"I can't do it," Bee said again just to remind herself and convince Alita.

"Who is this man?"

"Someone who I met at church."

"He is kind?"

"He seems so."

"He is patient?"

"Yes, definitely."

"He is handsome?"

"He's nice looking, yes."

"Marry him."

"Alita!"

Alita started laughing at her then. "I think you are waking up, Mrs. Bee. Go take a shower. I will make us both some tea." She started singing as she filled the kettle.

Bee stood in the shower for a long time, letting the water pelt down on her. She imagined the numbness washing away down the drain. She thought of her list and realized that she had not read it since Monday morning. "I promise I will read The List every day," she said aloud to herself.

Alita had the tea made and had toasted two English muffins for them. They both sat at the kitchen counter.

"Mrs. Bee, you don't have any trouble talking with me. When you go and see this handsome, kind, patient man tomorrow, pretend you are talking to me. I am beautiful and kind and patient. It shouldn't be a far stretch." Alita's eyes twinkled with mischief.

"He said 'this time', like there would be other times we would get together. I can't make it through a phone call. How will I make it through an entire evening, let alone other times?"

Alita shrugged her shoulders. "Do you worry about that when you talk with me and know that I will be here come hell or highest water in two weeks?"

Bee smiled at the ridiculousness of the question. "No, of course not."

"Why?"

"Well, I ..." Bee thought. "Because it's *you*. I know you. You know me. You don't expect me to be dazzling or witty or beautiful."

"Oh. So he has seen you dazzling and witty and beautiful already and you are afraid you cannot keep it up."

Hardly. "No, that's not what I mean. He certainly hasn't seen me dazzling and witty and beautiful."

"Then why has he spoken with you?"

"I haven't the foggiest idea."

"No? He's not said anything to you about what he liked about you?"

"He liked my car."

Alita frowned. "Mrs. Bee ..."

Bee sighed. "He said that I was hard not to notice."

"Was he over this morning then?"

Bee started to spit out a negative response and then caught the twinkle in Alita's eyes. She had a brief chuckle. "No, thank God."

"Why did he say you were hard not to notice?"

"I don't remember," she mumbled.

"I think you do. What did he say?" Alita persisted.

Bee remembered his words and was stunned to feel herself blushing. "He said I was lovely to look at, that I had a regal presence, and I 'exuded confidence.' She looked at Alita. "He said he's watched me coming and going in church and that I had a beautiful reading voice."

"Hmmm," Alita said after a moment of thought. "Do you think this man has a brother?"

Bee frowned. "Why would you ... oh ..." and she laughed out loud.

"Did you do anything to make him think these things? Have you had your eye on him hoping to catch his notice?"

"NO!" Bee exploded out. It was the most ridiculous thing to ask.

Alita shrugged. "So, you must be doing something right *without even thinking about it.* This man liked what he saw without you making any effort. Isn't that the easiest and best way?" Alita reached over and patted Bee's hand then stood up to resume cleaning. "Go to dinner with him, Mrs. Bee. Have a fun evening. Be yourself. If he hates you, fine. If he likes you, fine. While he is checking out you, you be checking out him. That's the way it works." She looked pointedly at her. "*You* might not think much of *him* after one dinner. One night out does not mean you are married. It means one night out."

Bee was supposed to pick Peter up at 7:00 p.m. She started getting reading at noon. She stood in her closet throwing things over her shoulder making new piles for more garbage bags. Too old. Too frilly. Too Jonathan. Too tight. Too loose.

The phone rang and Bee answered it still in her underwear. It was 3:00 p.m. Good God, she'd been at this for three hours already.

"Hello, Mom."

"Oh, hi Grace. How are you?"

"I'm fine. I just got home from work. You were on my mind today so I thought I'd give you a call. Would you like to come over for dinner tonight?"

Bee felt ashamed. She should be the one calling sometimes, not always the other way around. "Are you sitting down?" she said.

She heard the hesitancy in Grace's voice. "Yes …"

"I have a date."

"*A date?*"

"Yup, a date. And I've been standing in my underwear for three hours going through the things in my closet. I'm starting to get hysterical."

"Hmmm. How about that white blouse I got you for Christmas? Do you remember it?"

Bee padded over to the closet and searched through the racks. "Oh, here it is," she said. "Don't you think this is a little too young?"

"Well, no. I wouldn't have bought it for you if I'd thought that." Grace sounded hurt.

"What would I wear with it?"

"Do you have a pair of black slacks?"

"Yes."

"There you go. Who's the guy?"

"Someone I met at church."

"I thought you were becoming a heathen."

Bee smiled. "That was a few weeks ago. You've missed the belly dancer week and the Hindu week. I'm working on being the care-free swinging single this week."

"You have a good sense of humor, Mom. I've missed it. It's good to hear."

"I'm sorry, Grace."

"Why are you apologizing?"

"I haven't been much good to anyone lately and I know you've been worried."

"I love you, Mom. All I care about is that you know that and that you know I'm here if you need me. Okay?"

"Okay."

"Where are you going tonight?"

"No clue. He's planning, I'm driving."

"What's he like?"

"He seems nice. He's tall, wears glasses, and has a mustache. He said I've got a nice butt."

"Mother!"

"Still like my sense of humor?"

Bee could hear laughter on the other end of the phone. Finally, Grace asked, "Would you come to dinner on Sunday?" Grace had extended that invitation so many times and been rejected so many times that she'd almost stopped asking.

"I have good moments and bad days, Grace. Do you want to chance it?"

"Sounds like an improvement to me."

Bee nodded her head. "You're right, it is."

"Will you come?"

"Yes, I'll come."

"Zoe will be thrilled. I'll see you about 2?"

"2's great."

"Oh, and Mom?"

"What?"

"Ask questions tonight. I discovered it was a good way to keep the conversation going. If you think you need help with that, that is."

"How did you know?"

"I haven't been married *that* long. I remember that was the hardest part about a first date; keeping the conversation going. If you ask questions, it keeps him talking and the pressure's off you."

"I'll remember that."

She was twenty minutes late in the end because at the last moment her stomach was in such knots that she threw up. She had to brush her teeth again and fix her make up. To the white blouse and the black trousers she'd added repainted toenails (red again) and gold flip flop sandals. It was the best she could do.

Peter lived in a nice condominium community. He was standing outside when she pulled up, yanking weeds out of the border of his garden. He smiled and walked down the front lawn to her. She didn't know if she should get out of the car or not. *Great*, she thought, *indecisions already*.

"Give me a minute, I just want to run in and wash my hands." He held them up for her to see and they were covered with dirt.

"Okay."

When Peter came out she'd moved over to the passenger seat. He grinned. "I'm only spending time with you so I get to drive your car, you know."

"I figured as much."

"Italian, okay?"

"Sure." Bee had a wave of panic that it would be Max's restaurant, the one that was haunted with memories, but she realized they were headed in the opposite direction and relaxed.

"How was your week?" Peter asked her.

"Quiet. I did some rearranging in the house. Threw out some old stuff. It felt good." The enormity of what she was saying rose up behind her like a gigantic monster. She ignored it as best she could.

"I'll have to get you over to my place then. I battle pack rat tendencies regularly."

If only he knew. "How was your week?"

"Busy."

"Why were you home when I called you Monday?"

"I've got a home office. I spend about half my time there and half my time on site."

"Where do you work?"

"It's a company called CTW. I've only been there about three years. They had some things that I wanted and I had some things that they wanted. So far it's been a good match. That's what brought me to the east coast."

"Where were you before that?"

"Before I lived here in New Jersey, I was in Pennsylvania for a bit. Before that, for most of my life, California."

Bee gasped. Couldn't help it. Peter turned to her. "Is there something wrong with that?"

She managed a weak smile. "My son, John, lives out in California. Up near San Francisco."

"It's beautiful up there. How long has he been there? Who does he work for?"

She was amazed when they finally pulled up in front of the restaurant. Had they really talked casually the whole drive without her having to work at it? When he came around to open her door, she gave Peter a triumphant smile. *I lasted an entire car ride*, her head sang.

Bee realized that not only had she lasted the entire drive but that they'd driven quite a ways as well. It was a lovely restaurant with a wonderful atmosphere. He'd even made reservations. Their table was in a quiet little alcove with a fantastic view of the evening sky. She smiled at him with pleasure.

"You have a lovely smile," Peter said to her.

That made her self conscious and she didn't have a response.

"You're not used to compliments are you?" he said after a few minutes.

Bee sighed. "Truth be told, I'm not used to living much lately." She looked at him to judge how he'd take that honest admission.

Peter nodded almost with understanding she thought and that puzzled her. How could he understand?

"Were you ever married?" she asked suddenly.

"Yeah, I was married. I tried the divorce route as well just to make sure I got the whole experience." Peter tried to sound light about it but she all of a sudden *just knew*.

"You were hurt badly."

But Bee was wrong. Peter looked surprised. "No, *I* did the hurting. It's guilt you're seeing not pain."

She didn't know what to say but apparently her expression spoke volumes. Peter looked out the window and said in a tired voice. "I was a different man in my early years. Very driven, very focused. My priorities were screwed up. I was all work, work, and work. There was never time for children and eventually my wife got tired of the fact that there was never really any time for her as well. We divorced after twelve years of marriage."

Peter shrugged his shoulders. "You'd probably be horrified to know that initially when she brought up the idea of divorce I was relieved. I figured I could get on with what I knew had to be done and she could move on and stop being so miserable because of me and my failures in the husband department. But it didn't work out that way.

"She was just as unhappy without me as my ex-wife as she'd been married to me." Peter looked directly at her then. "If I'd taken the time to pay just a small bit of attention I would have realized that she was struggling with a lot more than just being unhappy with *me*. But I never did."

Peter looked out the window again and said quietly. "She killed herself two years after we divorced. Left me a long note explaining how I was responsible." He turned to Bee and smiled a sad smile at her. "It was very well written. Very detailed. She built an excellent case about my guilt. She was a lawyer you see."

He picked up the menu and made the motions to scan it. "I've been divorced for fifteen years." Glancing pointedly at Bee, Peter said,

"I've been *living* the past eight. I had some lost years in there while I sorted things out. I'm not done, but I'm close."

There were long moments of silence while Bee stared blankly at her menu and Peter stared impassively out the window. She wanted to take time and go off somewhere and ponder the fact that someone else could be so devastated with their life that they could get lost for a time just like she had. She glanced up at him and realized he had painted himself into quite a corner that was very hard to get out of. Where do you take the conversation from there? *Ask a lot of questions, Mother,* she heard Grace tell her.

"Do you like calamari?" Bee asked Peter.

He turned and looked at her, searching her face, she realized, for condemnation of some kind. Bee tried to just look hungry. Peter gave her a slow, quiet smile after a bit. "I *love* calamari," he finally said to her.

Peter was intrigued with the idea of her children. He asked lots of questions and she told lots of stories and they laughed over things she was able to remember. Indirectly it came out, Bee realized later, that a majority of her married life had been on her own with the kids. But he never asked specifics or whys and she was so glad of it. *Enough of dealing with scary ex-ghosts for one night,* her head said.

Peter insisted they decline dessert but they did have coffee – him - and tea – her - before they left. "I want to go someplace else for dessert, if that's okay."

They ended up sitting on a park bench under the late night sky eating ice cream cones and laughing at a family of Canadian geese. The geese were funny because the eight goslings were almost, but not quite, as large as their parents but still needed constant supervision and guidance. "Mine are *finally* out of that stage," Bee volunteered.

Still looking at the geese, Bee asked, "Have you always had a mustache?"

Peter seemed to think about it for a minute. "Just about. Grew one as soon as I could. Sometimes I do the beard thing, too. It's too hot in the summer though."

"I would imagine it would be prickly."

"I could kiss you and you could check it out."

Bee turned to smile at his joke but he was looking at her very seriously. "I've been wanting to kiss you for a while," he said.

Keep him talking, ask more questions, her panicked head screamed. "Since when?"

"Since you told me you were an embittered widow."

Bee snorted a loud, unladylike sound. "You did not."

Peter laughed out loud at her. "I certainly did. I thought, *now there's a challenge.*"

"I just barely started talking to people again. I'm definitely not ready for kissing," Bee said in absolute seriousness. She tried to sound firm and unbending, too.

Peter grinned at her. "You are fun to be with and talk with."

"Stick around, the real truth will soon make itself known."

"Now I am going to kiss you." And with that, he did. Right there on the bench, with their ice cream cones in their hands and the Canadian geese parents honking instructions to their wayward children.

It was a nice, firm kiss that just about made Bee's head explode. When was the last time she had kissed anyone? Even her children? She had no clue. She was conscious of his mustache – which *did* tickle – and the smell of his cologne and the way his hand reached around to the back of her head to hold her still. *It was nice.*

"You taste a little bit like garlic and a lot like chocolate." At Bee's furious blush of embarrassment Peter added with a grin, "It's a delicious combination."

"And that was your quota for the night. Don't get any other ideas," she said firmly and then popped the rest of her ice cream cone in her mouth while he laughed again out loud.

"We'll see ..." Peter said as he relaxed back against the park bench, stretched his long legs out in front of him and went back to his ice cream.

They walked the path of the park to work off dinner. "Can I sit by you in church?" Peter asked her after moments of comfortable silence.

Bee answered immediately, "No."

He looked at her. "Why not?"

"I don't know. It's too soon. People would talk. Sometimes I have crises in church ..."

"Crises ...?"

"It's a long story."

"I've got time."

"Not tonight you don't."

Peter sighed. "Okay, I won't sit by you. Can I look at you? Wave? Blow kisses?"

She laughed then. "Why did you speak to me in the first place?"

"I told you why."

"No really."

"You'll think it silly."

"I won't."

"Okay. God told me to."

"What?!"

"I told you you'd think it was silly."

"What do you mean 'God told you to'?!"

Peter sighed and put his hands in his pockets. "You read the scripture one Sunday. I was trying to pay attention but my mind was wandering." He looked at her, "I'm not one to sit still for long."

He shrugged. "You finished the reading, stepped down off of the altar and walked past me to take your seat. Clear as a bell in my head I thought, 'I think I'll ask her out for a cup of coffee.' As soon as I thought that, I felt such pressure to do just that!" Peter chuckled. "It was rather all consuming for a few moments. I sat there, so totally absorbed with the style and the technique and the logistics of the whole asking you out thing that I missed the whole sermon." He looked at Bee again. "And you cut out so quick I didn't even see you leave!

"It took me a good couple weeks to work up the courage to speak with you in the end, but I couldn't shake the need to do it. There have been a lot of things in my life lately that have happened that way. I've learned to trust my gut. For me, it's the way that God speaks to me."

"He talks to your stomach?"

When he turned to look at her Peter saw that she was teasing him and he relaxed. "Some people hear voices, some people dream dreams, some people have visions, and – this is the saddest I think – some people hear nothing. And me? I get indigestion." They both laughed.

They decided to call it a night. Bee drove home. Outside his place Peter sighed a big, deep, sorrowful sigh.

"What's wrong?" Bee asked concerned because she had thought it was a great evening.

"I've reached the limit of my quota," he said in a voice filled with regret.

It took Bee a minute to figure out what he was referring to as she stared at her hands holding the steering wheel. Then she remembered. When she looked over at him he was grinning and had leaned closer to her. "Do you think I could have an advance?"

"That's not wise financial planning."

"I wasn't talking about money." Peter kissed her again, and it was just as pleasant. It went on for a bit longer, too. When he finally pulled away, she reached up and touched his mustache with her finger.

"Should I cut if off?"

"NO!" Bee all but shouted. "Why would you do such a thing?"

"You seem a little bit too preoccupied with my mustache. I'd rather have you preoccupied with my kiss."

"It's all part of the package, I think."

"Hmmm," Peter said and he reached up and put his big warm hand against her cheek. "Thanks for asking me out to dinner."

"Thanks for being tenacious."

"It's all part of the package, I think." He got out of the car and walked up the lawn. Bee waited until he had the front door open and he'd given her a brief wave.

May those who love you be like the sun when it rises in its strength.⁷

The Fiery Woman's Faith

Peter didn't sit by Bee in church but she was completely conscious of him nonetheless. He did smile at her and sit two pews ahead of her. He couldn't sit behind her because she continued to sit in 'her' pew in the very back. He looked back at her briefly, once and arched an eyebrow as if to say, 'Is this far enough away?'

She gave him a brief smile and he seemed satisfied.

"Today's my last 'Woman of the Bible' sermon," Pastor Duncan began. He immediately held up his hands in a placating gesture. "Now, now, don't all look so upset." Everyone laughed. "Just so you know that I'm an equal opportunity pastor, I plan on doing a few sermons on some Men of the Bible. See if we can turn the tables a bit. Stay tuned."

He readied himself behind the pulpit, shuffling his notes. "The person I'm going to speak to you about today was a poet, a prophet, a judge, and a warrior." He nodded his head. "Yup, this person went to battle and led troops. In fact, the plan of attack was by this person's direction. And yes, this person was a woman.

"It's a stunning story. 13th century *B.C.* A time when the Israelites *didn't even have the capability of metallurgy.* They were so enslaved by their enemies that there was no trade, no travel, not even any farming. Things were really in a sorry state. Israel had no king at this time, either. It was a time of a lot of chaos, with the twelve tribes running around trying to survive each in its own style.

"Back in those days, there were no Bibles to refer to. No learned scholars to give advice. The way God worked things was when the time was right He'd speak to a specific person and tell him His thoughts and intentions. Then this person would relay God's words to the people and the people would then recognize this person to be a Prophet of God. In addition, God sometimes called up a specific person to act as a judge for the people. A judge specifically heard problems and complaints from the people and with God's guidance passed decisions and solutions on to them."

Pastor Duncan held up his Bible. "In this entire book we can count the number of women prophets on one hand. We can count the number of female judges with just one finger. The person we're going to talk about today was a truly remarkable woman because she was *both of these things.* Yes, she was a prophet and yes, she was the only female judge Israel ever had."

Bee found her mind beginning to wander and the tension beginning to slide out of her. *At last,* her head said to her, *a sermon that doesn't specifically talk to you.* Because Lord knew she *wasn't* powerful and she didn't have an ounce of leadership capabilities *or* desires.

"Prophet, judge, warrior, poet, wife … The Bible gives no record that she had children, but it does tell us that she called herself a 'Mother of Israel'. Who was this amazing woman? Her name was Deborah."

Bee looked up then at Pastor Duncan certain he would be looking right at her but he wasn't. Her gaze stayed riveted to him, waiting for him to glance her way. Pastor Duncan looked at his notes. "Once again, there are a lot of unanswered questions. There are even some commentators who question whether Deborah truly was even married. Apparently, the name of her husband – Lappidoth – means "fiery one" and some scholars believe that a better translation simply was that her name was Deborah, The Fiery One."

Pastor Duncan chuckled. "It's a great story. If you read it, you'll be in complete agreement that she be called 'The Fiery One.' Deborah called her general – his name was Barak – and told him to gather all the troops in Israel that he could. She told him that the Lord commanded that they must attack the city of Hazor which was led by the military commander named Sisera.

"Poor Barak. Being ordered around by a woman. Being told to attack the mighty city of Hazor that had no less than *nine hundred iron chariots* when he knew that Israel didn't even have *one piece of metal* in the entire nation! I'm sure he knew how scattered and unpredictable all the tribes were, too. As it was, not all of them showed up for the battle once they were called.

"Do you know what he said to Deborah? Barak said – and I quote," here Pastor Duncan picked up his Bible to read, "'If you go with me, I will go; but if you don't go with me, I won't go.'" Pastor Duncan looked at his congregation. "Are you getting the picture here? Guess what that fiery woman said ...?"

He looked down again at his Bible. "Deborah said, 'Very well, I will go with you. But because of the way you are going about his, the honor will not be yours, for the Lord will hand Sisera over to a woman.'" Pastor Duncan looked at the congregation and then walked out to stand in the middle of the altar. "What do you think? Did this woman have fire?" Bee saw people nodding their heads.

Pastor Duncan continued his account of the story. "The battle was a stunning success. Every soldier from Hazor, including the commanding general, Sisera, was killed. What I like to point out was that Deborah's prediction, about the honor of the battle being given to a woman does *not* refer to her. She spoke of another woman named Jael who was the one who killed Sisera."

Pastor Duncan stepped down from the altar into the congregation. "Okay, how many of you have some enemies you need to destroy? No?

How many of you are preparing to head off into battle? No? Oh, well then," he shut his Bible, "let's just go home."

He walked up the steps and turned around. "*Not.*" Everyone laughed. "Let me ask you this question: What was Deborah's strongest quality? What was it that gave her the power she had that overcame all the obstacles that she faced being a woman, being part of a subjugated nation …?" He waited and everyone was silent. "Come on," Pastor Duncan said to the audience, "someone have the guts to call something out."

"Her faith," Bee heard someone say and she knew without a doubt that it was Peter.

"Exactly," Pastor Duncan nodded. "It was her faith. A powerful, all consuming, righteous, inspirational faith. God spoke to her and she listened. It was as simple as that."

He looked out at the congregation. "Does God talk to you?" Pastor Duncan waited a moment and Bee heard Peter saying, '*I've learned to trust my gut. For me, it's the way that God speaks to me.*" And then she heard him saying, '*The saddest, I think – some people hear nothing*'.

Pastor Duncan said, "He does, you know. I guess it would be better instead to ask you, do you *hear* God talking to you? That's the million-dollar question. It all hinges on your faith. The stronger your faith, the louder God talks to you."

Pastor Duncan walked up to the pulpit. "Deborah was a magnificent woman because of her faith. Not because of any other reason. Her faith was so real, so strong, that she accomplished things *no other woman in Biblical history was able to do*." He looked out at the congregation and said earnestly, "There are still opportunities for *you*. *Today*. *Now*. It is a conscious choice we make to listen and follow or ignore and stumble. If you haven't made that choice, then I encourage you to do so. I encourage you to become a Deborah and lead a glorious life that is guided by your rock solid faith. It is each and every person's guarantee for success."

Pastor Duncan closed with prayer, the final hymn was sung and the benediction was given. Bee thought, but she was not positive in retrospect, that she stood and sat as the congregation moved but she wasn't exactly sure. As the people began to file out she stayed seated, unwilling and unable to move.

"Waiting for me?"

She recognized Peter's cologne and his hands even though she didn't look up at his face. She shook her head "no", not trusting her voice.

"Are you okay?" She could hear the concern in his voice and knew she'd have to speak then.

"Remember I told you that sometimes I have a crisis in church?" Bee spoke softly.

"Yes."

"I've just had one."

Concern edged Peter's voice. "Oh. What can I do?"

"Nothing, it's my own personal crisis, I don't want to share it."

He chuckled then and she looked up at him. "Is it a good crisis or a bad crisis then?" Peter asked when their eyes met.

What a ridiculous question Bee thought at first. She took a deep breath, inhaling the smell of him as he studied her intently. After a moment, though, she realized it really was a good question. "I guess, since you've made me think of it that way, that it is a good crisis."

He nodded. "Okay, then. Do you want me to send Pastor Duncan over to you?"

"Oh, he'll show up. I'm just going to sit here until he does."

"So you want me to go?"

Looking at him, Bee nodded slowly. "Just so I can have my own private time with this *good* crisis."

Peter reached over and touched her hand for a moment. "You know I'd stay if you asked me, right?" She gave him a weak smile, nodded 'yes', but stayed pointedly silent. And then he was gone.

She just sat there. Swirling around thoughts in her head. She took the time to look up the Biblical story of Deborah in the Bible, it took her a while to find the book of Judges. She finally, in frustration looked in the Table of Contents. Bee hadn't quite gotten finished with the full story when she felt Pastor Duncan sit next to her.

"I did it again, huh?"

"Big time."

"Wow."

"What's my name, Pastor Duncan?"

Bee felt him tense, uncertain where she was headed. She didn't look at him but instead stared straight ahead. "Your name is Bea Lawson."

"When I married Jonathan he used to tease me and call me 'Busy Bee' because I was always running around the house cleaning, cooking, decorating. I was like a whirling dervish it seemed. We laughed about it. He started calling me 'Bee' as a nickname." She looked at him then. "Especially after I got pregnant with John and in looking through the baby name books we discovered that the meaning of my real name was 'honey bee'."

Even Pastor Duncan looked stunned; he paled visibly and swallowed. "Your real name is Deborah," he finally said in amazed wonder.

Bee nodded and looked down at her hands. "Yes, my name is Deborah Lawson. I don't even think my children know that. It just got lost in my life."

"Deborah. It suits you, you know." Pastor Duncan extended his hand to her. "How do you do, Deborah Lawson? It is a *tremendous pleasure* to know you."

She started to cry then. Great gulping sobs that just poured out of her. He put his arm around her and they sat like that for quite a while. "God has great plans for you, Deborah. You know that now, don't you."

Bee sniffled and searched in her purse for a tissue in which she blew her nose very loudly. "It doesn't seem as if I have much choice," she finally said.

He laughed. "Oh, there are always choices. Whether you realize it or not, you've been making them all along, too."

She looked at him, stunned.

Pastor Duncan smiled at her. "You made the choice to continue to come to church, didn't you?"

She nodded, slowly.

"You did that despite great opposition, ... *Deborah*. A person of lesser faith would have let that be the first thing they packed in. But for you, it was the very last thing you had left to hold onto when things were going so badly. You maybe don't realize it but it is a tremendous spiritual statement. You think people still seek you out because of pity and obligation and a sense of decency, and yet the truth is that people are drawn to you because of the faith you have."

She sniffled, blew, and shook her head "no".

"Oh yes, Deborah. You have shown great faith your entire life, whether you realized it or not. Who got those three children to church each Sunday, even when Jonathan was traveling? Who still did Sunday School teaching and Vacation Bible School volunteering, and youth group activities and goodness knows what other things all the while she was holding down a home and being both mother *and father* half the time to those children? Do you know how many people fall away from the church when something bad happens to them? Do you? There are statistics I could bore you with but I won't. It's a huge percentage. People are quick to get the attitude of 'How could God do this to me after all I've done for Him?' You not only lost your husband - suddenly, but discovered after the fact a terrible secret that a woman of lesser faith would have been totally destroyed by."

Pastor Duncan waited patiently until she finally looked at him. "Being a Woman of Faith does *not* mean that you are unaffected by the harsh realities of life. It means, that when the harsh realities batter you down, you know that you have a secret weapon that is unbeatable. You hunker down, batten down the hatches, and ride out the storm. You know that in the end your ship will not sink. It might be battered. It might be barely able to float. But it will make it through the storm.

"And it seems to me, *Deborah Lawson*, that the way God communicates to you is apparently directly through my terrific preaching, so you better be sure you make it here each and every Sunday for the rest of your life."

Bee looked at him and his twinkling eyes, and couldn't help but smile back. "I'll have to trust my gut on that, Pastor Duncan," she said through her tears.

She went to Grace's for lunch and had a wonderful time. She read the kids stories and played baby dolls with Zoe and helped with their baths and dressed them for bed. Grace was all excited because she had only one more week of teaching before the end of the school year. Bee enjoyed talking with Grace and Neil and even took Neil for a spin in the car. As they sat drinking tea and she was getting ready to say good-bye, she noticed a family portrait.

"What a wonderful picture. When did you get it done?" she asked.

"A few months ago. It was Neil's idea. We are going to try and go once a year."

"Can I have a copy?"

"Sure!" Grace got up, went over to the drawer in the desk and pulled out an envelope. She handed her an 8 x 10. "Is this too big?"

"No. I'm doing some rearranging in the house and maybe I'll put some pictures up."

"Pictures up of family?"

"Yes, pictures of family," Bee said with a firm voice. She looked into Grace's eyes.

"Dad never liked to put photographs up. He always liked to put up paintings."

She looked at Grace. "Why do you think he did that, Grace?"

Grace looked at Bee and then at Neil and then back at her. "I-I don't know, Mom. Do you?"

Bee sighed. After a moment she said, "I don't think he liked to be reminded of his responsibilities."

Everyone was quiet for an awkward few moments. "Do you still miss Daddy terribly, Mom?" Grace asked in a quiet voice.

Bee felt the strength of being Deborah for a brief moment as she looked her daughter right in the eye. "No, not for a *long time*, Grace. Not for a long time."

Monday, mid afternoon, Peter called. He sounded uncomfortable. "I don't know if I'm supposed to call or not call."

"Can we make a deal with each other?"

He sounded hesitant. "Okay."

"Let's just trust our guts, okay?"

Bee could almost hear him smiling. "That's why I finally called."

"Then it was a good choice, I guess."

"Are you okay?"

"Yes," she said firmly, "I am okay."

There was silence. "Are you busy Thursday night?"

"Let me check my calendar. No."

He chuckled. "Do you have a calendar."

"No."

"I didn't think so."

"I do have a problem though."

"Oh?" He sounded concerned. Bee imagined him sitting up, gearing up, ready to try to help her with her problem. It was a nice feeling. "What is it?"

"You said that whoever did the asking, then the person being asked did the planning. If I do the planning then the most we'll do is sit here in this house and stare at each other."

"Has my quota been increased?"

Bee had to think for a minute. "Definitely not."

Peter sighed. "All right, I'll do the planning. But you owe me one."

"Okay."

"Are you adventurous?"

"No," she said with conviction.

He laughed. "Too bad. Look, dress casual, okay? No gold flip flops this time. Jeans and sneakers."

Good God, he'd noticed her flip flops. Bee was stunned. "Isn't it too hot for jeans?"

"It won't be."

"Do I need a parka?" she asked sarcastically.

He chuckled again. "No, I'll take care of the coat."

They discussed times, she gave him directions and they hung up.

Bee looked around her living room and debated seriously whether she wanted him to come into the house and see The List nailed over the fireplace. She realized with a sudden rush of delight that she didn't really care.

She puzzled over that all day. Why didn't she care if Peter read The List? It hit her in the late afternoon while she was sweating rearranging the furniture in the living room. The reason she didn't care was because her life didn't seem to suck so much anymore. She no longer felt so completely defined by the betrayal. The Truth that had just about destroyed her was now just simply one item on the wrong side of The List. She was, she realized with a start, much more than just the wife of an unfaithful husband. She was a mother. A grandmother. A friend. A *Woman of Faith*. She was *Deborah* Lawson now. Bee was gone. She was more than happy to carefully fold her old self away and more than ready to shake out the new self. Bee was determined to remain this new person. New and *improved*.

Wednesday, she drove to the local arts and crafts store and bought a whole collection of frames. All gold with different patterns and textures. She put the picture she'd gotten from Grace in one. She found Todd's college photo and John's, too. She went down The List trying to find representations for some of the things she'd written. She worked on it all day and by the end of the day she had something from everyone but Alita.

Bee remembered a plaque that Alita had bought her as a gift years ago from Costa Rica. She finally found it in the basement. It was lovely carved wood with a Spanish phrase carefully painted on it. But she had no idea what it said. *Ahora bien, la fe es la garantía de lo que se espera, la certeza de lo que no se ve. Hebreos 11:1.* She walked over to the phone, looked up Alita's number and dialed.

"Halo?"

"Alita? It's Bee."

"Well hello, Mrs. Bee. Are you well?"

"Yes, yes, I'm fine. I was wondering if you remembered that plaque you brought me back from Costa Rica a few years back."

She could hear the sounds of Alita's family in the background. "Yes, I remember."

"Do you remember what it said?"

"Read it to me."

"I can't read Spanish!"

"Give it a try Mrs. Bee. Maybe I can figure it out as you go."

Bee struggled with the pronunciations. Alita had the nerve to giggle twice. When she finished, Alita said, "Oh, I know that one by heart Mrs. Bee. It is from book of Hebrews in the Bible, chapter eleven, verse one. It says," Alita hesitated as she prepared to translate, "'What is faith? It is the confident assurance that what we hope for is going to happen. It is the evidence of things we cannot yet see.' That's what it says, Mrs. Bee."

"That's beautiful, Alita. Thank you."

"It is a true saying, too."

"Yes, I know it is."

"I knew that Mr. Jonathan didn't like things hung on his walls, but it was the thought that had to be counted."

"Yes it was. It was always the thought. Alita, can I ask you a favor?

"Anything, Mrs. Bee."

"Would you call me, Deborah?"

"Deborah? Call you Deborah instead of Mrs. Bee? You have decided to get a new car and now change your name?"

"Well, it is my real name. Bee is just a nickname."

"I would be honored to call you Deborah."

"I'll see you next week, then."

"Yes, you will."

By late that evening she'd arranged and hung all the pictures including Alita's plaque. She stood back to admire her work and was pleased. She'd taken her list down for all the pictures were now over the fireplace but was unwilling to put it away just yet. Instead, she tacked it on the refrigerator. In the late evening hours, she sat in her newly rearranged living room, sipping a cup of tea and admiring her continually improving decorating sense. *What is faith? It is the confident assurance that what we hope for is going to happen. It is the evidence of things we cannot yet see.* She thought of all the things she hoped for and they were too numerous for her to really list. Happiness, love, laughter, companionship, excitement, being valued, wanted, sought after … But rather than be saddened by what she had not achieved, she had a flash of excitement. If she was a Woman of Faith as Pastor Duncan said she was, then couldn't she dream of some things and have faith that she would be able to enjoy at least some of them? "Yes I can," she said aloud to herself in the living room. It was another very good feeling.

Bee was just tying her sneakers Thursday evening when the doorbell rang. Fifteen minutes early. She peeked through the spy hole in the door and was stunned to see the back of a tall, rough looking motorcycle rider standing on her doorstep. She was horrified. He sported a leather jacket, leather pants and even had a bright red bandanna tied around his head. Good Lord.

The he turned around. *Good Lord.*

She opened the door and stood there with her mouth hanging open.

"I asked you if you were adventurous."

"I told you I wasn't."

"I told you 'too bad'."

"Why do you look like that?" she sputtered out.

Peter looked confused. "It's what bikers wear."

"And you're a biker?"

He grinned like a delighted child. "Tonight I am."

He looked down at her feet. "Good, no gold flip flops. Come out and see my ride." He turned and walked down the steps and around the corner towards her driveway totally confident she'd follow. The curiosity just about killed her.

It was a gigantic, dark blue motorcycle. Bee stood there stunned and completely oblivious to all the motorcycle information Peter proudly imparted to her. *He expected her to ride on this?!* her head kept saying over and over.

"Isn't it a beauty?" she heard Peter say proudly to her.

She slowly walked around the monstrous thing. Twice. Bee finally looked at him. "Am I going to ride on this with you?" *Please say no,* her head said. *Please say you want to drive my car.*

He nodded ever so proudly. "But first you have to put this on."

Peter walked over and opened one of the side compartments of the bike. He took out a package and handed it to her. She took it hesitantly. They sat down on the steps while she slowly opened the bag and pulled out a beautiful black leather jacket. She looked at him, puzzled.

"I told you I'd take care of the coat," he said by way of explanation.

"I didn't think you meant it."

"I know. Try it on. I want to see how it looks on you."

It fit perfectly. "Peter, I can't accept this ..."

"Oh, you don't keep it. I save it and give it to all the women I give rides to."

She looked up at him with such an incredulous expression that Peter burst out laughing and then she smiled. He reached over and did up the zipper and hooks and said quite firmly, "*Yes,* you will accept this. It was a gut decision."

"God helped you pick out a leather biker coat for me?"

"Weeell, God has continued to encourage me in regard to you. I think this coat was my decision, though. I bought it because I knew you'd look great in it." He made her spin around by gently turning her with his hands on her shoulders. When she put her hands on her hips and stood still in front of him he looked at her thoroughly up and down. Peter nodded, seemingly satisfied. "I was right."

He reached over, unhooked a helmet and handed it to her. "Ready?"

"Give me two minutes. Do you want to come in?"

"Sure."

Following her in, Peter stood looking at her new picture arrangement while she rushed up stairs to modify her purse situation. She couldn't very well get on the back of a motorcycle with her pocketbook slung over one shoulder. Bee found a small wallet, put her license, credit card, and some cash in it and shoved it in her back pocket.

When she came down the stairs, he turned and smiled at her. "Tell me who all these people are."

Bee went through and named each one of them. She was impressed that he remembered funny anecdotes about the children that she had told him at dinner. She told him about the plaque and what it said. He nodded. "It's a good verse."

Before she knew it she was clinging to the back of him in a death grip roaring down the road. When they stopped at the first light, Peter turned to her and shouted through his helmet. "Are you all right?"

"Now is *not* the time to ask," she shouted back.

He stayed turned to her although Peter couldn't look at her directly. "If you're frightened, we'll go back. It's okay." She heard the disappointment in his voice even though he tried to hide it.

"If we go back, do I have to give back the coat?" she yelled.

She could hear him laugh through his helmet and then he nodded yes, "It's all part of the package."

"I'm okay," she finally told him.

"Honest?" he shouted.

"Honest," she shouted back.

"Only a little further and then we'll be on quiet country roads. It will be nicer."

He was right. They drove through miles and miles of winding country roads past quaint little towns and towards the colorful sunset occasionally visible through the trees. She relaxed against the back of him, growing accustomed to the motion of the bike and the sounds of the rushing wind. She lost track of time and was lulled by the beautiful sights and rhythmic sound of the bike's motor.

They stopped at a country store, bought sandwiches, chips, drinks, put them in one of the side compartments of the bike and drove to a small lake he knew about. They sat at a picnic bench and ate in companionable silence.

"How is it you know about all these lovely places and have only been here a short time and I've lived here all my life and know nothing?"

"How is it you have a house full of beautiful pictures of your children, family and friends and I have a house full of empty walls?"

She had nothing to say to that so she ate another chip. Peter looked like he wanted to ask her something and then thought better of it and changed his mind. "Go ahead," she said after a few moments, "ask. My daughter said that the best way to keep a conversation going is to ask questions."

"I'm worried that the question is too personal."

"Then I'll tell you it's too personal."

"How come there are no pictures of your husband hanging up?"

"Good question."

"I thought so."

Bee sighed. "I guess the easiest answer is to simply say that I didn't *want* any pictures of him up. In fact, I spent the better part of this past week working to eliminate his presence from the house."

"He hurt you."

"Big time."

"It wasn't a good marriage then?"

She smiled a smile that she realized was probably very brittle. "I wasn't aware of how bad it actually was until after he died."

Peter looked at her as he munched his sandwich. He didn't ask a question, he just watched her. She shrugged. "He traveled. A lot. It was a style of life that we all became accustomed to and accepted. It wasn't terribly bad, although it wasn't terribly good either. It's taken me a while to realize that his regular absences from the house made me a capable, independent woman." She smiled again, a real smile this time. "It's taken me a *long time* to be able to say something positive. That's *huge*.

"When he died I was a grieving widow. I went through all the motions and emotions that anyone would go through. The church was wonderful, the kids were wonderful, and family and friends were wonderful. I would have recovered, eventually."

Bee rolled up her sandwich papers and collected the rest of her food garbage into a tidy pile. "When the will was read, he left provisions for his *other* wife and two children who lived in California. That's pretty much the time I went off the deep end."

Peter didn't say anything for a long time. He finally reached out and took the pile of garbage she was slowly twisting into a knot and walked over and threw it out in the garbage can. Coming back, he straddled the bench with his big long leather-clad legs and sat next to her. Bee's hands were now clenched together and he reached over and pried them apart. He took her right one and enclosed it within his two big hands for a while and she let the warmth of his touch relax her. When Peter felt the tension slowly leaving her, he uncovered her hand in his and began to play with her fingers, touching them lightly and tracing the patterns of the lines in her palm.

"Do you hate him?"

Bee sighed. "Oh, I did for quite a while. Lately, though, I've just gotten too tired to keep it up. It's so all consuming."

Peter nodded in understanding. "It's difficult, isn't it? When you can't confront or talk with the person that's caused you all this grief and pain."

She told him then, about John and her discovery that he had known for such a long time. She told him about John's questions about whether he had done the right thing in not telling her and how she'd answered him.

"You're a great mother. You give much more than you take. You protected them even in your misery." Reaching up, he smoothed her hair and grinned. "You look cute with helmet hair." He kept his hand on her head but slowly drew her down so that she was resting her head on his shoulder. She didn't resist.

He kept his hand on the back of her neck and the pressure was nice. "In some ways I'm a lot like your husband," he said after a while.

Bee jerked up. "You are not," she said in a furious tone.

"Oh, yes I am," he said with conviction. "You could sit here right now - if it was possible - and have a lengthy discussion with my ex-wife and you two would no doubt agree on a *pile* of similarities."

She opened her mouth to argue and Peter looked at her with one eyebrow arched daring her to prove him wrong. Bee shut her mouth to organize her thoughts because she knew he already had his argument set.

She thought long and hard for a few minutes and then looked at him. "At another time, under different circumstances, perhaps there were similarities. I only know what you've told me about yourself. But I can make a critical distinction with your own words that *you* said to me only the other night. You said, 'I *was* a *different* man in my early years. My priorities were screwed up.' As far as *I'm* concerned that is all the difference I needed between the two of you. You recognized something in yourself that you decided to consciously change. That puts you in a completely different league entirely. What's past is past. What's done is done. What's now is *now."* She gave him a supremely confident *so there!* kind of expression and cocked *her* eyebrow at *him.*

And Peter kissed her then, longer and sweeter and with much more passion than the other night. He held her face with both of his hands and gave her the impression that he was *never* going to stop. And wonders of wonders, she realized she'd be quite happy with that, too. Bee formed a ridiculous picture in her mind of them covered in fall leaves, still kissing and it made her start to chuckle. That made him stop.

"*What* is so funny?" He frowned at her.

She reached up to smooth away the frown from his face and he closed his eyes and sighed, seeming to enjoy her touch. "Are my kisses that comical?" Peter persisted, still with his eyes closed.

"Your kisses are quite wonderful if you want the honest truth," she admitted to him. He opened one eye to peer at her, still waiting for an explanation. "I was giggling because I got thinking that I better up your quota or you're going to make your one kiss last all the way until autumn."

"I told you I was tenacious."

"Yes, you told me you were tenacious." And *Bee* kissed *him.*

In the driveway of her house, she stood next to him while he strapped her helmet securely on the back of the bike. "Can I make a rather bizarre request?" she asked.

Peter stopped working with the helmet and looked up at her absolutely serious all of a sudden. "Sure."

"Would you not call me Bee anymore?"

He sat on the bike seat, crossed his arms and grinned at her. "Are you going to give me a replacement name or can I pick one of my own choosing?"

She smiled. "What would you pick?"

"What an impossible question."

"'Bee' is a nickname. My real name is Deborah."

He leaned toward her and quirked an eyebrow. "And are you Deborah now? No longer Bee?"

What a question. What a question. Bee frowned in thought. Was she Deborah, no longer Bee? Was that the transformation that was making her no longer numb, solitary, bitter ... With delight she realized she couldn't remember the full list of depressing characteristics. Peter was watching her, patiently letting her sort through her thoughts. Finally she shook her head and smiled at him, "No, it doesn't seem as if I am Bee anymore."

"Deborah. Deborah. Hmmm, sounds good." He grabbed hold of the lapels of her leather jacket and pulled her to him and kissed her soundly. Keeping her close enough to rub his nose against hers he said softly, "You're a good kisser, Deborah."

"Aren't you going to ask me why?"

Peter gently let go of her, touching her cheek lightly and smiling. "I'm not a dope," he said sounding rather indignant. "I'm sure it had something to do with the 'good' crisis you had in church on Sunday. Right?"

She nodded. He shrugged. What had been huge to her was no big deal to him and she realized she was glad about that.

Peter got on the bike, turned it around, and started it up. Just before he put his helmet on he shouted over the engine, "How's my quota?"

"Full," she shouted back.

"Too bad," he said and pulled her into his arms to give her one more kiss. "Goodnight, Deborah." And he was gone.

I pray that every day I live Your heart will be pleased. [8]

The Greedy Man's Punishment

Sunday morning found her sitting quietly in her pew somewhat relieved that there would be no huge spiritual discoveries on her part today. Pastor Duncan's series on Women of the Bible was over, right?

"Pardon me, is this seat taken?"

She looked up into Peter's smiling eyes. "No."

"Oh, good. Hi, my name is Peter Gannon. And yours?" He extended his hand to her.

She played along with him rather than make any sort of scene. "Deborah Lawson."

"*Deborah Lawson.* It's a pleasure to meet you." He winked at her, settled in next to her, opened his bulletin and began to scan through it.

"How am I doing?" he whispered quietly out of the side of his mouth.

Deborah tried not to smile and just shook her head, ignoring him.

Peter had a nice singing voice her head registered. A rich, deep voice that was a pleasure to listen to. He read the responsive readings with the same confident style and actively participated in the Bible scripture reading by finding the passage in his own Bible. She enjoyed observing him – indirectly, of course.

"Today's story is a sad one," Pastor Duncan began. "I cannot in any way, shape, or form present it any other way." He walked behind the pulpit and came out carrying a magnificent layer cake. He walked to the center of the altar. "Looks good, doesn't it?" Everyone laughed when one little boy said, "YEAH!" very loudly and very fervently. Pastor Duncan smiled.

"Have you ever heard the expression 'You can't have your cake and eat it, too'?" He looked at the nodding congregation. "Of course you have. Well, today's story is about a man who had never heard that expression." He carefully placed the cake on the table that was used for communion. He hesitated, looked at the people, and then took a quick taste of the icing. He rolled his eyes in ecstasy. Everyone laughed as he walked back behind the pulpit.

"His name was Achan and he was traveling with the Israelites as they were wandering, headed to the Promised Land. We must assume that he had heard stories of the slavery by the Egyptians, the twelve plagues that Moses used to gain their freedom, and the dry ground of the Red Sea when it was parted. He was part of the huge Israelite force that was gradually cutting a path through the land of Canaan. He was actively involved in the many battles to claim the land that they had been promised by God.

"Joshua was in charge then. There had been numerous battles and despite the fact that the Israelites were literally *nothing* but a group of escaped slaves they had accomplished many stunning military victories. Because they were God's chosen people. Because they were following God's directives. Because they were being obedient.

"There were lots of rules. That's because they were God's *children*. Oh, I know they were adult in age. I know that they had many adult responsibilities. Some of you know how it was. How many of you were ever parents of a teenager? How about this; how many of you were ever teenagers?" There were quite a few chuckles.

"God had set them out a stunning list of rules and regulations they were to follow to remain obedient. Why the entire book of Leviticus was just procedures and instructions for how to do things right.

"Now I ask you, do your teenagers follow your every rule and piece of advice? I don't have teenagers yet, but I keep hearing cryptic comments such as, 'Just wait', or 'You think it's tough now …' or – my personal favorite – 'I'll talk to you again when they're teenagers'." Many in the congregation were nodding.

"Achan behaved like a typical teenager although in reality he was a full grown man with a wife, children, and full head-of-household responsibilities. Achan *wanted his cake but wanted to eat it all, too.*"

Pastor Duncan clasped his hands behind his back and walked out from behind the pulpit. He took a good long look at the cake. Then he looked out at the congregation. "One big rule was that whenever the Israelites attacked and destroyed the city *nothing* was to be taken from the city except silver, gold, bronze, or iron which was kept for the treasury of the Lord's house. There was to be no plundering. No soldier was to gain in riches through the destruction of any city.

"Joshua had already had his stunning victory at Jericho. Remember Rahab? He had so many victories under his belt that the Bible said his name had become famous throughout the land."

He nodded his head. "Even Rahab had known of Joshua. When she first talked with the two spies from Israel that she protected, she told them," here Pastor Duncan looked down at his Bible to read, "'I know the Lord has given you this land. We are all afraid of you. Everyone is living in terror …'

"When it came time for the Israelites to attack the city of Ai, they had little concern over their victory. *Everyone had witnessed their numerous victories.* They had a reputation that proceeded them and a name that lasted long after they moved on. They were *Israel: The God Jehovah's Chosen People.* Spies had been sent out to check out Ai and they had reported to Joshua, 'It's just a small town and won't take more than two or three thousand of us to destroy it. There's no need for the whole army to go.'

So the three thousand Israelites trooped off to Ai and it was a stunning ... *defeat.* The Bible says that the men of Ai chased the Israelites from the city gate and that the Israelites were *paralyzed* with fear at this turn of events. Their courage just melted away. The defeat was so shocking that Joshua knew right away that the Lord had *permitted* the defeat. And if the Lord had permitted the defeat, then that meant that something was terribly wrong in the nation of Israel. But what?

"Oh boy. When Joshua prayed and asked what was wrong did he get an earful. Besides specifically accusing certain Israelites of stealing, sinning, breaking promises, and lying, God said to Joshua, 'Now Israel has been set apart for destruction. I will not remain with you any longer ...'

"Joshua wasted no time. Each tribal head was brought before him and finally the Lord identified the tribe of Judah as the problem. Then each clan within the tribe of Judah was brought forward and the Lord made known to Joshua the clan of Zerah. Then the families were brought forward one by one and the Lord isolated out the family of Zimri. Finally, each and every family member, person by person, from Zimri's family was brought forward and the Lord told Joshua to single out Achan."

Pastor Duncan said quietly to the congregation. "What do you think Achan did? What could he have done that would have angered the Lord so much? What sin could Achan have *committed* that would have justified all of this? *Is anything you desire worth the loss of a life?"*

Pastor Duncan shrugged. "Achan 'fessed up. He'd taken a fancy robe, two hundred silver coins, and a bar of gold that weighed more than a pound. And he had it buried under his tent." Pastor Duncan went back to the pulpit. "Oh, when put on the spot did he confess! He was quite specific, even telling them that the silver was buried deeper than the rest of the stuff.

"Now what would you do if you had been Joshua? What do you think would be a suitable punishment? Remember, when Moses left Egypt - over forty years prior to this incident - they did a count and at that time there were over six hundred thousand *fighting age men.* This was a *huge* nation of people. The enormity of Joshua's responsibilities cannot truly be comprehended by us today."

Pastor Duncan sighed and shook his head. "I told you it was a sad story. They took Achan, and his precious stolen possessions, as well as his sons, daughters, cattle, donkeys, sheep, tent – everything he owned – some distance from the camp. And the Israelites stoned them all to death and then burned everything. They piled a great heap of stones over the remains. The Bible says that after that the Lord was no longer angry at them." Pastor Duncan rolled his eyes and mumbled almost to himself. "For a time, anyway. Remember, *they were just like children.*"

"It is not our place here and now today to debate whether this punishment was unacceptably brutal or not. We can't. We were not there, we simply could not possibly understand. It certainly seems to me – *if the stolen goods were buried under the family tent* – that this was a family affair."

Pastor Duncan walked over to the cake and picked it up. He carried it forward to the edge of the altar. "The purpose of this story is for us to examine our own lives. We are all like Achan. We all have desires for things that come in the way of our faith and what the Lord wants us to do. And yes, there are some whose passion for such forbidden things is so all consuming that it could destroy your family."

Still carrying the cake, he stepped down onto the floor of the congregation and stared out at the people.

"Alcohol.

"Drugs.

"Work.

"Love of money.

"Food.

"Possessions.

"Selfishness.

"Greed.

"Hatred.

"Anger."

He hesitated a minute. "*Need I go on?*

"How about this question: what would *others* say about you that you have in your life that is so all consuming that it has destroyed your family? For I will tell you this with absolute certainty: if you have anything in your life that is more consuming than your dedication and commitment to God, then you have already signed your family's death sentence. *Think about that.* What are your priorities? Your life depends on the correct order."

At the benediction, Pastor Duncan invited everyone back for coffee *and cake.*

Peter looked at her. "Looks like I might have a crisis or two over the next couple of Sundays," he said with a quiet smile.

"Oh, there's still room for me to have a few, too, I think."

He nodded and touched her hand. "Probably."

Deborah was surprised that it didn't seem to be such a big deal and said so. "Isn't that why we come here?" Peter asked her sincerely. "To gain insight? To have moments of personal reflection?" He leaned over and his warm breath tickled her neck. "To have God speak to us in a way other than indigestion?"

She laughed out loud and then quickly clapped her hand over her mouth. But everyone was busy talking and visiting and filing out and no one noticed.

Peter's smile was tender. "I like the sound of your laughter. When I hear it, that moment almost always becomes the best part of my day."

"I liked the sound of your singing voice. It's quite nice."

"Really? No one's ever told me that." He thought for a moment. "But then I've never sat in church with anyone who'd be inclined to let me know, I guess."

They stood in line waiting to file out with everyone. "What do you mean?" she said to him.

"This whole church - going, God - fearing, indigestion listening guy you see before you is relatively new. I was never much for church or God stuff. Certainly not when I was married."

"So I'm the first church - going woman you've asked out for coffee?"

He had the audacity to look embarrassed. "Well, no ..." Then he looked worried.

That made her laugh again and he relaxed. His eyes twinkled and she knew he was going to tease her. *Good grief,* her head said in shock, *you're learning his expressions* … "I make it a point to ask out all the attractive widows in every church I attend. I only stay long enough to work my way through the whole group of them and then I move on."

"What about the divorcees?"

Peter shook his head emphatically. "No, just the widows."

"Can I take you to lunch? My treat."

"Oh, you're one of *those.*"

"What's that mean?"

"Equal opportunity."

"I wouldn't have any idea. If you've been paying attention, I've never done this before. It simply seems to me that there's no reason why *you* should pay every time we go out and it seems to me that you have been."

"When you get feisty, you frown."

"*Feisty?*"

Peter nodded. "Yeah, feisty. Do you realize that this will be our fourth date?"

Deborah stopped and looked at him. "Really?" and then mentally counted. "You're pushing it to count the coffee."

"I've got to start somewhere. And I've decided to put you on the spot. If you're paying, you're planning." He looked at her and grinned. "You're frowning again."

"I'm concentrating."

She took them to a restaurant she remembered – vaguely and with a little bit of panic – she'd seen on the corner near the car dealership where she'd bought the car. They had a lovely lunch and on the spur of the moment caught a movie at the big cinema multiplex that was at the intersection as well. The conversation flowed well. They had a comfortable banter between them that neither seemed to have to consciously work at.

At the church parking lot where Deborah took Peter to get his car, he asked her, "Do you like baseball?"

"No."

He laughed. "Can you stand watching a game?"

"Yes." She smiled. "Both John and Todd played little league for years and I've watched hundreds of games."

"You've never gone to a *real* game?" When she shook her head Peter continued, "There's a minor league team that plays in its own stadium nearby. I thought I could get tickets for Friday evening. It might be fun."

"Can I bring a book?"

"*No.*"

They agreed who'd drive (him, and she was to wear jeans and sneakers again) and what time. Peter started looking all around suddenly and Deborah was puzzled. "What's wrong?"

"Well, I want to kiss you good-bye, but I don't want anyone to see me do it." He looked at her pointedly. "The gossips will have a *field day*, you know. Don't want to ruin my reputation here at church, either."

"You really have to work on the twinkle in your eyes when you tease me. It's a dead give away." She leaned into him and he put his arms around her and held her for a bit. "This is kind of nice, isn't it?" he finally said to the top of her head. She knew he wasn't just talking about the hug.

"Yes," she admitted, "this is kind of nice."

Monday, Todd called. "I sold the car."

"What car?"

"Dad's car, Mom."

"Oh. OH! Great!"

"That friend of mine bought it. It took him a while to get the money together. Can we come get it tonight?"

"Sure, do you want to come for dinner?"

There was silence at the other end of the phone. "Todd? I asked if you wanted to come to dinner."

"You're feeling better, Mom."

"I have good days and bad days, but the good ones are starting to outnumber the bad ones. It's about time."

"You haven't invited me over for dinner in ... jeez, I can't remember when, Mom."

"It's kept my food bill down."

"Will you make your fried chicken?"

Deborah had a wave a pleasure. "Sure, does your friend want to come, too?"

"I'll ask. What time?"

She had forgotten what it was like to have the sound of laughter and big boys in her house. The refrigerator door opened constantly, dishes were piled on the counter, and she tripped over an enormous pair of sneakers in the middle of the floor. Todd had brought three friends with him in the end, two to see the car and one because of the offer of fried chicken she suspected. Deborah made a huge platter full of chicken and at the last moment she'd made a double batch of brownies and a huge bowl of potato salad, too. There wasn't a speck of food left at the end of the meal.

They teased her a bit, too. When they finally went to look at Jonathan's car, the one who had planned to buy it made to get in her car. She laughed and he grinned. The look of longing was so profound on his face that she told Todd to go fetch the keys and take them for a spin.

"Really, Mom?"

Deborah shrugged. "It's just a car, Todd."

They all piled in and she sat down on the front steps. She had every intention of going inside to clean up once they roared away but it was such a nice evening. She enjoyed the sounds and the smells and the sights. It was peaceful. It felt *so nice* to be aware of it and not be numb. She had a flash of sitting on the steps and opening up the package with the leather coat in it. That led her brain off into an amazing series of wonderful memories. *And you've only had four dates,* her head felt compelled to remind her. She was still sitting there contentedly when they pulled back into the driveway. Todd's friend got out and said, "I'll take it!" and she laughed again.

The papers and the money were exchanged and hands were shook. The guys thanked her numerous times for dinner and one even offered to go in and do the dishes. That got a big round of teasing from the other three.

"Never mind giving him a hard time," she heard herself saying to all of them. "At least *one* of you was raised properly," and Deborah gave Todd a meaningful glance.

Todd smiled. "I'll stay and help clean up."

"No," she said and smiled, "I'm only kidding. What else do I have to do? I'm happy to do it."

Todd looked at the other three as they piled into Jonathan's car. "I'll meet you at Pete's?" They nodded, waved, and drove off.

"Who's Pete?" she asked as they walked inside.

"Not 'who', what. It's a sports bar we like to hang out at a bit."

"You don't drink and drive, do you?"

"I'm careful, Mom. You taught me well."

When Todd looked at her Deborah gave him her 'mother's glare' to see if he was telling the truth. He looked right back at her, his face serious and open. She was satisfied.

Todd walked with her up the front steps into the house. "Remember when you used to tell us that your 'mother's glare' could read our minds? God, that used to scare the crap out of me. I always tried to not look you in the eye when I was trying to pull a fast one over on you. It took me a *long time* to realize that the not looking you in the eye was what was giving me away. Not your ability to read my mind."

She chuckled. "Parent's can be so evil, can't we?"

"*Mothers* can. Dad never bothered one way or the other."

Deborah's automatic response was to defend Jonathan. She'd always done that. Always supported his work ethic for being away, missing holidays, family functions, school performances, ball games ... She could hear her words defending him, 'Your father works hard to support us so that we can live in this lovely house and have this comfortable life style. He's not any happier than we are to be away so much and miss so many things.' If she had said that once she had said that a million times. *What an idiot you were,* her head told her.

They were standing in the kitchen. Deborah looked at him, silent and unwilling to defend Jonathan anymore. Todd looked at her and quietly reached up and took The List down from on top of the refrigerator. "You left this tacked on the fridge, but I took it down when the guys and I got here. I thought you wouldn't want them to read it."

Heart hammering in her chest, Deborah took it from him. "Did you read it?"

"Yeah, I read it the other night."

She was stunned. "What other night?"

"I stopped by Thursday night to tell you I'd sold the car, but you weren't here. I let myself in, wandered around looking for you but I finally decided you were out. Drank a soda. Ate some stale cookies. Read a piece of paper on the fridge that said 'My husband was a lying, cheating, bastard', and then went home. I called John. He told me because I was so worked up. I told John I wouldn't speak to you about it because I didn't want to upset you."

"You weren't ever supposed to know." She held The List in her hand not knowing what to do with it and then finally put it in the phone book drawer.

"And just why did you decide that?" He was furious.

"What good would it do?"

"A hell of a lot!" he shouted at her.

"Like what?" she said quietly.

"Like explain why my father never seemed to love me enough or care enough. Like why it seemed that work took such a priority over me and John and Grace *and you*. Like why my father was always so furiously defensive if we so much as *hinted* that we'd have liked to have had him at a game or at a school performance or at a God-damned birthday party!" Todd shouted and paced around the kitchen, flinging his arms wide to make a further point at the top of his volume. "Like why he always seemed to only be partly here even when he was home," he finished quietly and went and sat down at the kitchen counter.

Deborah was speechless. Finally, she said, "I thought I did a good job -"

He looked at her furious. *"Don't you get it? IT WASN'T YOUR JOB!!* It was *his* and he chose not to do it. He chose to let you handle it. And when you couldn't completely do your job *and* his, he covered the holes with bluster and fury and righteous indignation about how we didn't appreciate all he had done and sacrificed for us!"

She went over and sat next to him. After a time she sighed and said, "You can listen to me or not, but hating him does you no good. It just saps all your energy and concentration and you loose the ability to really live." She reached up and brushed Todd's hair out of his eyes and looked at his profile. "I've had two years to deal with it though. John's been carrying the burden for four. Grace doesn't know. I suppose I'll have to tell her now. I don't want her to think I've purposely excluded her."

"It'll drive her nuts. She always thought Dad walked on water. He favored her."

"Really?"

Todd looked at her, exasperated. "*Yeah, Mom.* Big time. How many dance recitals did he make? He called her 'his princess'. Hell, he even managed to be an assistant coach the one year she played soccer."

She didn't remember everything, but Deborah did remember the fight they'd had over the assistant coach position. Jonathan had said he'd help coach and she'd been furious; fearful that he wouldn't show and it would be another thing she'd have to cover for. It had upset her that he'd been willing to do that and not something with the boys, too, and just a little jealous that he'd make the effort for Grace and no one else. "I guess I did know," she whispered almost to herself after a time.

Todd sighed and put his head down on his arms. She reached around and hugged him. Tight. "I love you, Todd. You read the whole list, didn't you? You saw your name on the side that was the wonderful things that God has given me."

"Yeah, I read the whole thing, Mom," his voice was muffled. "It still doesn't keep me from dreaming of ways I would have preferred his death to occur." Todd looked up at her and Deborah saw tears in his eyes. "*What was he thinking, Mom?* How could he do that? To you, to us. Even to the other family …"

Deborah was quiet for a long time with her thoughts "You have a good heart, Todd, that you can even think about them, you know. That aspect never even occurred to me until you just said it."

Todd snorted. "Good thing you don't know some of the ways I imagined him dying." His voice sounded so bitter.

She sighed. "Can I tell you something?" He looked at her and nodded. "I didn't mind Jonathan being away so much. My life was better without him than with him. I know that sounds rather pitiful, but it was the truth. Without Jonathan, I was independent, decisive, sure of myself, in control. Heck, I think I was even more fun. Those weeks that he was home here with us I seemed to fade away and just wait until he left again to reemerge. It's taken me almost two years of hell, but I've just recently begun to discover that I am and always was better off without him." All of a sudden, Deborah had a thought. "And do you know something? If I hadn't found out that he had been unfaithful, then I might just have worn 'the grieving widow personality' the rest of my life. Instead, I got so righteously pissed off at him that I fell off the deep end – but for just a few years." She grinned at Todd. "I thought of that just now." She shoved him with her shoulder. "Heck, I really *must* be getting better."

Deborah stood up and started putting the dishes in the dishwasher. Todd helped. The silence between them was companionable, both of them lost in thought. When they were finished, she looked at him, put her hands on her hips and said, "Go to Pete's."

Her son looked at her lost and sad. Deborah was so glad that the sight of him no longer reminded her so much of his father. He was just her baby who was showing no inclination to leave. She went over and gave him a hug. She came up to his shoulder. He gave her a big tight bear hug. "How about you come to dinner again on Wednesday? You can bring the guys again. Maybe I'll ask Grace and Neil, too."

"Will you make your spaghetti, meatballs and garlic bread?"

Deborah grinned against Todd's chest and nodded her head.

"Okay."

Deborah wasn't sure, but she was almost positive that Wednesday night was the very best night of her life. She made three pounds of pasta, three dozen meatballs, sauce, had three loaves of garlic bread, and two homemade apple pies. The house was wild with Grace, Neil, the kids, Todd and four friends all laughing and talking at once. It was wonderful chaos. One of Todd's friends brought her a huge bouquet of flowers – beautiful pink Shasta daisies with blooms almost as big as Zoe's head. And

Zoe, true to mischievous form, managed to go upstairs to Deborah's bedroom unnoticed in the confusion and come down wearing Deborah's make up, shoes, and a goodly amount of her jewelry. Grace was furious, Neil was horrified. Deborah smiled and told Zoe that she looked fabulous.

As Deborah crawled into bed that night, she lay there for a long time wide awake. It seemed to her that in whatever direction she looked she was surrounded by people who loved her and cared about her and wanted her to return to the land of the living. The pain, so long her best and only friend, was thankfully being replaced. *At last.*

Thank you, God, her head said with a grateful sigh. *Thank you for my life."*

She woke in the middle of the night, drenched in sweat and trembling. Good grief. Some horrible nightmare she couldn't recall. She got up and in the dark, changed her damp nightgown and splashed cold water on her face. She'd go downstairs and get a drink of iced cold water. How many times had she run up and down those steps over the goodness knows how many years she'd lived in the house? But she misjudged the start of the steps in the pitch dark and started to fall. She cried out first from the shock and put her hand out to break her fall. Then she yelled in pain. It was a slow motion fall for her, and she was aware of the motions as she rolled head over heels down the long flight of steps. Ow, her back! Ow, her hip! Ow, her head! Ow, her arm! The fall ended in blackness when her head hit the wall at the bottom of the stairs.

Suddenly, Jonathan was there. Looking highly put out it seemed. He always looked put out should anyone feel brave enough to disrupt his schedule or to voice the truth. He had his hands on his hips and he was frowning something fierce.

"Yes?" Deborah said to Jonathan in a carefully neutral voice. It was always best to mask your emotions around him when he was in a mood because any emotions other than Jonathan's in an argument always made things significantly worse.

"What have you gone and done this time? I can't always fix your problems, Bee. You know how busy I am. You know that I can't be in two places at once."

"I'm doing the best I can, Jonathan."

Jonathan snorted a disgusted snort. "Obviously *not*. How could you be so clumsy as to fall down the stairs? What's the matter with you? Why are you always so awkward? You'd think you'd at least be able to walk down a flight of stairs."

"Go away, Jonathan," she said in a firm voice. "Go buy a ticket and fly back to California. Maybe there's a family out there that needs you more and appreciates you more."

Jonathan's face got purple with fury. "*How dare you.* I flew all the way back here as soon as I was informed that you were hurt and *this is the thanks I get?!* Do you realize the enormity of responsibilities that I have in California?! It's not something I can just drop at a moment's notice!"

"Look, let's make a deal. If I need you, Jonathan, I'll call you. Please make sure that no one has your phone number on the way out." Deborah chuckled at her own humor.

"You can't make it on your own, Bee. *You need me.* You've got three children. You don't have a job. You've got financial responsibilities. Don't be so flip with me or I will take you up on your ungrateful suggestion. Then you'll be sorry."

She tried to turn to look at him, but was too tired to bother. "You're a fool, Jonathan. I *have* been making it on my own. I *don't* need you." Deborah smiled again at the coming joke. "And I *don't* have to worry about financial responsibilities and the children because with you or without you, you'll still have to take care of that. Yes, I think I'll keep everything *except* your pants. You can have them."

As Jonathan turned in fury and began to stomp out of the room, she called him back. He turned to look at her. "And one more thing. My name is Deborah."

Are you going to stay again tonight?

Yeah, if that's okay with you.

Sure, that's fine. I'll go home, check on the kids. Todd said he'd come in the morning to relieve you.

Okay.

Thanks for saying you'd stay.

It's all part of the package.

Deborah's head hurt. Oh my God in heaven, but her head hurt. She tried to reach her hand up to touch the pain but didn't have the strength to move her arm. Panicking, Deborah made an effort to try and sit up. Oh God, every single inch of her hurt.

Easy there, girl. Rest. You've got company here to watch over you. I hope you can hear me. Shall I sing a song to you?

Jonathan was back. Good grief. Couldn't he take the hint? And standing next to him was Peter. My, this was a bit awkward. Deborah felt compelled to introduce them. It was the least she could do. "Peter, this is Jonathan. Jonathan, this is Peter."

Peter extended his hand. "Hi. Never thought I'd get the opportunity to meet you. I understand you're a lying, cheating bastard," he said in an easy-going tone of voice.

Jonathan frowned. "Hello. Who in God's name are you and what have you got to do with my wife? Besides, I heard that you're a selfish, egotistical son of a bitch."

Peter nodded agreeably. "Yup, that's me. But I don't particularly think I have to answer the question about "your wife". Heard you got away with bigamy. Two wives. Five children. Two homes. Kept it up for over twelve years."

It was Jonathan's turn to give a weary nod. "Yeah, no one ever knew until I died. It was fantastically complicated keeping both lives separate. The stress was incredible. No one has *any idea* how difficult it was to keep everything balanced *and* provide financially for them all." Jonathan shook his head in dismay. "Hell, even in death I provided well for them. I was quite a guy. I heard, though, Gannon, that you were so self-centered and work obsessed that you totally missed your wife's serious depressed state and she committed suicide as a result. Man, if you'd only just taken a few moments to try to find her some help ..."

Peter stiffened in anger. "You've got a hell of a nerve! I was busy building my little start up company into a major corporation that was publicly traded on Wall Street! At the height of our business, I had 120 employees – as well as God knows how many family members - that were completely dependent on me and my expertise! My ex-wife never appreciated the magnitude of my responsibilities and obviously neither do you. Maybe I should introduce the two of you. You might get along famously."

Holding up his hand, Jonathan shook his head saying, "No thanks, two wives was more than I could handle. You have no idea how difficult holidays were. *Oh my God!* Everyone whining and complaining and pulling me in every direction. Do you know that one Christmas, I was so sick and tired of all the complaints and the guilt trips that I took a trip *all by myself to Hawaii?* It was the best Christmas I ever had." Jonathan smiled, lost in remembrance."

"My ex never let me forget that we didn't have kids. I wish I had a dollar for every time I heard about my failure in that department." Peter reminisced. "It wasn't like I had been dishonest with her. When we were first together, I was already a very busy man. I *told her* children were not a priority with me. She enjoyed the perks; nice car, nice home, designer clothes, and exotic vacations when I could find the time. Her life wasn't all misery, although she liked to say so."

Jonathan reached over and slapped Peter companionably on the back. "Your life wasn't a piece of cake either, I guess. Seems like we could almost be brothers," he chuckled.

"That's not true!" Deborah finally shouted in a strong voice.

"Who asked you?" they both say in unison almost surprised to find her still there.

"Peter, tell him. Tell Jonathan how you're different. *Tell him,"* she said earnestly.

"Tell me what?" Jonathan demanded. "What does she know that I don't know?"

Peter grinned a brilliant smile and looked at Deborah. He winked. Then he looked at Jonathan. "Oh, she knows that I'm *forgiven."*

How was she last night?

Pretty quiet. She got upset at one point and I was able to calm her down.

What did you do?

I, well I ... sang to her. She told me last Sunday that she liked my singing voice.

Well, I won't sing. I sound like a fog horn.

Just talk to her. She seemed to like that almost just as much.

Deborah opened her eyes and looked up at an unfamiliar ceiling. Strange patterned tiles. Odd wallpaper and border. And who chose those curtains? There was a sound in the corner and she turned. What was Todd doing sitting in that chair reading a magazine?

"Hey."

"Mom!" He jumped up and pulled the chair over to her bedside. "So, you're awake at last, lazy bones." He smiled, but she knew he was up to something.

"Could I have a drink of water?" Deborah licked her parched lips. Yuck.

"I don't know. Let me go get a nurse." Todd was gone in a flash. Nurse?

Within minutes there were not one but two nurses, checking her pulse, her bags of medicine, taking her temperature, touching her arms ... One brought Todd a Styrofoam cup of ice chips and he gradually began feeding them to her. The ice tasted like heaven.

"What's going on?" she finally managed to ask.

"You fell down the steps, Mom."

Deborah remembered then. "It was dark. I had a nightmare. I was going for a drink and ... I misjudged the step."

"Alita found you Thursday morning sometime. You've got a fractured skull. You've been out of it for five days. It's Monday."

"Five days?"

"You've given everyone quite a scare. Even John's here. He flew out Saturday morning. We're all taking turns staying with you."

"I'm sorry I'm so much trouble."

Todd smiled and shook his head 'no'. "It's about time we got the chance to pay back all the bedside attending you've given us."

"How long do I have to stay here?"

He shrugged his shoulders. "No clue. You'll have to talk to the doctor ..." That was the last thing she heard before she fell asleep.

It was dark when Deborah was alert the next time. John was slumped over in the corner in the chair, his long legs propped up on the heating vent.

"John?"

He just about fell out of the chair. "Hey, Mom, how are you doing?"

"Go home and sleep in a proper bed."

He chuckled. "You don't wield a lot of power lying all broken up in a hospital bed. Maybe I'll sleep in a proper bed tomorrow night. You'll have to be satisfied with that. Here, Todd said you were thirsty when you were awake last time." He held a Styrofoam cup with a straw and she drank deeply of the nice, cool water.

"Oh, that's paradise," she sighed.

"How are you feeling?"

"I don't know, really. My head hurts. Every part of me has an achy feeling to it and my body feels like it weighs about a million pounds."

"You've got a fractured skull and sixteen stitches in your head right here," John motioned up towards the right part of her hairline. "I'm not sure where the fracture is up there. Boy, when you fall down the stairs, *you fall down the stairs.*" He grinned at her.

Deborah sighed. "I always was clumsy."

"Says who?"

She hesitated. "Jonathan."

"Who else?"

She thought. It made her head hurt. She couldn't think of anyone else and said so.

"Then we'll just dismiss that opinion, okay?"

She smiled and made the massive effort to reach her right hand up to touch his face. He grabbed her hand and held it. "We were all very, *very* worried about you," he said.

"Well, I decided you've been worrying so much about my state of mind, I'd move on to make you worry about something else instead. It was the least I could do."

It had begun to get light out in the brief few moments they had talked. "Looks like it's morning," she said.

John turned around to look out the window. "Yeah, Todd usually takes the morning shift, Grace comes in the afternoon, and Peter and I have battled over who gets to sleep through the night here and who goes home."

"Peter?!"

John smiled and nodded. "Yes, *Peter*. Go back to sleep, Mom. I'll see you this evening." He carefully put her hand down by her side and brushed his hand against her forehead. She slept.

Deborah missed Todd completely and woke in the late afternoon as Grace was gathering her things together and Peter was standing there waiting to relieve her. "Don't leave without saying goodbye," she managed.

"Mom!" Grace came over and gave her a quick kiss on the cheek. "I'm so glad you're awake."

"You poor thing. Sitting here all afternoon. Who's watching the kids?"

Grace grinned widely. "*Are you kidding?!* I've just had a glorious number of afternoons, sitting quietly, reading and doing *nothing*. It's been great! The kids are making me nuts and I've only been home on summer break a little over a week!" She laughed. "And Todd's watching the kids. The house is a complete disaster when I get home each day, but Zoe and Max think he's the greatest thing. Max screams *when he leaves* not when I do!"

Grace looked at her watch. "But I've got to go. Todd's been working the night shift so that he can be here in the morning and I don't want him to be late." She turned and looked at Peter. "Are you staying tonight?"

With hands on his hips, Peter said in a surprisingly determined tone, "*It's my turn*. I know better than to let John challenge me with arm wrestling this time. He'll just have to play fair this time."

Grace laughed. "I'm not getting between the two of you. I'll definitely see you tomorrow though?"

"Absolutely."

"I love you, Mom." Grace gave her a quick kiss and was gone.

Deborah watched Peter walk across the room, choose and drag a chair over by her, reposition it by her bedside and settle himself in. "This chair is *much* more comfortable than that one," he motioned with a twist of his head.

"You're not staying the night."

He sighed. "You've been alert for approximately," he looked at his watch, "eleven minutes and you're already giving me a hard time. What's that all about?"

She smiled. "What are you doing here?"

He leaned forward and rested his arms on the railing of the side of her bed. "I'll answer your question with one of my own: if things were reversed, what would you be doing right now?"

It was easier, Deborah decided, to ignore the topic. "I must look a fright."

Peter nodded. "You do."

"That's not what you're supposed to say!"

He smiled. "At least you know when I say you're hot, I mean it."

"I'm never hot."

He reached in and gently took her hand in his. "Oh yes you are, but I refuse to argue about this subject either. Besides, the only opinion that matters in that category *is mine*. How do you feel?"

"Tired. Achy. Stupid."

"Do you want to try to sit up a bit? I could reposition the bed." They spent a few hysterical moments with Peter trying to do the controls and not jar her to death. Her head spun when she was finally sitting up a bit, but once things settled she felt better.

When Peter had finally settled down next to her again and reclaimed her hand he said, "Some people will do anything to avoid a baseball game."

"How did you find out I was here?"

"Oh, you're not going to like that, so let's change the subject." His eyes twinkled.

She gave him her Mother's Glare.

Peter laughed. "Grace called Pastor Duncan. Pastor Duncan called me."

She felt her mouth drop open in stunned amazement. "How did Pastor Duncan know to call you?"

Peter leaned over and whispered in a very conspiratorial tone. *"He saw us hugging in the church parking lot."* Deborah gasped and he laughed, absolutely delighted. "You should know he's been here at least three times to see you, too. He even brought us all donuts one time."

That made Deborah almost laugh but she caught herself because it made her head hurt too much. "What's so funny?" Peter asked.

"He only brings donuts because *he* loves to eat them," she said smiling.

Peter nodded and chuckled. "Yeah, he told us that."

Dinner arrived and Deborah managed to eat a few bites. In between mouthfuls, she asked, "Did you sing to me?"

Peter looked so uncomfortably embarrassed that she knew immediately that he had. Reaching up, Deborah touched the side of his cheek, his mustache, his hair … He caught her hand again and kissed her palm.

"You'll have to get me to tell you about some of my funny dreams," she said to break the silence.

"Was I in them?"

"One you were. You and Jonathan had a long conversation."

He looked incredulous. "They gave you quite a bit of medicine for the pain and everything. It's a wonder you didn't have pink elephants and flying monkeys in your dreams." She yawned then, a huge, highly unladylike yawn.

"You should go to sleep again. I'll be here if you need me."

"I want you to go home. I'll be fine. The nurses are here."

"Yes, the nurses are here but so am I." Peter tried to look fierce and unbending when he saw her starting to speak. "Deborah, I won't argue with you about this. I'm staying. Hell, *it's my turn*! You work on convincing John tomorrow night if you want." He motioned over to the floor. "I've brought my computer and my cell phone. I can catch up on a pile of stuff that I never seem to find the time to do. *This is what I want to do* so give me a smile, say, 'Thank you' and then say, 'Good night.'" He tried to look fierce again but failed miserably.

She smiled anyway. "Thank you. Good night." But kept her eyes open looking at him. He arched his eyebrows at her willing her to obey him. She whispered very quietly, "Would you sing to me again?"

He looked almost like he was in physical pain. "I can't do it when you're looking at me. I get too embarrassed. If you'll close your eyes … *I'll try*." He was blushing something furious.

Deborah closed her eyes and fell asleep listening to Peter's lovely voice.

Fear God and obey his commands, for this is the duty of every person.

God will judge us for everything we do, including every secret thing,

whether good or bad.[9]

The Foolish Man's Triumph

Wednesday the nurses got Deborah out of bed. She had only mild dizziness, which passed quickly, and it felt glorious to be sitting up in a chair. Wednesday she also tried to make Todd promise that he would speak with *all involved* and have them stop the forced bedside vigil they had all taken on. "I'm not dying," she said to him in a feisty tone.

"We know that *now*." He was not deterred by her orders.

"I feel uncomfortable with all this fuss and bother."

"I'm sorry about that."

She sighed. "Please? Look you can all come visit me, but I'd like you to get on with some sort of normalcy in your lives. Please?"

"You can't stand all this attention, can you? That's the whole root if it. You're quite happy fussing about others, but when the tables are turned, you can't handle it."

Deborah thought for a moment and answered Todd honestly. "Part of that is true. But there's another part of me that for the past *two years*, Todd, has been solitary and private. Now that I'm awake and coherent, I'd like some of that solitary time back. That part of me has been able to sort through this whole tangled mess that my life has become and finally make some sense out of it. It's been important for my healing. Maybe someone would have been able to do it faster or more efficiently, but at least I got it done."

"Or maybe someone else would have gone stark raving mad."

She smiled. "Yes, well, maybe someone else would have gone stark raving mad. Please? Will you speak with everyone and get them to just come for a *visit* and not *move in*? I'd like some private time."

Todd gave her what she could best describe as his Son's Glare and she looked at him openly. "I don't know if I can trust you," he mumbled in frustration. "You're too good at this."

She chuckled then and reached up to hold her head as a result. "I'm not being deceitful. You can trust me."

When he finally made the motions to go he had contacted everyone and he assured her that they would be coming in later in the afternoon for a *visit*. He stood hesitantly at the door seemingly unable to leave. Deborah took pity on him. "Do I need to do a dance? Sing a song? Tell a few jokes?" she said with forced enthusiasm.

"No, you just need to let me look at you a few more minutes. Do you know how much we love you, lady? Do you know what a fright you gave us? Do you know that *none* of us can get along without you?" Todd was almost shouting when he was done. She could see real fear in his eyes.

"Of course you could all get along without me! I've prepared you all superbly. All three of my children are strong, capable, smart, and independent. I've spent my *whole life* working on that! Don't you *dare* imply that should I disappear you'll be unable to cope." She spoke as loudly as her head would allow.

Todd grinned at her. "What about Peter?"

The change in topic startled her. "What about Peter?"

"He needs you."

Deborah snorted. "He most certainly does not."

"I'll let him have that argument. But I'll tell you this: *he's a good guy.*

"I know he's a 'good guy', thank you very much. And I'll thank you to mind your own business where my lov -," she broke off abruptly, embarrassed with what she realized she was just going to say.

Todd laughed and finished her sentence. "Where your love life's concerned?"

She blushed. "This is *not* a conversation a mother has with her son."

"Why not?"

"I don't know, Todd! Don't you think it's a bit odd?"

"Not at all. And you should know that *all three of us* like him. We've had lots of time to talk with him and check him out and come to our own personal conclusions. And we all agree, too."

"What do you mean?"

Todd looked around the hospital room. "Take a good look, Mom. It's pretty tight in here. It's been a stressful situation over quite a number of days. If that doesn't show everyone's true colors, then I don't know what does. We liked what we saw."

"Oh …"

He came over, squatted down and kissed her gently on the forehead. "I love you, Mom. You know that, right?"

"Yeah, I know that. How could I not?"

He looked pleased with her answer and was still smiling when he walked out the door.

She thought, although she didn't exactly time it, that she had exactly seven minutes of private time before Pastor Duncan strolled in with his obligatory bag of donuts and coffee. She groaned.

He looked suitably stunned by Deborah's lack of enthusiasm at his arrival. He stood in the doorway and said, "Is this a bad time?"

"What kind of donuts did you bring?"

"Chocolate frosted."

"Okay, you can come in."

He settled himself down, handed her a cup of *tea* (he seemed pleased that he knew enough about her now to know that she didn't drink coffee) and passed out the donuts.

"I hear you've been here quite a few times."

"A few," he said. "How are you feeling?"

"Better. It feels good to be sitting up at last."

"Have they told you when you're going home?"

"No, not yet."

In companionable silence they munched the donuts and sipped their hot drinks. "Did someone tell you that chocolate frosted were my favorite?" Deborah finally asked.

"Well, you didn't eat the cream filled the last time I brought them."

"And what, you just gradually work through the different types until you hit on a successful match?"

Pastor Duncan chuckled. "Well, sometimes. Grace mentioned the other day that she thought she remembered that you always enjoyed chocolate frosted so I filed it away in my memory banks."

"You have a mental list of what donuts your parishioners like?" Deborah teased.

He surprised her by looking quite pleased. "Yup."

"You're not kidding me."

He looked startled. "No, I'm not."

That made Deborah laugh and he smiled. "I missed your sermon on Sunday. Have you arrived to give me my own private telling?"

His mouth was full of donut. He even had a splash of chocolate frosting in one corner of his mouth. He shrugged, smiled and nodded, not wanting to talk with his mouth full. When he swallowed and wiped his mouth with a paper napkin he finally said, "Sure if you want ..."

"Who'd you preach on?"

"Judah. I called my sermon 'The Foolish Man's Triumph'."

She took a sip of her tea. "Why was he foolish?"

"Oh, loads of reasons. *Loads*. He was one of twelve sons of Jacob. Remember him? He was the one that was the husband to Leah, the Unloved Wife?"

She nodded.

"Well, as you might have expected, there was enormous dysfunction in the family. Jacob didn't learn from his mistakes in favoring one wife over another and went on to favor one son over all others."

"Was it one of Leah's sons?"

"No. Rachel's. The favorite wife did finally have a son. That was the one he favored."

"What a bastard." Then Deborah looked embarrassed at her language.

But Pastor Duncan laughed. "Jacob certainly was no prize, I'll give you that. But don't forget, he *was* God's chosen man, Deborah." He took another bite of donut and chewed thoughtfully. "I personally like that all these important Biblical men and women that God established all of his great covenants – promises – with were so flawed." He smiled. "It gives *me* hope about *myself.*" He looked at her. "Do you want me to really tell you the story?"

She nodded.

"Well, there ended up being twelve brothers in the family. Rachel died giving birth to her second son which sent Jacob into a tailspin of grief and forever elevated both her sons above the other ten. There was profound hatred between the brothers and Joseph, Rachel's oldest child. Jacob made things worse by giving Joseph the coat of many colors, not making him work with the other brothers, and, I suspect, he educated him differently as well."

Pastor Duncan shook his head. "What a family. The daughter Dinah was brutally raped and some of the brothers retaliated by slaughtering an entire city of men. Rueben, one of the other brothers had an affair with one of Jacob's wives. And in their hate and jealousy, the brothers sold the favored brother Joseph to slave traders. They then lied and told their father he'd been killed by a wild animal and Jacob swore he'd never recover from that sorrow.

"In the midst of all this chaos and dysfunction was Judah. His entire life seemed to be one foolish decision after another, hence the title of my sermon. He was there when his brother was sold into slavery. In fact, it was his idea. The brothers were originally going to just kill him but Judah said, 'We don't want guilty consciences with his blood on our hands,' so they sold the boy to slave traders instead.

"Judah married a foreign woman." Pastor Duncan looked at Deborah. "That was a big no-no. He went on to have three sons. The first son was so wicked, the Bible simply said that God took him. Can you imagine?"

She shook her head, totally absorbed in the story Pastor Duncan was telling.

He continued, seeming to enjoy his rapt audience. "It was the custom in those days that if a man died without leaving an heir – a son – and if the wife was still of child bearing age *and* the man had a brother then the widow would then become the wife of the brother. The brother's duty would then be to get her pregnant so that there would be an heir to inherit the dead man's birthright."

"You're kidding."

Pastor Duncan smiled at her. "No, I'm absolutely serious. Aren't you glad you didn't live back then?"

"And how."

"So the wife of Judah's first son, ended up the wife of Judah's second son and, surprise, surprise, he was no good either. God took him, too." Pastor Duncan looked a little bit uncomfortable. "You can read the Biblical account to get the details," he said with a faint blush on his cheeks.

"Now Judah had a third son. But he was young and Judah had already lost two sons with this woman, so he didn't want to risk the last one. He sent the poor woman home to her family. She returned home, surrounded in disgrace and forced to wear widow's clothing until she married the third son.

"I don't know if that young woman knew all along or if it finally dawned on her that Judah had no plans of allowing her to marry the third son, but she finally figured it out. She came up with her own solution to the problem. She dressed in prostitute attire, sat by the side of the road and seduced her father – in - law as he went by on the way to town."

"This story *cannot* be in the Bible!" Deborah exploded and Pastor Duncan laughed out loud.

"Oh yes it is!" He grinned and nodded at her. "Genesis, chapters thirty seven and thirty eight! It's there, it's there! People don't realize that the Bible is *full* of stories that make our lives sound mundane and tame in comparison.

"Now remember, Judah thought this young woman was safely tucked away in her parent's home dressed in widow's clothes. Then he found out she was pregnant. *And Judah was furious!* He demanded that she be taken out and *burned.* I love how she let her father – in - law know who was responsible. As she was being dragged to the stake she sent a message to her father – in - law. She said, 'The man who owns this identification seal and walking stick is the father of my child. Do you recognize them?'

"I can't begin to imagine Judah's reaction. For, of course, they were *his* identification seal and walking stick that he had paid the prostitute with when he hadn't had any other way to pay her for her services."

Pastor Duncan tapped his chin. "The Bible doesn't say, but I think that this moment in Judah's life was definitive. I believe that it was at this moment that Judah stopped becoming The Foolish Man." He looked at her and shrugged.

"He publicly took responsibility and even acknowledged that she was more in the right than he was because he hadn't kept his promise to let her marry his third son. That took guts, I think." Pastor Duncan looked at Deborah and winked. "And he became the father of *twins.*

"In the meantime, there was the brother they'd sold into slavery, remember? That was all within God's plan and Joseph went on to become second in command answerable to only Pharaoh himself. When famine swept through the land, the brothers were forced to travel to Egypt because it was the only place that had food. The brothers didn't recognize Joseph, but he recognized them. Joseph questioned them about his family, forced them to bring his younger brother Benjamin to him and put them through a number of stressful trials to determine if they had changed from the selfish, hateful, murderous brothers he'd remembered.

"It's Judah that brings Joseph to tears in the end, offering to take the place of his younger brother, Benjamin – who's been accused of a serious crime – rather then break his father's heart *again* with the news of

Benjamin's impending fate. The speech Judah gave to Joseph in defense of Benjamin and at great peril to himself personally has been called by commentators as 'one of the noblest pieces of natural eloquence'."

Pastor Duncan shrugged and smiled. "When Jacob died, he blessed each of the sons, but to Judah he gives the choicest piece. For it is through Judah's line that Jesus Christ will be born. Jacob tells him, 'The scepter will not depart from Judah, nor the ruler's staff from his descendants, until the coming of the one to whom it belongs, the one whom all nations will obey.' King David and King Solomon are his descendants as well. So The Foolish Man Triumphs in the end."

Deborah was quiet for a bit after he finished. He finally looked concerned. "I've gone on for far too long and you've been too polite to stop me."

She *was* tired, but smiled at him just the same. "Politeness is *not* my strong suit, Pastor Duncan. Yes, I'm tired, but that's not why I'm quiet. I was just thinking of Judah."

"It's a story that has numerous lessons that we can all learn from. It's never too late to change. No mistake is so big that it can't be forgiven. The right decisions are rarely the easiest. God rewards you for wise and honorable choices. We could go on and on."

"But not everyone will embrace those lessons will they?"

Pastor Duncan looked at her seriously. "No, not everyone will learn from them, Deborah. I'm sure a majority of my congregation heard this story on Sunday, thought it was a highly interesting account, and then never gave it a second thought. Part of being a true child of God is being able to realize not only our constant proclivity towards sin but also our constant need to examine ourselves, ask for forgiveness, and pray for *ongoing* guidance and correction."

"That's what separates the women from the girls and the men from the boys," Deborah said grinning at him.

"You've got that right."

"Jonathan never understood that lesson."

Pastor Duncan sighed a great, world-weary sigh and looked out the hospital window. "There is one thing that I am *so thankful* for each and every day of my life."

"What's that?"

"That when we get to heaven, I'm not in charge of the gates of admission." He looked at her. "I didn't know Jonathan well. I had only just arrived and begun ministering to our church and then he died. He never spoke with me and so I don't know his heart." Pastor Duncan gave her a sad smile. "He's a lot like some of these Bible men and women in that he will be remembered *by us* solely on his failures and mistakes. I *do* know that the Bible forbids us to judge one another so I won't go any further."

He took her hand. "You are *so much better* now than that morning I sat in your living room a number of weeks back and you told me the awful secret you'd been bearing all on your own. It is almost as if the Lord has reached down, gently picked you up, dusted you off, given you a loving kiss, turned you around 180 degrees from the direction you were going, stood you back on your own two feet *and* given you a gentle push to get you to start moving in the right direction. You are smiling, and talking, and interacting, and *living* again." He chuckled and shook his head. "And I'm saying this to you sitting by your hospital bedside and you with a fractured skull! How ridiculous is that?"

Even Deborah chuckled. "I know what you are saying, though. The numbness that I worked so hard to keep with me at all times has just faded away. I *am* living once again."

Pastor Duncan looked at her then and Deborah realized that he was a very wise young man. "And perhaps the greatest reason for this well being is that you have put the hate and bitterness away. You have chosen to focus on *Deborah* and her life rather than Jonathan."

She looked down at her hands and after thinking for a bit, she nodded. "Yes," she said quietly, "you're right. The hate's gone." Deborah looked up at Pastor Duncan and said sincerely, "It never did *me* any good, just robbed me of living."

Pastor Duncan nodded. "You've got to forgive him, eventually, too, you know. That will make your healing complete. I'm not saying that you have to approve of what he did, - no one should - I'm simply saying that you have to acknowledge that all of what he did was *his life*, his blame. His choices were not your choices, your fault, your responsibility. You have to give them to Jonathan, sweep your house clean and continue to look forward.

"I have been praying earnestly for you, Deborah. I've prayed you into church and I've prayed your gradual healing. Mind you, I'm not taking any of the credit. That belongs to God. But people don't realize that the most powerful weapon we have is prayer. It changes things. You are living proof of it.

Pastor Duncan stood, gathering up the empty donut bag. "You are a strong woman, Deborah. It's a continual pleasure to know you and spend time with you."

She snorted at him.

"And I forbid you to call me an idiot this time."

She laughed then. "Could you go and get a nurse and tell her I'd like to get back in bed?"

"Absolutely."

She noticed, once they had her settled in bed that there was less pain in the movement and said so.

"You're healing nicely," the nurse said. "We should be able to kick you out of here very soon."

"Thanks for coming, Pastor Duncan."

He came over and patted her hand. "My pleasure, Deborah. If I was a betting man I'd guess that you'll be asleep before I get to the elevator. Pleasant dreams. I'll check on you again soon."

"Pastor?"

"Yes?"

"Thanks."

He looked at her in surprise. "It's my duty to visit my parishioners when they're in the hospital."

"No, I meant for calling Peter and telling him I was here."

"Oh, *that*." He grinned and bowed. "My pleasure."

Deborah slept the afternoon away until they all showed up around dinner time. They'd brought subs to eat and Zoe had brought Deborah a beautiful drawing to hang up by her bedside. As they passed around the subs, there was one extra one. "Who's that for?" Deborah asked.

Grace looked surprised. "Peter. He should be here any minute," she said looking at the clock. "He always gets here about 6:00." Grace smiled at her mother. "He's nice, Mom."

Deborah was blushing when Peter walked in. He arched his eyebrow at her and gave her a smile and a wink. When he walked over to her she thought she would explode with embarrassment, mortified that he would kiss her in front of the kids. He seemed to know this as he walked over to her and grinned at her. Deborah had a start when she realized Peter seemed quite delighted with her discomfort. He took pity on her though, and just reached over and gently cupped her cheek with his hand. "Have you had a good day?" he said leaning over quietly to her. She realized then that with everyone and everything going on in the room no one was even looking at them and she relaxed a bit.

"Yes, I had a good day. I'm ready to go home, though."

"I bet you are. I'll get one of the kids to speak with the doctor and get some answers, okay?"

She nodded.

"Are you still in much pain?"

"I still have a slight headache, but I sat in the chair all day and being moved wasn't nearly as bad as I thought it would be."

"Good." Peter carefully selected a chair, dragged it over and sat down next to her. He seemed to be claiming his territory.

They all munched their sandwiches. Deborah didn't talk much but watched the interaction between Peter and the kids. They seemed comfortable and easy with him; enough such that there was a goodly bit of teasing back and forth. She realized that while she had been out of it for a bunch of days they had been forced to get to know each other, whether they liked it or not. She smiled then. They seemed to like it better then not.

"What's so funny?" Peter had glanced over and seen her smile.

"Not funny. Nice."

"Is this too much?"

"*This* is absolutely perfect."

"Okay, then."

Deborah came home on Friday after she was able to prove to the doctors and nurses that she could at least get to the bathroom on her own and care for her personal needs. She found it a little bit comical sitting in the hospital bed with John, Grace, and Todd all hovering around her listening and asking questions while the doctor spoke with her and gave her final instructions.

All three escorted her home. "Mother," Grace began and dropped her voice so that no one could hear her speaking. They were both in the living room while John made Deborah a cup of tea and Neil and Todd ran around with Zoe and Max in the backyard. She could hear shrieks of delight filtering in through the open windows. She tensed a little bit because every time Grace had something serious to discuss with her she called her 'Mother'.

"Yes?" Deborah was sitting in the living room in one of the wing chairs with her feet tucked up underneath her.

"Todd's moved back into his old bedroom here for the time being in case you need something in the night. Grace rushed on, "Peter has insisted on setting up his home office here, wanting to spend the days with you ... Is that okay with you?"

"I don't need a babysitter."

"No, but you need someone close by for the first few days just in case." Grace smiled at her mother and touched Deborah's arm. "*We* all agree about that, even if you don't. What we came up with seemed like a logical solution ... If there are any days that Peter has to go on site I could make certain to be here. You wouldn't get much peace and quiet if I was here with Zoe and Max. John will have to get back to California, and Todd has to work ..." Grace looked uncomfortable. "*We* like Peter, you know. A lot. He's impressed us with his kindness, his no nonsense approach to things, and, above all, his dedication to you. But you and I have never talked except to decide what you were going to wear on a date with him! I realized as we picked you up at the hospital and brought you home that we've not really asked you *your* opinion of this arrangement. We were so wrapped up in coming up with a plan that would work, we forgot to ask *you*." She took a deep breath. "If you're unhappy with the way we've planned things out then it's easy to change."

"He's cute, isn't he?"

"*Mother.*"

Deborah chuckled and patted Grace's hand that still rested on her arm. "It's a fine arrangement, Grace. We've only been out a few times but it has been very easy and comfortable."

"Okay, then."

Deborah sighed. "He's a *nice man*, Grace. He's not made any effort to portray himself as perfect, though. In fact, he's gone out of his way to make sure I know that *he's not*. But it seems that everything that comes out of his mouth is refreshing and every action he does is kind and thoughtful."

She gave Grace a smile. "He's a foolish man who's making every effort to triumph. And I'm more then happy to have his company."

Deborah could tell Grace didn't quite understand her little speech but she didn't care. She was alive, she was surrounded by those who loved and cared about her, and there wasn't a speck of numbness. Despite all of her aches and pains, *she felt very good.* Very good indeed.

John brought Deborah and Todd breakfast Saturday morning and to say good-bye as he had a one o'clock plane to catch. They sat in the sunny living room, her comfortably seated on the couch all propped with pillows. *This is the life,* her head said.

"I hope you won't have any trouble with your job missing the whole week," she said to John.

"They were very understanding, Mom. I took a few vacation days and a few personal days and I've done a lot of stuff through email. It's okay."

"Thanks for coming."

"I'm not my father, Mom," John said with a sharp tone.

There was an awkward silence for a time between the three of them. "All right you two," she finally said, "you need to know that one of the main reasons I'm feeling so much better lately is because I've finally been able to put my hatred for Jonathan aside. I think you two should work on that, also."

"It's not that easy, Mom," Todd mumbled, studying the collection of pictures over the fireplace.

"You're telling me that?" she asked maybe a little too abruptly.

Todd looked at her uncomfortably. "No, I mean yes ..." He sighed. "I need time, Mom."

"Part of your problem is that you've *always* had issues with Jonathan, even before all of this stuff came out. You all but said that to me the other day when we talked in the kitchen. I don't know how to help you with that except to tell you that whatever anger you have toward him in regard to *me* you need to put away. I'm okay. The woman that I am now is a result of the life I've led. I'm not perfect or as strong or as confident as I'd like to be, but I've still got time to work on those areas. Make sure whatever issues you've got with Jonathan are your own personal ones, Todd. Don't add me into the mix."

"Why?" John said a little strongly. "Why can't we be indignant for what he did to you?"

Deborah was quiet while she organized her thoughts. She shrugged finally. "Because it's over. Done with. Water under the bridge. Spilled milk. *We can't change it.* Pastor Duncan says I'm to look forward and that until I can forgive Jonathan I'll never be completely healed."

"*Forgive him!*" Todd exploded. "He's got a hell of a nerve telling you that."

"You know," Deborah said, "I would have had the same reaction a few weeks ago. But now ..." She was at a loss as to how to explain it to them. "Oh, I don't know!" she finally exclaimed in frustration. "You can pick at a scab over and over and make it sore and cause a scar or you can just leave it alone, let it heal, and pretty soon you can't even remember where the cut was. All's I know is I feel *so much better* just letting it all go. There is still hurt, and confusion, and anger but it's not choking me anymore. Do you know that my throat used to hurt from the effort it took to keep myself from screaming?"

Both of her sons looked at her and were silent. "Do you go to church?" she finally asked them.

"No," they both said together, suddenly flashing identical deer-in-the-headlights expressions.

"Why not?"

John said, "I'm too busy. I've got stuff to do on the weekends that I can't do during the week."

"Like what?"

He looked uncomfortable.

"Like sleep late?"

John grinned. "That's a *very good reason*," he finally said and Todd laughed.

"What's your excuse?" Deborah turned, focusing in on Todd.

"Sometimes I have to work."

"Uh hmmm …"

"Sometimes I like to sleep."

"Got any other excuses?"

"Sometimes I … forget." Now it was John's turn to laugh.

"I want you to make me a promise."

"Oh, brother," Todd said, rolling his eyes and then glancing at his brother for ideas on escape.

"Don't 'oh brother' me, I want both of you to give me your word that you'll make it to church at least twice a month.

"That's all? I don't have to go every Sunday?" It was Todd, acting like he'd just gotten a reprieve from the death sentence.

"There's got to be more to this promise," John said looking very skeptical.

"Nope, that's it," she said.

"Why is this so important to you, Mom?" John finally asked.

"Because *I'm* better for going and I think it will help you, too. All you have to do is go to the building. But I do insist that it's a sound church, one that teaches real Bible truths. If you can't find one, I'll get

Pastor Duncan to give you a list of ones near where you both live. Once you get in the building God and I will take care of the rest."

They both looked at each other and then back at her. "What are you going to do once you get us in the building, Mom?" Todd asked, struggling not to laugh.

"Pray. And then you're in for it, *big time.*" She smiled and knew she looked rather smug. "Come on, I want your promise. At least two Sundays a month to a *good* church."

With a marked lack of enthusiasm, they both promised. Deborah knew she looked triumphant.

"Now, a last word. You and I were not responsible for Jonathan's choices. *He was.* And since he made them, only he could explain them. And since he's not able to explain them, then they'll all just have to fade away."

Both of their faces took on that hard look of anger with the mention of Jonathan. "Learn from Jonathan's mistakes," she said as earnestly as she could. "Don't let them destroy you. He wasn't perfect and neither are we."

"Who wasn't perfect?" Grace asked walking into the living room.

John looked at his watch. "Crap," he muttered under his breath, "I had hoped it was time for me to head off to the airport." Todd gave him a 'ha-ha you're stuck' look.

"Why's everyone so serious?" Grace asked breezing in and collapsing on the sofa.

"Neil and the kids here?" Todd asked hopefully, desperate for an out for the coming discussion.

Grace shook her head. "Nope, just me. He took the kids to the park and I came over for a quick kid-free visit."

"Crap," Todd muttered under his breath to John. "Now we have *no* chance of avoiding this."

"Would someone tell me what's going on?" Grace said in a strident tone. She looked at all three of them, expectantly. The boys turned and looked at their mother. It was all Deborah's show.

Suddenly, Deborah was profoundly nervous. Fearful that the good feelings within the family, so newly discovered, would be shattered into a million pieces and lost should The Truth come out. But *The Truth was out*, her head reminded her, and incompletely at that. Deborah realized there was more potential for hurt should she leave things the way they was. *Help me*, she heard herself pray, *give me the right words*. She felt a bit more peaceful then.

"I need to tell you some things, Grace," she said, and Grace, now fully agitated, sat up rigidly on the edge of the couch.

"I have been meaning to speak with you about this, and now is as good a time as any. Will you let me talk without interrupting and then, when I'm finished, I'll answer any questions you have?"

Grace looked nervously at John and Todd and then slowly nodded. The boys' expressions were closed and serious.

"You know that I have been struggling since Jonathan died. His death was so sudden and unexpected. But what you don't realize was that there were things I discovered after his death that caused me even more heartache and pain. It was those additional things that I discovered that almost pushed me off the deep end." Deborah sighed, trying valiantly to lighten the heavy gloom that sat in the room with them like a gigantic fire-breathing dragon. "For me, it's taken almost two years to come to terms with what Jonathan did and I have finally, only very recently, been able to set aside my anger and grief and ... hatred and begun to live again."

Grace opened her mouth to speak but Deborah held her hand up to keep her silent. "Let me finish. I'm afraid I'll loose my train of thought and this is very difficult for me. I want to get it right." She shook her head. "No, I want to get it *perfect*." Grace closed her mouth reluctantly it seemed.

Deborah got up – carefully for the dizziness was still there - and went into the kitchen. She got out The List from the phone book drawer and came back in to where her children all continued to sit in miserable silence. "I was ready to give up on every*one* and every*thing*. Remember when I told you I was even going to give up on God and become a heathen?

Grace nodded her head, slowly, still uncertain and confused.

"But God, didn't give up on *me*. He has worked diligently over these past weeks, proving to me that I am worthy, loved, fortunate, and *alive*." She held The List up. "God's given me more things the I could possibly need to get through all of this." Deborah hesitated and had a wave of panic that she was making a complete mess of everything. She sighed and smiled at Grace. "I sit here today with you and can honestly say that *I have never felt better in my whole life.*

"I had intended on keeping these private things – between Jonathan and I –," Deborah shrugged and looked down at the list in her hands, "just between me and him, and God, I guess. But that is not the way it has turned out to be. And as John and Todd have found out, it is only fair that you know, too.

"Grace," it seemed as if everyone in the room took a deep breath simultaneously, "Jonathan, when he died, left another wife and two children in California. In his will, he left provisions for them as well as for me.

"The boys, still have a lot of anger towards him and you walked in when I was telling them that rather then hate Jonathan, they should learn from his mistakes. None of us are perfect."

The silence was deafening in the living room. Deborah had never understood the expression until that very moment as all four of them sat there, unmoving and barely breathing.

"I want to say that it can't possibly be true," Grace finally said, frowning and glancing at her brothers for some sign of agreement.

No one said anything. The silence went from deafening to damning.

Grace stood up and began to pace around the living room. "Who is this woman? Where is she now? What is going on with the children? Did she know about us? Was she a home-wrecker or was she an innocent?" The questions, when they finally came out of Grace's mouth, had the force of a shotgun blast.

Deborah pondered the questions for a few moments. Odd, but Grace asked questions that she had never even thought of. She shook her head. "I'm sorry. I can't answer a single one of your questions, Grace," Deborah finally managed.

Grace stalked over to John and Todd, stopped in front of them and said accusingly, "You knew?"

Deborah felt compelled to answer before either of the boys could. "John found out by accident almost four years ago. He's suffered with the secret the longest. Todd found out accidentally just recently."

Grace studied both of her brothers, her gaze boring into them. Both looked profoundly uncomfortable but silently stared back. Grace turned to her mother, then, near tears. "I always thought he was such a good husband and father ...!" It was just as Todd had said it would be for Grace and Deborah's heart broke then for her daughter.

"He never was *either*," Todd ground out through clenched teeth.

"Todd ..." Deborah tried to say the necessary words to keep the situation from exploding but it was if Todd had struck a match and dropped it into an open can of gas.

While they shouted accusations and hurled their fury and hurt around the room, Deborah sat silently and watched. Suddenly, she was *so* tired. The sorrow welled up in her, like a long lost companion and close behind danced her very best friend, numbness. Sitting on the couch, Deborah slowly felt all the characteristics slowly attach again to her like leeches; anger, hatred, sorrow, misery, bitterness, loneliness, despair. Hell, she might as well shoot for the moon. She added old, and broken, and stupid and clumsy ... The list went on and on.

The List, the voice in her head said. *Read The List*. She looked down at the crumpled piece of paper in her hand and as the fury and sorry and numbness swirled around her she meticulously read The List. Then she looked at the pictures she'd carefully hung up over the fireplace that represented only part of the wonderful things that God had given her to not only survive but to *succeed*. And still the shouting swirled around her, her three children were now facing each other, fists clenched at their sides shouting things about past and present and future wrongs and misdeeds.

"Shut up or get out!" Deborah finally shouted loud enough to be heard above their angry voices. When the three of them looked at her, silent at last, Deborah spoke through clenched teeth, "You're dragging me back down and I can't have it! I won't allow it! *You've got to get out.*

"I'm not saying you're not entitled to your emotions, but I am saying you can't drag them out around me. If you want to fight and scream and rail at each other go to another location. *But don't do it here.* I can't have it. I won't have it."

Fiercely, Deborah said to John, "You're going to have to work on the guilt. I've told you quite specifically you did the right thing in not telling me. You've known the longest and therefore suffered the longest. I'm sorry for that and that's the only bit of *anger* I still carry in me towards Jonathan."

Deborah turned to her youngest, the spitting image of Jonathan. "Todd, you've got to work on your fury. You were angry with Jonathan before all this was made known to you and you remind me now of a dry forest that's just had a match thrown into it. You've turned into a raging inferno. *Don't let it burn down your entire wood.* I've told you that. That's the only bit of regret I still carry in me towards Jonathan."

Deborah turned to her daughter's mascara streaked face, "Grace, you've benefited from more of Jonathan's love than any of us here. That's a fact that perhaps you weren't aware of but all of the rest of us were. I'm glad you've got that treasured memory to hold dear. At least one of us has some fond memories of Jonathan. But don't deny any one of us the emotions we feel as a result of this betrayal. They are ours to do with as we please. That's the only bit of *sorrow* I still carry in me towards Jonathan; in that in revealing his deception it will somehow cause division among us."

Suddenly exhausted, Deborah wandered over to the couch and sat down. She felt like she was one hundred years old. "We *need* each other. *You are what God has given me to get through this.* And *we* are what God has given each of *you* to get through this, too. None of us are perfect, but together, if we hold on to each other tightly enough, with God's help we should be able to keep each other from falling apart."

"Who's falling apart?" Peter asked as he carefully shut the front door and walked into the living room.

No one spoke. He came over to stand by Deborah as she sat on the couch and rested his hand on her shoulder. He looked at everyone's faces and then said quietly, "Ahh, the truth is out."

"*He* knows, Mother?!" Grace's voice was furious.

"Yes, Grace, Peter knows," she said quietly. "It's my right to be able to speak and tell anyone I wish about my life without gaining your permission." Peter squeezed her shoulder and she looked up at him. He brushed her cheek with his knuckles.

"I've shared private things with her about my life, too, Grace," Peter said to Grace quietly. "You can't begin to understand and care about a person until you learn about what makes them tick. And when you get to be as old as we are, there's usually a hell of a lot of mistakes and lessons worth telling."

Wiping away her tears with the back of her hand, Grace looked at her watch. "I'm going to go. Neil's waiting for me."

"Yes, okay," Deborah said thinking perhaps enough had been said for one visit.

Grace looked at Todd, still visibly furious and then John, standing miserably by the window. "Have a good flight, John," she managed before she rushed out the front door.

"Told you, Mom," Todd said with frustration.

Deborah sighed. "You're so wise and all knowing, Todd. Did it ever register with you that I never disagreed when you said the truth wouldn't go over well with Grace? You can't blame me for still having some far flung hope though …"

"I've got to go, too, Mom," John said. "I should have left fifteen minutes ago."

"Go, I'm fine."

John knelt down by her. "No you're not, but you are okay, aren't you?"

"Yes," Deborah leaned over and kissed him, "I *am* okay."

"I love you, Mom, and I'll keep my promise."

"You better, or I'll be forced to fly out there, move in with you and monitor you." John kissed her once more and was gone.

Deborah looked at Todd then. "Don't you have anything better to do then to stand there and glare?"

He looked at her, lost and upset. "It will get better, I promise," she finally said to him quietly. "At least I'm pretty sure it won't get any worse than this."

"God, I hope not," Todd said. He looked at Peter. "Will you be here for a while?"

"I DO NOT NEED BABYSITTERS!" Deborah shouted.

Both totally ignored her. Peter nodded, "Yeah, I planned to stay the afternoon, or until she kicked me out."

"Okay, you still have my cell phone number?"

"Yup."

"Okay, call me if I'm not back before you need to go."

"Fine, but I'm not in any hurry."

Todd kissed his mother and Deborah took a moment to hug him and whisper that she loved him. He gave her a weak smile and left.

Peter sat by her on the couch. He looked at her in silence for a long time. Grace had helped her wash her hair last night and it was a curly mess all over her head she suspected. The bandage over the stitches was just above the right side of her hairline. His staring at her made her self-conscious and she instinctively reached up and tried to smooth her hair. Had she even put any mascara on this morning? Who knew?

"You did well," he said after a time.

"What do you mean I did well?" she said.

"I was listening."

"For how long?"

"I pulled in right after Grace got here. I saw her walk in the front door."

"And you *eavesdropped?*"

Peter shrugged, completely unrepentant. "Well, I had every intention of coming right in but things heated up nearly immediately. I almost left and then I thought I'd hang around in case you needed me. You know, the whole knight in shining armor coming to rescue the damsel in distress thing."

"It was hard," Deborah finally said.

"For most people, it would have been impossible."

"I prayed I'd have the right words …"

"If I'm any judge, I'd say you did."

"I wanted them to appreciate that I've *moved on* and am so much better because of it."

"You did communicate that. In fact, as far as I'm concerned there's only one thing you forgot."

"What?!"

"You forgot to tell them your name is Deborah, the fiery woman. If you'd done that from the start, I don't think you would have had to shout at the end." Deborah didn't have a response to that.

They were quiet for a bit and then Peter said, "You have no idea how much you frightened all of us." He leaned forward and gently touched the bandage on her head. "Does it still hurt?"

"Yes, a little." He took Deborah's face in his hands and ever so very gently leaned over and lightly kissed the bandage that covered the stitches. The warmth of his hands, the smell of his subtle aftershave, the very *presence* of him made all the chaos of the last few minutes fade away into oblivion. He looked at her and smiled a sweet smile and then dropped his hands and sat back and looked at her.

"My neck hurts back here, too," and Deborah pointed to a spot at the base of her neck just where her hair ended. Peter shifted closer, leaned over, slid her around and lifted her hair off her neck. She felt his warm breath and mustache kiss her gently there, too, and her body was immediately covered with delicious goose bumps.

"And my shoulder hurts here," she said quietly, pointing. He hooked his finger in the neckline of her tee shirt and pulled the edge of it away to bare her shoulder and slowly and carefully kissed her there. She let out a contented sigh.

"And here," she breathed pointing to her wrist and felt wonderful chills again all over as he caressed the length of her arm and then kissed her wrist and her palm. She remembered he'd kissed her palm like that in the hospital …

"And here," she said and pointed to underneath her chin and he gathered her close in his arms and kissed her neck and, without her having to point it out, the hollow by her ear, just in case she supposed.

"How about here?" Peter finally said and touched Deborah's mouth ever so softly with his finger. "Does it hurt here?"

"I can't seem to remember ..." she said in a dreamy voice and he chuckled a very satisfied chuckle.

Above all else, guard your heart, for it affects everything you do.[10]

The Man Who Lived The Saddest Story Ever Told

"I'm going to tell you the saddest story in the Bible today," Pastor Duncan began. Deborah was seated between a highly uncomfortable Todd, who sat tensely to her right and a relaxed Peter who sat to her left.

"Relax," she whispered to Todd, "no one's going to attack you or anything."

"I'm afraid the ceiling might cave in because I'm here," Todd whispered out the side of his mouth.

"It's not been *that long*," she said.

"Oh, yes it has," he insisted.

"If it didn't collapse when I first walked in many years ago, I *can assure you,* you have nothing to worry about," Peter leaned over and whispered. He grinned at Todd. "It's nice to have you here. Do what your mother says and relax. I'm the one that should be nervous."

"Why should you be nervous?" Deborah asked him but he ignored her question and just smiled and took her hand in his.

Pastor Duncan stood at the pulpit and put his finger to his chin as if in thought. "Let me see, I could tell you about Prince Jonathan. Oh, that's a sad story. He was such a good guy. I would say he was one of the best examples of loyalty in the Bible. But he had a tragic life. He was a prince that never became king, he was a son that was ignored and unappreciated by his father, his best friend was given his birthright, his son was crippled in an accident, and he died a horrible death beside his father, King Saul, in battle. His enemies *nailed his corpse* to their city wall."

Deborah stole a look at Todd and was pleased to see that he seemed to be listening to the sermon. *Please keep him interested,* she prayed.

"Or, I could tell you the story about Samson. His mother was barren. She was visited by an angel and told that the child she would conceive who would go on to do great things. Samson did do great things for Israel, but he made great mistakes in his life, was captured by his enemies, blinded, made a slave, and he too died a horrible death.

"Or, I could tell you about Prince Absalom. Handsome, smart, popular with the people, but who was so consumed by revenge, hatred, and greed that he *also* died a horrible death and never achieved his potential.

"But no, the saddest story in the Bible, in my opinion anyway, is none of these. The man I'm going to tell you about was so loved by the Lord, that he was given a private, special name – Jedidiah – which meant 'Beloved of the Lord'. He so pleased God in his early years, that the Lord personally spoke to him and offered him *anything.* God literally said to this man, 'What do you want? Ask, and I will give it to you!' *Can you imagine?'*

Pastor Duncan stood at the pulpit and quietly said, "What would you have asked for?" and then waited a minute for everyone to think.

"This man, so beloved of God, gave God an answer that was pleasing. And because of that God gave him other things that he *hadn't* asked for; riches, power, prestige ... God told him, 'No other king in all the world will be compared to you for the rest of your life.' This man was Solomon, and his request from God was for wisdom. Not wealth, not power over his enemies, not honor, but simply wisdom to have an understanding mind so that he could govern God's beloved people well and know the difference between right and wrong.

"People came from all over the world to talk with Solomon and gain benefit from his insight. Let me read to you about him." Pastor Duncan gathered up his Bible and began to read.

"'The people of Judah and Israel were as numerous as the sand on the seashore. They were very contented, with plenty to eat and drink. King Solomon ruled all the kingdoms from the Euphrates River to the land of the Philistines, as far south as the border of Egypt. The conquered peoples of those lands sent tribute money to Solomon and continued to serve him throughout his lifetime. The daily food requirements for Solomon's palace were 150 bushels of choice flour and 300 bushels of meal, ten oxen from the fattening pens, twenty pasture-fed cattle, one hundred sheep or goats, as well a deer, gazelles, roebucks, and choice fowl. And there was peace throughout the entire land. Through the lifetime of Solomon, all of Judah and Israel lived in peace and safety. Solomon had four thousand stalls for his chariot horses and twelve thousand horses. God gave Solomon great wisdom and understanding, and knowledge too vast to be measured. He composed some 3,000 proverbs and wrote 1,005 songs. He could speak with authority about all kinds of plants, from the great cedar of Lebanon to the tiny hyssop that grows from the cracks in a wall. He could also speak about animals, birds, reptiles, and fish. And kings from every nation sent their ambassadors to listen to the wisdom of Solomon.'"

Pastor Duncan looked up at the congregation. "Wow. Some guy, huh? How many of you know the story of Solomon?" Many people raised their hands. Pastor Duncan nodded. "He built the magnificent Temple and Palace, right? He was wise and rich, and brought the nation of Israel to its greatest heights."

Pastor Duncan walked from behind the pulpit carrying his Bible. He stepped out to the center of the altar. "Wisest of the wise, richest of the rich, revered, sought after ... Listen to one of the last things he wrote."

He looked down and read again from his Bible, "'Don't let the excitement of youth cause you to forget your creator. Honor him in your youth before you grow old and no longer enjoy living. It will be too late then to remember him, when the light of the sun and moon and stars is dim to your old eyes, and there is no silver lining left among the clouds. Your limbs will tremble with age, and your strong legs will grow weak. Your teeth will be too few to do their work, and you will be blind, too. And when your teeth are gone, keep your lips tightly closed when you eat! Even the chirping of birds will wake you up. But you yourself will be deaf and tuneless, with a quavering voice. You will be afraid of heights and of falling, white-haired and withered, dragging along without any sexual desire. You will be standing at death's door.'*²*"

Pastor Duncan stepped down into the congregation. "Does he sound like a happy man to you?" Deborah saw many people nodding their heads 'no'.

Pastor Duncan shook his head 'no', too. "No, at the end of his life when Solomon wrote this he was miserable. As wise as he was, he didn't follow some of his best advice nor did he heed God's warning when God granted him that wish in the early years of his rule. God had said to him, 'Follow me and obey my commands as your father, David, did.'"

Pastor Duncan's voice dropped to almost a whisper. "Do you know why this is the saddest story every told? Solomon died distant from his beloved God. The nation of Israel, at his death, *immediately* divided, never to be united again. In less then five hundred years, both parts: Judah to the south and Israel to the north, would become captive slaves of foreign powers. The people chosen by God, whom God choose, loved, freed, rose up, taught, encouraged, protected ... drifted far from Him, confused by the mixed signals that Solomon not only permitted but embraced himself; for Solomon's *seven hundred wives* and *three hundred concubines* brought idol worship and pagan rituals and beliefs into the very midst of this young, impressionable nation and they succumbed to all the temptations that were put before them. Solomon, the wisest man in the world, watched the disaster grow larger and larger around him and *surely had to know* what was coming and that it was most certainly all his fault, but *he did nothing*.

"*And God allowed it.* The wisest man in the world must have been one of the greatest of disappointments to God. Solomon was a classic example of someone who believed that he alone could be the exception to the rule. Solomon believed that he was the one person who could break God's law without suffering the consequences."

Pastor Duncan looked pointedly at the congregation. "And I'll tell you something, *we are all guilty of the same sin.*"

Pastor Duncan then did something Deborah had *never, ever* seen him do. He looked directly at her. But it turned out it wasn't Deborah he was looking at. "Come talk to us, Peter."

Peter squeezed Deborah's hand, released it and then he stood and walked forward to the front of the congregation. Standing beside Pastor Duncan, they had a Mutt and Jeff quality about them for the Pastor was on the smallish, short of stature range while Peter was just the opposite. "I don't know," Pastor Duncan began, "if all of you here know, Peter Gannon. He's been attending here, what? about six months, Peter?"

Peter nodded and smiled at the congregation. Deborah's heart was hammering so hard in her chest she thought surely her blouse must be moving in rhythm with it. "Do you know what he's doing?" Todd whispered out of the side of his mouth.

She shook her head 'no' but didn't say anything. She wasn't sure if her voice would be heard over the thumping of her heart.

"It has been my pleasure to get to know Peter and I asked him to share a little bit of his life's story with us and he has graciously agreed." Pastor Duncan motioned to the congregation, "They're all yours," he said to Peter with a smile and then went and sat down at the first pew.

"He's a little sneaky, our pastor," Peter began with a smile. He made no move to go up behind one of the pulpit spots but stayed down on the congregation floor and clasped his hands behind his back. He looked comfortable and at ease like he did this every darn day of his life. Deborah, on the other hand, thought she was beginning to hyperventilate. "Pastor Duncan told me who he was preaching on and thought my testimony would fit nicely with the story." He shrugged his shoulders. "I thought, *Oh, great! I'm going to be compared to the great King Solomon.*" Peter rolled his eyes and everyone laughed. She heard Pastor Duncan's shout of laughter over everyone else's.

"I was raised in profound poverty. Maybe the term 'abject poverty' is better ... Welfare, hunger, fear of survival ... There was abuse, too – neglect, intimidation ... I had parents that couldn't seem to get their life together well enough to provide for themselves let alone their *seven* kids. From an early age I developed an all consuming determination to distance myself as far and as fast from the reality of the way I was raised. Nothing else was more important. Nothing else was worthy of my time, energy or passion. I watched and learned. If I saw a person I was impressed by, I studied them until I figured out what it was about them that impressed me and then I worked to assume that quality. If I saw someone that I perceived to be successful, I studied them, trying to gain as much insight as possible to apply to myself and my future." He looked at the congregation. "*Every speck of information or ability I could acquire was one step away from the life I was determined to escape.*"

Peter shrugged. "I was smart, quick, persistent. *Tenacious* is a great word to describe me." Deborah could hear him saying, *I'm rather tenacious when I set my mind to something.* "The teacher's all loved me. I got a scholarship to a prestigious private high school in a nearby town and worked with determination to be top of my class to get into the desired college of my choice - and succeeded."

He paused then. "I *think* that at the moment I accomplished that goal - of getting accepted to the college of my choice on full scholarship - that I realized that I could accomplish just about anything I put my mind to." Peter looked seriously at the congregation. "When I left for college, I severed all ties with my family. They did not even know where I went. I never saw either of my parents ever again. For them, it was one less mouth to feed, one less problem to deal with, I guess. For me, it was the start of my master plan: to be successful, rich, respected, sought after ..."

Peter grinned then and looked at Pastor Duncan. "I'm beginning to see a big similarity here ..." Deborah could see Pastor Duncan nodding.

"God didn't offer and I didn't ask, though. I don't think I actually denied God's existence, but His importance in my life did not even warrant thought. But still and all, everything I touched seemed to turn to gold."

He looked earnestly at the people. "I don't tell you this to gain your admiration. But you need to know the man I *was*.

"I formed a company. I became rich. I became powerful. I became sought after. I had a magnificent home. One year, I remember I spent $26,000 just on spring landscaping." Deborah heard someone near her gasp. "I was totally consumed with being bigger, richer, more powerful, and more sought after. I never knew the feeling of satisfaction or contentment. Those two words were not within my understanding. I married but never had time to foster that relationship and had no desire to have a family." He looked at Pastor Duncan. "No 1,000 wives and concubines for *this guy.*" Some people chuckled.

"Like Solomon I seemed to have everything anyone could dream of and just like Solomon I was *so unhappy.*" He sighed and smiled. "I really can't pinpoint a turning point for me. It could have been the multimillion-dollar buy out of my company that left me - for the first time in my life – with free time on my hands. It could have been my divorce. It could have been my ex-wife's suicide." Deborah heard another person draw in a quick breath of shock. "It could have been the profound feeling of worthlessness that I struggled with for a number of years – I call them *The Lost Years.* It could have been all of those things or none of them, really. But the point was, *unlike* Solomon, God guided me, purposefully and clearly, to Him."

Peter smiled. "I stand here, today, before you no longer rich, no longer powerful, no longer avidly sought after in high level business circles. My goal is no longer to achieve any of those things but rather to be a *man after God's own heart.*" He looked at Pastor Duncan. "That was how they described David, wasn't it?" Pastor Duncan nodded. "I have come to learn that the things we should value, are the things that God values and to do that brings happiness, contentment, and peace like you cannot comprehend. There are no treasures here on earth of any value that can overshadow what is of Godly importance. Luke 12:34 says, 'Wherever your treasure is, there your heart and thoughts will also be.' I have to remind myself of that every single day of my life.

"I've learned to be patient and content with my life. I've learned to go slow and approach everything with prayer. I've learned to put the things that worry and upset me in God's hands." And for the first time since Peter had begun speaking, he turned and looked at her. He made direct eye contact with her, locked his gaze with hers and said, "I've learned to guard my heart and only let the things God would choose enter in to it. And I've learned to delight in the precious things that God sees fit to send my way that bring me happiness and laughter, whether I deserve them or not." He paused for the briefest of moments and then looked back at the congregation and smiled. "I pray that my story will help you in some small way. If it can make the difference for *just one person* then that's enough for me. Thanks for listening."

Todd had taken her hand when Peter had looked at her and she had gripped it tightly. Peter walked briskly back to them and everyone stood and began to sing the closing hymn. Deborah gave him a sidelong glance and he'd been waiting for her to look at him. Although he didn't look directly at her, he grinned through his singing and winked at her.

"*You* are not supposed to give me a crisis in church, only Pastor Duncan is," she said just loud enough to be heard over the singing. "Why didn't you tell me?"

Peter leaned down to her and said in her ear, "I was afraid you wouldn't come to church and then I wouldn't be able to sit with you."

Deborah looked up to catch his teasing look but he was absolutely serious. She sighed. They finished the last stanza of the hymn with her leaning against him.

As the people filed out, Peter grabbed hold of her hand and wouldn't let go. She tried to pry it loose, but aside from making a scene, was not successful. He stood at the end of the pew, with both of his hands behind his back and hers tightly clasped inside them. She listened to the sound of his voice respond to the polite comments of praise from the people and then remembered Todd. She turned to him. "What did you think?"

"It wasn't so bad, Mom."

"Are you just saying that?"

"No, it didn't kill me. The roof didn't collapse in. The minister didn't point directly at me and scream 'sinner!' I think, all in all, it was an okay visit."

Deborah chuckled. "Will you come to lunch with us?"

"No, you guys go ahead."

Peter turned around in between people stopping to speak with him. He'd obviously been listening. "Why?" he said to Todd. "Got a better offer?"

Todd grinned. "Actually, I do. And she's a lot prettier than either of you, too." Then he looked sheepish. "No offense, Mom."

"Good grief. I'd certainly hope that anyone you took out on a date looked better than your mother!" They both laughed.

"Okay, we'll let you off then," Peter said again over his shoulder, "but you owe us one."

"It's a deal. You'll bring Mom home?"

"Only if she makes me."

"*Peter!*"

Todd burst out laughing.

In the end, she pleaded tiredness and a headache – who would have thought that one brief morning could exhaust her so much? – and they drove to her home. Peter left again, once she was settled, and then came back with a pile of rented movies and take out Chinese food.

As they sat in companionable silence on the couch eating and watching a movie Deborah finally said to him, "No one has ever done anything as sweet as what you did today in church."

"What do you mean?"

"You know exactly what I mean."

Peter grinned his big wolfish grin. "No, tell me. How sweet was I today in church? What did I do? What did I say?"

She got embarrassed then. What if she'd misinterpreted his look? What if she'd heard what she wanted to hear and not exactly what he said? All of a sudden she felt hugely foolish and insecure. She was being a big dope. Deborah couldn't look at him anymore and instead looked down at her cashew chicken examining it as if she was preparing for a major science evaluation. "Nothing. Never mind."

"Okay."

She looked up at him then and Peter was looking at her very seriously. "What did I say today in church, Deborah? What did I do that was so sweet?"

She looked down, still unable to speak. Peter purposefully pried her dinner plate out of her hand, placed it on the coffee table, reached over, caught her chin and made her look up at him. "Tell me what you saw and heard today, Deborah. *I need to know if you got my message.*"

He was looking so damned serious. Her insecurities played riot with her thoughts. "You said ... I heard you say ... Oh, I'm a dope." Deborah was horrified with herself because she all of a sudden wanted to just start crying. She pulled her chin out of his grasp and looked down again at her empty lap.

"That's definitely not the message I was trying to get across," and Deborah could hear the teasing smile in Peter's voice.

"I know that," she muttered.

He sighed. "I think I said something like, I was driven, self centered, egotistical, and, in general, a bastard most of my life."

"That's *definitely* not the message you got across."

He chuckled. "Well *that's* a relief."

She still didn't look up at him.

"Did you hear me speak of my heart at all?"

Deborah nodded.

"Did you hear me speak of my need to guard it?"

She nodded again.

"Did you hear me say something about delighting in the precious things that God has sent me that bring me happiness and laughter – whether I deserve them or not?"

She nodded again.

Peter reached up and put his hand under her chin and made her look at him again. "Did you hear me mention your name?"

She shook her head 'no'.

"Did you know that I meant you?"

Deborah just looked at him, disbelieving that this wonderful man could be sitting there in her living room, on her couch, telling her what he seemed to be telling her. She couldn't shake her head 'yes', but she couldn't shake her head 'no', either. Her eyes felt like they were going to explode with the pressure of tears. She closed them shut. Tight.

"I've told you that God told me to speak to you."

Deborah felt a tear slip out.

"I've told you that hearing your laughter is almost always the best part of my day."

She tried to pull away but Peter wouldn't let her. Another tear slipped out.

"I've told you how much I enjoy being with you."

The tears began to fall in earnest now and it seemed that the harder she squeezed her eyes shut, the more spilled out.

"Tell me what you saw and heard today in church, Deborah. I want to know if you got my message."

Deborah looked at him then and the tenderness in his expression made her want to melt. She took a deep shuddering breath and tried to find her voice. "You told me," she said in the quietest of whisper voices, "that you loved me."

"Ahh," Peter smiled at her, "so you *did* get the right message," and pulled her tightly into his arms. "Thank *God*. Yes, I love you, Deborah Lawson. I have for quite awhile now."

They stayed like that for the longest of times. Finally, she couldn't resist asking, "Since when?"

Peter chuckled. "It certainly started when you had the guts to climb on the back of my motorcycle. I knew you were terrified. Remember how I asked you at the light if you wanted to go back?"

"You sounded so disappointed. I couldn't tell you 'yes'…"

"I wasn't disappointed! I was feeling guilty that I was ignoring your obvious feelings of terror and expected imminent death. Do you remember what you said?"

Deborah laughed just a little bit, still leaning against his chest with his arms around her. "I tried to be funny. I asked if I had to give back the coat."

"That was when."

"Then?!"

"Yup."

"Oh."

He sat up then and looked a bit sheepish. "I'm still hungry. I'm going to warm up my Chinese in the microwave. Can I do yours, too?"

She nodded. As he walked over to the microwave, and began to push buttons Deborah asked, "Do you have any contact with your brothers and sisters?" Then qualified, "Now it's your turn to say if a question is too personal or not."

"Deborah, you can ask me anything you want. I'm happy to answer your questions. No, I don't have any contact with them. At least not directly."

"What's that mean?"

"Well, I know where they all live."

She waited for him to elaborate, but he didn't. He carried their now steaming dishes back over to her and settled himself down. "Be careful, I think I made it too hot." He started to munch his food and appeared to be quite absorbed in the movie.

"*And?*" she finally said.

"And, what?"

"Peter ..."

He grinned. "It's fun to exasperate you. You get this little wrinkle right here ..." he leaned over and kissed her right between her eyebrows.

"It doesn't make sense."

"What doesn't?"

"The man you are *now* would have made the effort to settle things with your brothers and sisters."

Peter arched his eyebrow at her. *She* liked when *he* did that but she wasn't going to get off the track and tell him that now. "You think so, huh?"

"I know so."

"But you forgot a big piece of the puzzle. *I'm* different. *They* aren't."

"Oh."

He seemed to take pity on her and shrugged. "Both my parents had died by the time I was professionally established. Even though I ended up settling in California – I was born and raised in Pennsylvania – a few of my brothers and sisters found me. During my," he paused and then seemed to have a flash of an idea, "*Solomon years*," he winked at her, "they seemed to feel that I owed them things by right of family obligation. I don't think I remembered to say that I was the youngest this morning, did I?"

Deborah shook her head 'no'.

"Well, I was. Despite that, most of them seemed to have an opinion that it was only right that I *share*. Hell, when they first found me and made contact they made it quite clear that they *all* felt they deserved a complete free ride courtesy of *me.*"

"Did you?"

"No."

"Oh."

He sighed. "I got divorced. I sold the company. Janet killed herself. I got lost for some years. When I came out the other side of the long dark tunnel, one of the things I did was seek them out." Peter closed his eyes at the memory of it all. "*God,* that was *hard.* I think that took me almost six months …"

He looked at her then. "Each of them lives in a home I purchased for them. Paid free and clear with their names on the deeds. No one said thanks and I told them to consider all obligations met." He took a bite of his food.

He seemed uncomfortable. Deborah leaned over and kissed him on the cheek. "Hmpf. I *knew it.*"

He glanced at her out of the corner of his eye and smiled a sheepish smile. He took a deep, cleansing breath. "It's *so nice* that you always seem to expect the best of me. Not everyone does you know."

"I'm not everyone."

"No, you're not."

He looked serious. "Put your food down, I want to kiss you."

Deborah heard herself actually giggle. "No, it won't taste good heated up a third time."

"Does this couch have stain guard on it then?"

"I was an only child."

The change of subject didn't seem to faze Peter in the least. He leaned over and kissed her, just to make a point Deborah supposed - without spilling a bit of food. He kissed her nose, too, before he stood up. Having finished his plate of food, he got up and poured them both a fresh iced tea. From the kitchen he said, "Was that good or bad?"

Deborah shrugged. "Don't know. It was all I knew. Daddy was a very dominant, in-control guy. Mother was very quiet, submissive. She kept a lovely home, dinner was always on the table at 5:30. I was always dressed properly. It was a very traditional, 1950's style existence, I guess. A very *Leave it to Beaver* or *The Donna Reed Show* style of life. I don't remember a lot of love and affection displayed. It was all about what was proper, right, acceptable, *done*." She all of a sudden realized the picture she was painting and hurried to qualify. "I had a happy life, I don't mean to imply I didn't. I knew I was important and cared for."

"Did you know you were loved?"

She hesitated and thought. When she went to open her mouth, he held his hand up. "You just answered my question," he said.

"No, really. I *did* feel loved. By both of them. They each had different ways of communicating it to me even if I never heard them say it. He was a college professor and she was a homemaker. They both gave me the best they each had to give. Mother taught me all about being a good wife and mother and Daddy taught me the value of an education and pursuing excellence in oneself. I was expected to go to college, of course, and the suitable occupation for a young woman was to be a teacher. Of course, eventually, I was expected to marry and have children and then stay home."

"Do you realize how nontraditional your upbringing really was? Do you realize that you've described what should have been acceptable for our *grandparents* traditional roles?"

She looked at Peter. "It's all I knew when I was growing up. There was a lot of interaction with adults because my father and mother were always entertaining college colleagues. I didn't have much to compare to, really."

"Didn't you have friends?"

Deborah sighed and frowned trying to remember. "There was one girl, I think I was in 5th grade ... I can't recall her name ..."

Peter sounded furious. "It sounded like they kept you a virtual prisoner!"

"No! No! It wasn't that way *at all*. We just did everything together, as a family. There wasn't a lot of room for anything else. We went on glorious vacations. I traveled to Europe, Canada, all over the U.S ... Daddy worked hard to supplement my public school education with subjects he felt were vital." She looked at Peter. "They dedicated they're whole life to me. Don't you see? They didn't say they loved me, but they *showed* me. Why, when Daddy decided I was to become a teacher -"

"Your father chose your profession?" Deborah could hear the incredulousness in his voice.

She nodded. She sighed. Better get it over with. "Daddy chose Jonathan, too."

Now Peter was speechless.

"Jonathan was one of Daddy's students. Very bright, very polite. Daddy brought him home for dinner. That's how we met."

"How old were you?"

"I'd just started college, so I was almost eighteen."

"When did you get married?

"Two weeks before my nineteenth birthday."

"So much for your father thinking an education was important and encouraging your choice of profession." Peter's voice dripped with sarcasm.

"Oh no! See, that's where you're so wrong about Daddy. He sat down with Jonathan and I and he made Jonathan give him *his word* that he would make sure I finished college *and* have an opportunity to teach for a while before we began to start a family."

Peter took his glasses off then and rubbed the spot on his nose where they rested. Then he ran his hands through his hair. Finally he put his glasses on and looked at her. "I *cannot* absorb what you're telling me, Deborah. What kind of a man was Jonathan that he would allow his life to be dictated so?"

Deborah looked smug. "I told you that you two were nothing a like."

He snorted. "It just doesn't make sense … Where did you live when you were first married?"

"Here."

"In this town?"

"No, here the house I grew up in."

"This was your parent's house?"

Deborah nodded. "Remember our first date, when we went for coffee by the college? My father was a professor there for thirty-nine years," she said proudly.

"Did Jonathan attend there?"

She nodded.

"And you did, too." Peter was no longer asking questions, he was just stating what he already knew to be fact.

She nodded.

"So, you married the man your father chose, attended your father's college, and lived in your father's home your whole life."

Deborah nodded again, beginning to feel like one of those bobble-head dolls.

"And how long did you teach?"

She sighed. "You know, even though Daddy encouraged me to become a teacher, I think, had I been able to choose, I would have still become a teacher. Peter, *I was good at it."* She sighed at the fond memory of it all. "It was through teaching that I gained self confidence and discovered myself. I seemed to come alive in that classroom. I would walk in and it seemed in the blink of an eye the day would be over. I couldn't believe I got paid for it, either. For the first time in my life, I discovered I had my own opinions about things. I spoke out. I didn't always follow the rules. That's when Jonathan started calling me a maverick."

"Did he mean it as a compliment?"

Deborah thought for a moment. "I don't suppose so, now that I think about it." She grinned at him. "But I took it as one, anyway."

"You didn't answer my question. How long did you teach?"

"I got pregnant with John when I was twenty-five. We'd been married for about six years and I'd been teaching for about four."

"And once John was born, you stayed home."

"Yup, I had Grace before John was two and then Todd before Grace was two." She smiled. "It was a good time, for me, Peter. Jonathan began traveling right around the time I became pregnant with Todd. It was hard being on my own so much, but it was good, too. I took that little spark of self-confidence that had flared when I was teaching and put it to work as a stay at home mom. *I was good at that, too.* The outspokenness that had begun as a teacher, stayed with me as a Mom." Deborah looked at Peter. "Jonathan did *not* like that trait. He told me so on more than one occasion."

"I bet he didn't."

"But seriously, how could I be the meek, subservient, little wife he wanted so much when he wasn't here half the time? At some point, whether Jonathan was pleased or not ceased to matter to me." She looked at Peter. "Don't get me wrong. We were always polite and civil to each other. We behaved like a family."

Peter just looked at her. She looked back. "And your parents?" he finally said.

"At some point, they moved to a retirement community not too far from here. Daddy died right after Todd was born. I was glad he got to see his grandchildren. Mom died just about four years ago. John told me that at her funeral he already knew about Jonathan …"

Peter shook his head then. "I don't know which one of us is more pitiful."

"What do you mean?"

"The two of us had such a screwed up life." Peter thought of something. "Where did the church attending come from?"

Deborah thought for a few moments, searching back in her memory. "My mother. She started to attend a church by her, right after my father died. When I asked her about it, she said, 'It gives me courage.' I remember thinking that it was such an odd thing to say … But she did get more opinionated as she got older. *My* memories of her are of a meek, soft-spoken woman, but I would bet my kids have a different image of her. Mother championed me to do things *I* wanted to do rather than what Jonathan thought I *should do*. I guess I liked the change I saw in her. Dad died, Jonathan was always traveling, Mother visited, but not all the time. By the weekend, I was *desperate* to have some adult interaction of any kind. Church had a nursery. I got at least one hour of peace to myself." Deborah looked sheepishly at Peter, "Not the best reason to attend, I guess."

"It got you there."

"Yeah, it got me there. Jonathan reluctantly began to attend with me on the Sunday's he was home. *Appearances*, you know. I told him I was going to go with him or without him." Deborah remembered then. "Mother encouraged me to take that stand ..."

She shrugged. "So that's me. That's my life. I've spent my whole life being just what everyone else wanted me to be. I've been polite, respectful, kind ..." She shivered at the description she was giving of her self. "Yuck, I've always been so *well-behaved*."

Peter reached over and touched her face then. Starting at the top of her hairline, where the bandage was still covering the stitches and then slowly down the side of her face to her neck. Deborah sighed at his touch, closing her eyes in delight of the moment. His hand traveled down to rest on her breast over her heart. It stayed there. She opened her eyes and looked at him.

"You have a good heart, Deborah. You are a well-behaved woman with a good heart." His hand traveled back up and traveled around to the back of her neck. He drew her close for a kiss but stopped just a breath away from her mouth. She was still looking into his eyes. She could feel his breath and *almost* feel the tickle of his mustache. *Almost,* but not quite. "The good heart I wouldn't change for anything." Then Peter grinned that great big wolfish grin. "But we've got *plenty of time* to work on changing the well-behaved part."

Tuesday morning, when Todd came down she told him to go home to his own place. He stood there in his boxer shorts and his hair sticking up all over his head. "How come, Mom?"

"I don't need a baby-sitter. In fact, I'm driving myself to the doctor on Thursday and I hope he'll take the stitches out. I'm just about back to normal. Go home."

He walked over to the fridge and peered inside. "The food's better here," he mumbled. She watched as he drank directly out of the orange juice container and then wiped his mouth on his shirt sleeve. He looked over at her and gave her his Son's Glare. She stared right back at him. "Okay, I'll go home. The guys miss me. Besides," he got a wicked twinkle in his eye, "I'm sure you and Peter would like to be alone."

"Oh, you think so, huh?"

He began to take another drink of orange juice and winked at her.

"You sleeping here didn't stop us last night."

The orange juice exploded out of Todd's mouth as he coughed and spluttered. Deborah laughed and laughed, finally leaning against the counter to stay upright. She couldn't remember the last time she laughed so hard. It was *wonderful*. She got up, got a wet sponge and started wiping the orange juice up off the floor and the wall next to the fridge. Todd still kept choking and couldn't get his breath. When he finally was quiet she sneaked a peek at him and he was standing there in the middle of the kitchen looking at her.

Deborah took pity on him. "I'm *kidding*." She felt compelled to point out, however, "*You* started it."

He relaxed. "I can't deal with this stuff so early in the morning," he muttered and went upstairs to get dressed. He came down with a garbage bag filled with his clothes.

"Are they all clean?"

Todd shrugged. "Clean enough."

"Leave the dirty stuff here and I'll wash it. Why don't you come for dinner tomorrow night?"

"Will you cook stuffed peppers?"

She laughed. "Yes, I'll cook stuffed peppers. Bring the guys."

"You sure you're up to it?"

"If something changes, I'll call you. Okay?"

He shuffled over and kissed her on the cheek. "I love you, Mom."

"You didn't eat breakfast. Did you even brush your teeth?"

"First shift always meets at a local diner to start off. Don't worry. *Yes,* I brushed my teeth." He opened his mouth to prove it. She laughed again.

"I love you, too, Todd."

Peter called at about 9:00 a.m. and said he had to visit a site unexpectedly. When she assured him that she'd be fine on her own, he said, "Call Grace."

Groaning in exasperation, Deborah ground out, "I don't need a babysitter! How many times do I have to say that to all of you?"

"I didn't mean call Grace *for you,* I meant call Grace *for Grace.* She can *think* she's coming over for you, but we both know the truth."

She sighed. "How can you be so wise and not have had any kids?"

"You're rubbing off on me, I guess."

"I'm cooking stuffed peppers tomorrow night. Will you come?"

He was silent for a minute and Deborah felt compelled to ask, "Peter, is something wrong?"

"I was wondering what you were cooking for dinner tonight and if I can come, too."

She laughed, absolutely delighted. "Yes, you can come to dinner tonight, too."

"I might be late, though. I'll call you, all right? Don't go to any trouble. We'll go out ..."

"Okay."

Deborah called Grace. She didn't lie, but did let Grace think that she wanted her to come by because *she* needed *her.* Deborah assured Grace that she'd love to see the kids, too. She could tell by Grace's tone that she was still upset. Sighing, she hung up the phone knowing it could be a very long afternoon.

They arrived after lunch, Zoe wearing a bright green neon Tinkerbell dress and matching high heel plastic shoes. Grace rolled her eyes. "She slept in it, too. It's her latest favorite."

"She looks great. What's the big deal? Choose your battles wisely I always said."

Deborah had filled three buckets with water and put measuring spoons and cups and bowls out on the deck. "I thought we could sit outside and let the kids have some fun."

"Oh, that's a great idea, Mom. I worried that there wouldn't be anything to amuse them and they'd make us both nuts."

In the end, they convinced Zoe to take off her dress so it wouldn't get soaked. Before long, both of the children were stark naked and having a blast.

"I used to do this with you guys. Do you remember?" Deborah said with a fond smile.

Grace nodded. "You used to even bathe us out here, didn't you?"

"Yup. It was fun, it was easy. You spent most of your early summers almost completely nude." They both chuckled.

"I'm sorry about Saturday, Mom."

"Grace, let's get one thing straight before we talk about this. Each one of us has reacted to the truth about Jonathan in our own very personal way. We can't, for one minute expect anything less or more. Okay?"

"I told Neil."

Deborah nodded. "I had expected you to."

"He wasn't surprised."

She looked at Grace. "*Really.*"

"Really. We had a huge fight over it. He had the same perception of Daddy that Todd and John did. That he'd been a lousy father and a lousy husband." Grace looked a little sheepish. "I hadn't expected him to react like that. It sort of pushed me right over the edge."

"But he'd never said anything to you about it?"

"I asked him about that. I wanted to know why he'd never voiced his opinion before then. You know what Neil said?"

"What?"

"He said, 'And just what good would that have done, Grace? Name one person that would have benefited from my voicing that opinion.'" Grace sighed. "I slept on the couch Saturday night."

"Oh, Grace. I'm so sorry."

"No, it was good. Sometimes I need time to think. I didn't really sleep much. I just kept puzzling over and over in my head how I could have had one opinion of my father and everyone else had another."

"Did you come up with an answer?"

Grace looked at her mother. "I decided that the reason I had that opinion was because my father went to the effort to make sure I *did*. And when I came to that conclusion, then I had to admit that if he chose to make that conscious effort with *me* then he must have made an equally conscious effort to *not* do it with any of you. That's when I started to cry. Why do you think he did that, Mom?"

Deborah thought for a long time. "I don't know, honey. But there isn't much I can explain about Jonathan. We were married for almost thirty years, but it seems that we were almost complete strangers. How could *that* be? Perhaps if I'd been a different type of person it would have been better." She looked at her daughter. "But it could have been much worse, too, I think.

"That's why I've finally come to the conclusion I'm not going to loose anymore time over this, Grace. I don't think I'll ever know why Jonathan did what he did. And for me, now, that's okay. Alita gave me a good saying, 'Don't let the tail wag the dog.'"

Grace laughed. "I like that."

"Don't feel guilty because Jonathan gave you something that he chose not to give as much to me or the boys. You're a mother and a wife and a capable, outspoken woman. You're married to a lovely man. Pastor Duncan says that when bad things come our way, instead of saying 'Why did God let this happen?' we're supposed to look around and see what God sent our way to see us through. You're rich like I am, Grace. You're surrounded on all sides by a wonderful support system. God's blessed you tremendously."

Grace looked over at Zoe, who had somehow managed to color herself and Max with bright blue ink. "*Zoe! Where did you get that pen?!*" Zoe, matter-of-factly pointed to Grace's purse sitting over by the door to go inside. "God help me, Mom!" she said and rolled her eyes. They both laughed.

"I'm glad you called and had me come over." Grace looked suspiciously at her. "You don't seem like you're in much need of care, though."

"I didn't say I was."

"I thought …"

Deborah looked pointedly at Grace. "I just wanted your *company*, not your care."

"I love you, Mom."

"I love you, too, Grace."

Peter took her out to dinner on Tuesday. She cooked stuffed peppers for ten on Wednesday night. Thursday, she was up and dressed and rushing around to get out for her doctor appointment at 10 when Alita showed up.

"Well, what do you have to say for yourself, Mrs. Deborah?" was the first thing out of Alita's mouth. Alita stood there with a thunderous expression on her face and her hands on her hips.

Deborah stood there in the kitchen with a half chewed English muffin in her hand. She swallowed. "What do you want me to say?"

"All's I have to say, Mrs. Deborah, is that if I come over to this house *even one more time* and find you lying in a pool of blood at the bottom of your stairs, *I QUIT!!*"

Deborah went over and hugged her. "I'm sorry you had to be the one to find me. But thank you for your quick thinking. They told me that you were the one that called the ambulance and all the kids, too."

Alita eyed her suspiciously. "You were not trying to 'end it all' were you?"

Deborah shook her head. "No, throwing myself down the stairs isn't very efficient if that's what I was planning."

Alita seemed satisfied with her answer after she studied her for a moment or two. "That was my way of thinking, too." Her eyes gleamed then. "I met that man of yours."

"Peter?"

"Yes, Mr. Peter. He is *very nice*." Alita gave her a knowing look and went over to the linen closet humming under her breath.

"How did you meet him?"

"I saw him only one time, really. At the hospital. He didn't see me, though, he was in too much of a rush."

"I didn't know you came to the hospital."

Alita nodded. "Just the day the ambulance brought you in. I followed in my car. I didn't want you to be by yourself so I waited until someone came that you knew." She looked at her pointedly. "That Mr. Peter was the first one to show up, you know."

"No, I didn't know."

She nodded sagely. "I guessed as such. He is sweet on you, I'm thinking."

"I think I'm sweet on him, too."

"That is a good thing."

"Yes, it is a very good thing."

"He came running into the hospital and they told him that because he wasn't family he wouldn't be allowed in to see you. I was waiting in the waiting room because they had told me the same thing." Alita chuckled. "He looked that little, teeny, tiny nurse right in the eye and shouted so that *everybody* heard, 'I'm in love with that woman and you can either give me permission to see her *now* or you can call the cops to have me dragged away from her bedside because I'm going in whether you like it or not!'" She thought for a minute and then nodded. "Yes, that's just what he said. I worked hard to remember the real words because I knew you'd want to hear them one day or another."

"What did the nurse say?"

Alita chuckled. "Oh, that little, teeny, tiny nurse took one look at your Mr. Peter and said, 'Oh, you didn't tell me you were in the *love* category. Go right on in'. Then your Mr. Peter relaxed and got polite again. He said his thanks and that was the last I saw of him."

Alita looked at her and with complete seriousness said, "What are you going to do with that man, Mrs. Deborah?"

With twinkling eyes, Deborah said, "He says he is going to work on getting me to be less well-behaved. I think I might let him."

"Ahhhh," Alita said with a satisfied gleam in her eye. "I *knew* I liked him. Did you tell me he had a brother?" Deborah was still chuckling when Alita began to sing and clean.

Blessed is he who has regard for the weak; the Lord delivers him in times of trouble.

The Lord will protect him and preserve his life; he will bless him in the land.[13]

The Hero's Reward

"**T**oday's guy is a good guy," Pastor Duncan. "My wife pointed out to me that there hasn't been many stellar Biblical examples in the men category so far …" He looked at the congregation and in a conspiratorial whisper said, "It is *so tough* living with your greatest critic …!" Everyone laughed.

"We don't know much about this gentleman's early life. We don't know if he was widowed or never married, there's no record of stunning battle victories, or amazing spiritual gifts. He was just a quiet, well thought of, wealthy farmer. His name was Boaz."

Deborah sat next to Peter who'd actually picked her up so they could drive to church together. He didn't specifically make a comment about it when she said yes to his offer, but he'd arched his eyebrow at her waiting for her to give him a hard time and bring up the issue of appearances. She surprised him by telling him she liked when he did that thing with his eyebrow. That confused him. She discovered she liked doing that a little bit, too. Todd had called first thing that morning. Mumbled something about a late night and he'd try to catch church another week. Taking pity on him, Deborah simply told him she'd miss him and thanked him for calling and letting her know. He sounded relieved that he didn't get an earful.

Pastor Duncan stood behind the pulpit. "When the story opens in the Bible it's harvest time. Now, the Israelites - remember how I said they had so many rules and regulations - had made provisions for the very poor. During harvest time, after the owner of the field had done his harvesting, the poor were allowed the gather up what little was left behind for their own use. And the poorest of the poor were childless widows. You know, there's a term for them, it's "liminal". It means they lacked any level of social status. It means quite literally that they were barely perceptible. And in Biblical times, a woman's social status depending on her husband's or her son's social standing. If her husband died and she was childless, then she just about literally ceased to exist. With no one to look out for them, provide for them, or champion them, they faced the bleakest of futures.

"Anyway, what Boaz didn't know was that a distant relative of his by the name of Naomi had recently returned to town. She'd had an enormous run of hard times. Her husband had died. Her sons had died. And rather then stay and be miserable and poor in a foreign city, she returned to her hometown. Now Naomi had *had* it. She was in such a deep state of depression, she wanted to change her name to 'Mara' which meant bitterness.

"She'd tried to send both of her daughters – in - law back home to their families before she traveled back to her own country because both of the young women were foreigners – not Israelites. One of the women had been cooperative and listened, returning to her family. But the other one, Ruth, had refused to leave Naomi and begged Naomi to let her stay with her. So these two widows – one old and one young – returned to Naomi's hometown of Bethlehem.

"Ruth was industrious. In addition, Ruth loved Naomi, had learned about Naomi's God, and had embraced Him as her God as well. Ruth took it upon herself to go glean – that means gather – the leftover wheat as the poor were allowed to do in an effort to keep starvation away from their door. When she told Naomi what she planned to do, Naomi had the presence of mind to advise her to go to Boaz's field – a distant relative – and therefore probably the safest location."

Pastor Duncan looked a little embarrassed. "In my mind, I imagine Ruth to be quite beautiful, although the Bible doesn't describe her physically. If you read the Biblical account, I think you too would come to the same conclusion. The Bible *certainly* described in great detail her inner beauty. She was spiritual, kind, loving, patient, helpful, obedient, loyal … And Boaz noticed her that very first day she went to the field.

"I don't think this was a lustful thing. He was a good man, with a kind heart. He instructed his gatherers to leave extra behind in the field for Ruth to collect and not to give her a hard time. Boaz encouraged her to come over and drink from the refreshments he had provided for his workers, offered her food at lunchtime, and told Ruth not to go to any other field but his. When he spoke to her, he even complimented her on her devotion and kindness to Naomi. Her lovely spirit had been noticed by others."

Pastor Duncan chuckled. "When she got home to Naomi that first night, Naomi was ecstatic over the amount of grain Ruth had managed to bring home and was thrilled to hear how well received she'd been by Boaz. That got Naomi thinking. You see, there was another rule about widows. It was the 'Kinsman Redeemer Rule'.

"A kinsman redeemer," Pastor Duncan walked out from behind the pulpit, "was a male in a family who was responsible for protecting all manner of rights for a family. It was a rather complicated rule, but partially related to the concept we talked about when we learned about Judah – when the widow would marry the brother of her dead husband to carry on the family line and keep the inheritance properly distributed."

Pastor Duncan chuckled again. "That Naomi! She pulled herself out of her depression and came up with quite a plan. She had Ruth bathe, put perfume on, dress in her best clothes, and then sent her over to where Boaz was now threshing the wheat that had been gathered." Pastor Duncan held up his hands. "Please bear in mind that Naomi was *not* trying to initiate a sexual act between Ruth and Boaz. Things were very ritualistic and precise back then. These two women needed to somehow communicate to Boaz that they wished him to act in his role as kinsman redeemer. They had *no one* to act as intermediary for them, so they had to do it carefully and precisely.

"But there's not *one doubt* in my mind that Boaz, should he have been inclined, could have taken complete advantage of Ruth. He didn't. Ruth waited until he'd fallen asleep and then quietly went into the threshing place – which was filled with other sleeping men whom I'm *sure* had had more that a few skins of wine. Naomi had instructed Ruth to lay down at Boaz's feet and wait for him to notice her, so that's just what she did."

Pastor Duncan went back behind the pulpit. "I've called Boaz the quiet hero, because what he did was not known by many, but was still a gloriously honorable and noble act. He was tender and kind with Ruth that night, acknowledging her request, treating her with respect, sending her home before first light mindful of her reputation and the fact that she'd been in a threshing shack all night with only men for company. Rather than jumping on what must have been a very favorable opportunity, Boaz first approached another family member, whom Naomi didn't realize had a closer claim on the family land. You see, Boaz would have been required to marry Ruth and offered this relative first opportunity to assert his rights. When Boaz was certain that it was right and proper by all concerned, he went ahead and married Ruth."

Pastor Duncan smiled and sighed. "It was such a happy ending! The book of Ruth ends with Naomi caring for Ruth and Boaz's infant son, Obed. The Bible records the women of the town saying to her," here he looked down at his Bible and turned a few pages, "'Praise the Lord who has given you a family redeemer today! May he be famous in Israel. May this child restore your youth and care for you in your old age. For he is the son of your daughter-in-law who loves you so much and who has been better to you than seven sons!'"

He looked up at the congregation, "And one last thing I cannot help but add. The book of Matthew lists Jesus' lineage. Guess who was Boaz's mother? *Rahab,* the heathen with the good heart we talked about a few weeks ago.

"This man, this son of a redeemed woman became the redeemer of another person in similarly desperate straits. This man, a quiet hero, received no public acknowledgement, no riches, no fame, and no glory. Yet, when we read Boaz's story we are *so impressed* with the good person he was. We sigh in wonder and doubt we could be as honorable. We mentally aspire to achieve the noble heights he reached. We dream of being just as happy and just as content. We personally think 'if only I could achieve just a piece of what they had …'

"And you know what? It's available to every single one of us. Boaz, was a person who made wise choices, prayed wise prayers, and followed God's wise words. It is as simple and as difficult as that."

After church Peter seemed a bit preoccupied and she mentioned it. He looked apologetic. "I've got problems at one of my sites and I'm going to have to go out and deal with it today. I should have gone this morning, but I didn't want to miss going to church with you." He gave her a smile and reached up to touch her cheek. "Especially since you agreed to let me pick you up and drive you there."

"Do you know that I have no idea what you do for a living?"

He looked surprisingly uncomfortable. He sighed. "I've been purposely vague."

Deborah was stunned. "What do you mean you've been 'purposely vague'?"

"I didn't want you to know. Not yet, anyway."

She was hurt. And confused. He'd been so completely open with her since they'd met. Hadn't he? Doubts rumbled in her foundation like the beginning trembles of a major earthquake. "You've told me all kinds of private things about yourself and yet you didn't want me to know what you do for a living *now?*"

Though Deborah thought it sounded absolutely preposterous, Peter shocked her by nodding his head and saying, "Yup, that's about the size of it."

"Why?"

He looked off away from her, thinking. He didn't answer her.

"Are you embarrassed at what you do?"

He still didn't look at her. "No."

"Then why can't I know?" The curiosity welled up in her like a tidal wave.

"It's not that you *can't* know. It's just that, I was waiting until the right time to tell you. *Show you.*" Peter shrugged his shoulders then and looked profoundly awkward and uncomfortable. "It's complicated."

"This is the first time I've ever seen you this way."

"What way?" he asked and finally looked at her again.

"Unsure, uncertain. Not confident or sure of yourself." Deborah had a sudden thought. "Are you worried about *me* and how *I'll* react?"

Peter didn't answer at first and when he finally went to open his mouth Deborah put her hand up like he had done to her only a few days ago. "Don't bother, I've got my answer." She started walking to his car and he followed.

They drove to her home in silence. When he stopped in the driveway he looked at her, at an apparent loss for words.

She finally spoke, unable to stand the silence a second longer. "I can't *imagine* what you would do for a living that would cause you to doubt me and my reaction to it. I know only one thing for certain. I don't want to know what you do until you are comfortable enough to tell me. Because when you do that, then that will tell me that you give me *more credit then you do now.* If there is *one thing* you should have gotten out of your time with me it is that I hate deception and secrets. I've lived with it for far too long to tolerate it any longer. And I won't now."

She was on a roll. Stuff was pouring out of her mouth that she had never consciously thought of but it sure as hell sounded good. Deborah knew her voice was raised, too. *So what,* her head said, *go for it.* "I want someone who treats me like an equal. Who values my thoughts and opinions and perceptions – *whether we agree or not.* I want someone who will teach me things but will also learn a few things from me. I want someone who will strengthen my weaknesses and champion my strengths. I want someone who trusts me." *Hell,* her head said, *shoot for the moon.* She felt her throat tighten as she fought back tears. Her voice sounded husky with the strain when she said, "I want someone who wants to be with me as much as

I want to be with them. Who misses me when they're away from me. Who can't think of a better place then being *right beside me."* She got out of the car and walked into the house without looking back. And Peter let her go. He never called her back or chased after her. She was conscious of his car idling in the driveway and then, when she put the key in the door, she heard him shift into reverse, back out of the driveway and drive away.

Her heart felt like it was going to break into a million pieces. She stood in the front hall, leaning against the closed front door and cried and cried, until there were no more tears to shed.

Deborah struggled all day Monday trying to recall the numbness, but it was no use. Even more horrible, she felt worse then she ever remembered feeling after Jonathan's death. It was like she had fallen to the very bottom of a pit, managed to almost climb all the way out and then slipped and fell back in again. She was twice as sore, twice as miserable.

To make matters worse, she was afraid to leave the house because she was certain Peter would call – soon – and she didn't want to miss the call when it came. She *couldn't* miss the call when it came.

By Tuesday, Deborah was angry. Really angry. With herself, with him, with anyone and everyone. To hell with them all! She made her self get into her car and she drove around making herself do errands. She went to the food store, stopped and got gas, went to the post office and bought stamps. By the time she headed home she was in a frenzy to get home to the phone and the answering machine. *Surely there would be a message from him.* There wasn't.

Grace called Tuesday night to say hello and to find out how she was doing. Deborah tried to sound bright and casual and suddenly had a thought while they chatted. "Grace, did Peter ever describe what he did for a living? You mentioned when you brought me home from the hospital that if he had to go 'on site' that you would come and stay with me. Did he ever elaborate more then saying that?"

Grace was quiet for a minute, thinking. "No, I didn't think twice about it, Mom. He talked so casual about it, I assumed you understood. Why?"

Deborah tried to sound light and casual. "Oh, no reason. It was just a thought that popped into my head."

By Thursday she completely doubted herself and her recollection of anything that had happened on Sunday. She'd probably been unreasonable. She had no right to demand he tell her things he didn't want to tell her. She should have been supportive not confrontational. What right did she have rattling off a list of things she expected and wanted in a relationship? Who did she think she was? She heard voices from the past - her father's, Jonathan's, even her mother's - correcting, cautioning, advising, and rebuking. The anger was gone, replaced by profound despair. Worse still, all confidence had disappeared, replaced by a profound need to grovel and plead.

Deborah sat by the phone that night with her hand on the receiver. She'd call Peter, apologize, make an effort to sound casual and bright. She'd invite him over for dinner and not *let* him talk about the argument. Why, she'd tell him it didn't matter what he did for a living, that she didn't want to know and further more, never wanted him to tell her.

Who's lying now? her head asked her. Sitting with her hand on the phone, it was that question that stopped her from calling him. Because it *was* a lie. She *did* want to know. She *needed* him to trust and confide in her. The pain of the separation from him was horrible. But the memory of what Jonathan had done to her coupled with the fear that the same thing could possibly happen again with Peter was beyond her comprehension. A second time would kill her. She couldn't live through that heartbreak of deceit again. And she wouldn't. As she took her hand away from the receiver she began to cry again, sobs that seemed to have no end.

"What do I do?" she prayed finally out loud. "I don't know what to do ..."

Friday morning she was awakened by the phone. She looked at the clock before she picked up the receiver. 6:54 a.m. Good grief. Who would call so early? "Hello?"

"You're not awake yet." The wave of relief to hear his voice on the phone was so profound that she felt a rush from the top of her head, down her arms and legs right to the tip of her toes.

"No, I was out late last night drinking and carousing."

"Me too."

There was a silence for a few moments. Then Deborah spoke. "Keep talking. I need to hear your voice some more."

"So you missed me then?"

"No, not at all."

"I'll be over to pick you up in a half hour. Can you be ready?"

She sat up. "Where are you taking me?"

Peter sighed. "To work with me. Dress casual; jeans, tee shirt, sneakers."

"Okay."

"Deborah?"

"Yes?"

She could hear him sigh again on the other end of the phone. "I missed you so much it just about killed me this week." And he hung up.

She was sitting on the front steps eating an apple when he pulled into the driveway. She had on her leather jacket, unsure if he was picking her up on his bike. She stood up when she saw him pull in and before she could get down the steps he was there pulling her into his arms. He didn't say anything, just hugged her tightly. Deborah took a deep breath of the scent of him. "You smell good."

Peter looked at her and then kissed her. "You taste like heaven."

He told her to leave the coat home and that she didn't need her purse. Although she was profoundly puzzled she didn't ask questions. *No sense courting disaster,* her head said.

They were headed to Pennsylvania. It took her a while to figure that out. The drive was more silent then conversational and she continued to worry about asking questions that shouldn't be asked, but she did ask one. "Are you annoyed with me?"

"No."

"Honest?"

"One thing you should realize about me, I may be evasive, but when I'm put on the spot I'm always honest."

"Did I say that you were evasive?"

"No you said that I was deceptive and secretive. I changed it to evasive. It sounded better."

"Oh."

After a while Peter asked her a question. "Are you mad at *me*?"

She was silent for a long time sorting through her thoughts. She finally looked at him and said, "Don't assume anything because I'm quiet. I'm trying to get my thoughts just right."

"All right." He sounded sad.

"I think I'm mostly confused. And confusion is bad because it opens the door to other bad emotions like doubt, insecurity, defensiveness ..." She smiled a tiny smile. "Yeah, anger's in there, but it's way down on the list."

"Don't doubt me, Deborah," Peter said earnestly. "Not one thing I've said or done is subject to doubt. I swear it."

She reached over and touched his leg. "Okay."

He took her hand and held it for the rest of the trip.

She knew their destination was Philadelphia only when he exited the highway. Deborah's curiosity grew with each mile. Anxiety grew, too, as she watched the neighborhood deteriorate rapidly. There were burned out buildings that were boarded up and other buildings that people lived in that *should* have been boarded up. Peter knew where he was going, though, confidently driving through the streets, and waiting at traffic lights calm and casual as could be.

Well, maybe not so calm she decided. When they left the highway Peter had let go of her hand and as she studied him out of the corner of her eye she could see the hand draped on top of the steering wheel nervously tapping the dashboard. And he looked tense, too, she decided.

They parked in the worst possible neighborhood in front of a brownstone that was surrounded on both sides by boarded up buildings. The car they parked behind had no rear tires and the front and back windshield was completely shattered. There was not one living soul walking the streets. The traffic was minimal. Once Peter had turned the car off, he turned and looked at her. "I could have told you, rather then show you, but I think this is the better way. It's always pretty hectic, once I get inside, so can I promise to answer any questions you have once we're on our way home? That way I won't have to worry that I'm not giving you my full attention."

Deborah nodded.

"Okay, then. Let's go."

He rang the bell and within a few moments the intercom came to life. "Who is it?"

"Peter." She heard a buzzer release the lock, he opened the door and walked in.

As Deborah walked into the front hallway, she was uncertain as to what she had expected, but she was pleasantly surprised. It was a little bit like stepping back into time she supposed. Old-fashioned tiny black and white tiles covered the floor, sparkling clean and reflecting the muted light of the glass chandelier hanging from the ceiling. A stairway wound it's way along the left side of the wall to the upstairs and a huge, heavy wooded door, complete with the old style glass door knob was on her right. The wood ceiling and floor trim, the wood stair rail, and even the wood door were all a glorious dark polished wood that spoke of age and class. There wasn't time to comment or compliment, because immediately the door opened.

An attractive black woman stepped out. She wore a brilliant smile, jeans and a green polo shirt with the insignia *CTW* embroidered on it. "*Peter,*" she said and walked forward to grab his hand. "Thanks for coming."

Peter did the introductions. He introduced the woman as Kalliopi Winston and explained that she was the supervisor here at the 'Philly Site'. Kalliopi extended her hand, "Welcome, Deborah. It's such a pleasure to *finally* get to meet you."

The room they entered, Deborah supposed at one time had been a first floor apartment, but it now had more of an air of a common room. A desk, computer, and bookshelves filled one corner, kitchen equipment – including a large table and chairs - in another, and the rest of the space was filled with a casual collection of comfortable chairs and couches. In another corner was a large television in front of which sat three children who where fully engrossed in a video game. It was large, open, airy, spacious, and very welcoming.

"Come in and sit down, I'll make some coffee." They headed over to the kitchen area and Deborah and Peter sat down at the table.

Kalliopi pulled a jug of bottled water out of the refrigerator. "We can't go another day without water, Peter. The kids are thrilled of course to not have to wash, but the rest of us are going nuts. I've called at least a dozen companies and none will come out here to even *look* at the repairs." She sighed a huge sound of discouragement. "It seems as if it's not one thing it's another. I still worry that we should have picked a different site."

Site. There was that word again.

A movement caught her attention out of the corner of Deborah's eye. It was the strangest thing. Something appeared to be wiggling just above the top of one of the couches. It took her a moment to figure out it was hair. Braided in tiny tight braids, so tight that they stood straight up off the top of a tiny head. Gradually, a pair of black eyes appeared, too. The hair and eyes traveled the length of the couch, to the end and then a leg appeared over the arm of the couch, followed by another leg and the soft "thump" of small bare feet connecting with the floor. It was a little girl, no more than 2 ½ she guessed. One hand had a thumb firmly imbedded in her mouth while the other hand clutched a stuffed animal. She peered closely. A stuffed bunny. The little one gradually, slowly, silently, took tentative steps towards the kitchen. She eyed Deborah with great wariness and Deborah tried to smile to reassure her. The child never made eye contact with her again. Deborah was mesmerized by the entire steady advance the child made. It soon became obvious she was headed directly for Peter.

Peter and Kalliopi were in a deep discussion about plumbers. Papers were spread all over the table as well as two phone books. "I think you'll need to step in," Kalliopi said. "As much as I hate to admit it, I think some of these companies need to hear a man on the phone *or,* better yet, have an *angry man* show up at their doorstep."

"An angry man with money more like it," Peter said.

When the child was about two feet away from Peter she turned and put her back to him. Neither Peter nor Kalliopi had acknowledged the child in any way. Now Deborah was really curious. Was the child upset because she was being ignored? Should she interrupt Peter and Kalliopi and point it out? Had they even noticed her? Just as Deborah was about to say something, Peter, without looking at the child or pausing in his conversation with Kalliopi, put his arm out. The slow steady progression, *backwards now*, resumed until she bumped up against him. He picked her up, settled her in his lap, and the child rested her head against his chest.

"We've got to get someone today or we're doomed. No one will be available over the weekend," Peter muttered in frustration.

Kalliopi nodded in agreement. "Actually, there's a Spanish outfit on Lamington that seems to do business 24/7. I've heard okay things about them but they wouldn't even answer my messages."

"Okay, I'll drive over." Peter seemed to look at the child and notice her for the first time then. "Hey, where did this lump come from?" he asked and jiggled her by moving his leg.

Deborah saw a tiny smile behind the thumb.

"Niesha has something to show you, Mr. Peter," Kalliopi said.

"Oh she does? What's that you've got to show me? Is it that wet, sticky thumb?" He tried to pull it out of her mouth and she smiled and giggled. Niesha won the tug, the thumb stayed in.

"Come on, Niesha, show Mr. Peter," Kalliopi encouraged.

Niesha sat up. She took her thumb out of her mouth. She looked directly at Peter. She stared at him for a few moments. Then she said, "Hi," stuck her thumb back in and snuggled back against his chest.

"*She talked?!*" Peter looked at Kalliopi and seemed absolutely incredulous.

Kalliopi beamed. "Yup, Tuesday morning, sat at the table here and said 'Hi' clear as a bell. I broke my favorite mug. Dropped it in shock."

Peter gave the child a big bear hug. All you could see was the sticking up braids. "Good for you, Niesha! Next time I come, maybe you'll be talking even more. What do you think?" When he released her from his hug she looked up at him, studied him seriously for a moment then gave him an elaborate shrug. "Ah well," he said to her, "you think about it." He kissed the top of her head.

Peter looked at Deborah for the first time since they'd sat down at the table. "I'm going to have to drive over to this place and see if I can get anyone out here. I think you should stay here, okay?"

Deborah nodded.

"She'll be fine, Peter," Kalliopi said. "I'll show her around, give her the grand tour." Kalliopi looked at Deborah then. "We've heard all about you, but I haven't been able to convince him to bring you out here. I'm glad you're finally here. It's about time."

"You've heard about me?" Deborah said in a stunned voice.

"*Oh yes,*" Kalliopi said grinned with delight, "We've heard about you. All nice things, too." She deepened her voice to mimic Peter's, "'Deborah says...', 'Deborah did ...', 'Deborah and I...'" Kalliopi rolled her eyes. "Oh yes, *we've all* heard about you."

Peter was flushed absolutely scarlet when Deborah looked at him. She struggled to not smile. "I knew I shouldn't have brought you out here," he muttered. "There's nothing but trouble to be found in a house full of women."

Kalliopi laughed, delighted. She gestured toward the boys lying in front of the television. "See if you can find some company to take with you."

Peter stood up and carried Niesha back to the couch. Then he walked back to Deborah, leaned down and kissed her quick. He looked her right in the eye. "Remember, I'll answer any and all questions on the way home. *And don't* believe everything Kalliopi tells you. She lies all the time." Kalliopi laughed again and winked at Deborah behind his back.

"All right," Peter shouted in a booming voice across the room and she saw two of the boys jump, "I've got room for three trouble makers in my car. Who's coming?"

One boy stayed behind in the end. "That's Randall," Kalliopi quietly explained glancing over at him. "He and his mother, Katrina, are new here so he doesn't know Peter too well yet."

Deborah looked at Kalliopi. "What is this place?"

Kalliopi looked annoyed. "I *knew* it. He hasn't told you a *thing*, has he?"

Deborah shook her head 'no'.

Standing up, Kalliopi said, "Come on. I will give you a tour. The best way to describe this place is that it's transitional housing for *formerly* homeless women and their children." She looked at the couch where Niesha had started from and where Niesha currently was back to. "Hey there little girl," she called and the hair and eyes popped up over the couch again. "I'm going to show Miss Deborah around the place. Are you coming or are you staying?"

Niesha gave her the wary look again. "She's afraid of me, I think," she said quietly to Kalliopi.

Kalliopi answered just as quietly, "No, she's not afraid of you, she's terrified of you. But she's terrified of everyone. We're working on it." In a louder voice she said, "Well, girly? What's your decision?"

Niesha glanced at Deborah one more time and then pointed to the couch.

"Okay. We will be right back. Randall?"

The boy looked at her. "I'll be right back, I'm giving Miss Deborah a tour of the place. Niesha's there on the couch. Where's your mom?"

"Studying in the library."

"Okay. If you need something you know what to do?" He nodded.

The building had four floors and six apartments that currently accommodated six women and thirteen children. They were in the Great Room, and Kalliopi explained that it was available for all to make use of. "That room," she pointed to a closed door, "leads to the library." She shrugged, "It's not much but it's more than we had before. And that room," she pointed to another door, "is a private office that visiting doctors, etc. make use of." She shrugged. "It can be very difficult to find privacy in a place like this."

Down the hall from the Great Room was another large room that was fully equipped with school supplies. "This is for the women as well as the children. We have volunteers that come in and provide additional teaching opportunities." She looked at Deborah pointedly. "When you are hungry, frightened, and homeless, education often comes far down on the list of priorities. We try to repair that oversight."

Downstairs was a laundry room, a play room and an exercise room. Upstairs were the apartments. Each apartment had a living room, two bedrooms, it's own kitchen and bath. "When the women arrive here, they're given an opportunity to start fresh. Most stay here for at least a year, sometimes two. There is no set time limit, but it's not a free ride. *They work hard.* They must get schooling or some professional training, take parenting classes, and look for employment and then secure and hold down a job. While rent and utilities are covered, they are responsible for providing their own food and clothing. Free legal advice, child care and personal counseling are also available. We try to do everything possible to get them back on their feet so that when they leave here both the women and their children are better prepared to face the world and all it has to throw at them."

"How do you find the women?" Deborah asked.

"Good question. Sometimes by word of mouth. Sometimes by referral from other churches or agencies. Sometimes they just show up at our door." Kalliopi sighed. "Those are the toughest ones because we don't always have the space. Like right now, we're full."

"What do you do if that happens?"

"Try not to tell Peter," Kalliopi said with a chuckle. "He goes *nuts* if we have to turn away someone. We make every effort to find a place for them. We call around. Check some of our other sites to see what they have to offer. But we don't like to send the women too far, because most want to stay in a familiar area."

"How many sites are there?"

"Three. Peter's determined to have four soon."

"*Three?* This size?"

Kalliopi smiled and nodded with pride. "Yup, three. This one here in Philadelphia, one up in Easton, and one in Trenton. I've not been to the Trenton site, but I know all of the Supervisors. We all deal with the same issues so we talk a lot in the hopes that we can share solutions. Each site is right in the heart of the city. The theory being that rather then abandon you reclaim."

"And Peter manages them all?"

Kalliopi looked at Deborah. "Maybe you better sit down before I answer that question." They were just going back into the Great Room, having gotten permission from one of the women to see her apartment. She'd even been given a tour of the backyard that despite it being surrounded by an eight foot high chain link fence was full of toys and was still a wonderful world of play and imagination.

Deborah sat. Kalliopi asked if she wanted tea or coffee and when Deborah her tea and Kalliopi fixed her a cup. "I never served you this before, did I? I'm always doing that, offering someone coffee or tea and then getting distracted and going off to do one of the nine million things that needs to be done."

Kalliopi sat down with her own cup of tea and looked directly at Deborah. "Peter doesn't manage the sites, he owns them."

"He owns them?" Deborah managed to say in a stunned voice.

"See? I knew as soon as I left you, she'd be telling you a pile of lies." Peter came walking in with the three boys trailing behind him, each a sticky mess of ice cream.

"Were you successful?" Kalliopi seemed to be holding her breath.

He sat down at the table and searched Deborah's face while he answered Kalliopi's question. "They'll be here within the hour. As soon as I told them I would pay them immediately after everyone in the building was showered and clean, they couldn't get here fast enough. Deborah and I will hang around until they show, okay?" He looked at Deborah. "*I don't own them,*" he said in a firm voice and then glared at Kalliopi.

Kalliopi seemed totally unconcerned with Peter's obvious displeasure. She offered Peter a cup of coffee. "Would you try speaking with Katrina? She's in the library. Things aren't going so well with her and Randall."

Peter sighed. "What do I need to know?"

"She's angry, afraid, skeptical. Did you know that she's been homeless for over *three years?* She's also got two children younger then Randall who were taken away under charges of neglect. She's refused to take advantage of anything we're offering except the apartment and the other women are starting to get fed up with her attitude in general. I've talked to her until I'm blue in the face." Kalliopi sighed. "Just like the plumbers, I think she needs to get it straight from an angry white man."

Peter looked at Kalliopi and tried his best to glare at her. "Stop telling Deborah lies." Then he stood up and walked into the room that held the distinction of being the library.

Kalliopi grinned. "He'll tell you that he set up a trust fund that supports the three sites and he manages the fund. But the fund came from *him*. It has a board of directors and is attached to a world wide charitable foundation known as Care For The World. It's religiously based, but they try to be nondenominational in their approach."

Deborah didn't know what to say. "He's accomplished all this in the three years he's been out here?"

Kalliopi thought for a minute. "You're going to have to ask him that one. I've been here two years since this site opened. I *think* he began this stuff from where he lived out west. I don't know for sure though."

"Do you and Niesha live here?"

Kalliopi shook her head vigorously. "No, I'd go nuts. I can't work here all the hours I do and then sleep here, too." She looked profoundly proud. "But I used to be just like some of these women. Seven years ago, my four children and I were homeless. With the help of God and a few caring individuals, I got an education, a job, and finally a career. I'm the on site counselor, supervisor and the day to day disaster relief coordinator." She tapped her chin and thought. "I guess I'm also babysitter, custodian, grounds keeping, chauffer, and secretary." She grinned. "Give me a few minutes and I'll probably come up with a few more titles. I love my job, honest I do."

Peter sat down at the table. "I told you not to lie to Deborah." Kalliopi laughed and she smiled. "Am I ever going to get that cup of coffee you offered?"

Kalliopi looked at her. "See? I always offer but everyone knows I never remember to serve it. What did Katrina say?"

Peter shrugged. "She just can't believe it's all true. She's been disappointed so many times, why should this be different? I did my best to reassure her. And I did make her laugh. I told her that in all honesty, we only let her in because we heard she makes one mean blackberry pie. And that the next time I showed up, if there wasn't a sample for me, I *would* throw her out."

Kalliopi looked at him. "How did you know that she makes blackberry pie?"

"One of the boys told me on the way to the plumbers."

The intercom buzzer rang and there was great commotion at Kalliopi, Peter, and three curious boys bounded to the front door. Niesha peeked over the top of the couch but stayed where she was.

While everyone trooped downstairs with the plumbers, Deborah watched Niesha's expression gradually grow in panic. Deborah got up and went and sat down on a chair opposite Niesha's couch. The couch was literally full of small stuffed animals. There were so many that some had spilled onto the floor.

Deborah picked one up and began to have a silly conversation with it. Asking it questions and having it answer her. She rambled on and on. Out of the corner of her eye, she watched Niesha relax and gradually focus on the silly talk. All of a sudden another stuffed animal landed at her feet. Deborah picked that one up, too. "Well, who do we have here?" She began a three way conversation between herself, a stuffed dog and a stuffed rhinoceros.

By the time that everyone returned to the Great Room, Niesha was on Deborah's lap with bunny and five other stuffed animal friends and Deborah had a headache trying to keep all the personalities that she'd made up straight. "Niesha," Deborah had finally said, "I keep getting confused. You do bunny's voice, okay?"

Niesha nodded. "Hi," she said making the bunny talk.

When she turned around, Kalliopi and Peter were standing in the doorway with their mouths hanging open. Niesha held up her bunny. "Hi," she said again.

Deborah held up a stuffed elephant. "Hi," she said to Kalliopi and Peter.

"Hi," the both said back in stunned unison. She and Niesha smiled at Peter and Kalliopi.

In the end, they ate dinner in the Great Room with Kalliopi and Niesha. Just simple spaghetti with jar sauce but there was lot of laughter and good conversation. Kalliopi kept trying to get Deborah to tell her things about herself, Peter, and dates they had gone on. Peter worked diligently to change the subject each time and not to blush. He wasn't successful in either category. By the end of the meal Deborah was quite certain that Kalliopi's true goal was not to gain information but just to give Peter a deliciously hard time.

There was a collective cheer throughout the building when the water came on. Toilets flushed. Showers happened. Dishes got cleaned. Only the kids were disappointed as baths were ordered for all.

"Thanks," Kalliopi said to Peter and gave him a hug. "I couldn't have done it without you."

"It's nice to know I'm appreciated."

Kalliopi rolled her eyes. "Men. They always need constant reassurance."

Deborah laughed.

Kalliopi looked at Peter, her eyes filled with mischief. "You're right. She does have a nice laugh."

"It's time to go," he said blushing furiously again.

Deborah laughed again.

They were both silent in the car until they were back on the main highway, having worked their way past blocks and blocks of desolated neighborhoods.

Peter spoke first. "Aren't you going to say anything?"

"Is Kalliopi Niesha's mother?"

"No. Believe it or not, Kalliopi's Niesha's granddaughter."

"She doesn't look old enough to be a grandmother! She can't be more than thirty five!"

"Kalliopi's thirty-eight. She was a teenage mother and her oldest daughter was a teenage mother. The child was severely neglected and abused when Kalliopi got custody of her. She's four you know."

"*No!*"

Peter nodded. "Four and a bit. You should know that not only is "Hi" her first word but *you* are the first person besides me and Kalliopi that she's allowed to touch her. Even with me she's tremendously hesitant. The whole ritual you saw of her making her way over to me … Well, if I even glance at her then she'll run, hide and start all over again. So I have to not look, listen, and then know just when to reach out to her." He smiled. "I've gotten pretty good at it."

"Yes, you have." Peter looked very proud of her praise. How could he look proud over himself about something like that and try to keep the three sites a secret from her? That was her next question.

Shrugging, Peter said, "What was I supposed to say? 'Hi, I'm a magnanimous millionaire who's just the greatest guy in the world because of all the good things I've done. Come see what I've got to show you.'"

"So, you chose not to tell me because you thought I'd interpret it as bragging?"

"I was pretty certain you'd know better then that."

"Then why?"

"I was going to tell you the whole story. I was honest with you. I told you that I worked for a company called CTW and that it was a good match because we both had things that the other wanted. I just didn't elaborate that they had a good cause and I had a lot of money."

Peter sighed. "Things have gone faster between us then I ever imagined, Deborah. It seemed like one minute I was struggling to get up the courage to stop you long enough to ask you out for a cup of coffee and the next minute I was dreaming dreams about you."

Deborah was quick. "What kind of dreams?"

"None of your damn business," he grumbled.

She laughed out loud, delighted again to see him blush. "You've blushed more times today than I've ever seen since I've met you. Why, I didn't even know you *did* blush."

That didn't cheer him up at all. "I *never* should have told Kalliopi about you. Never."

"I know. That's the reason you didn't want me to come and see where you worked." She teased.

He blushed again.

"Oh, Peter. Have you told other people about me?"

"I had to."

"Why?"

"They asked. They wanted to know what was up. They noticed I was different. I innocently said I had met someone and all hell broke loose. The phones were buzzing." He mimicked a woman's voice, "'Peter's dating someone! Have you seen her? No! Have you? Find out what she looks like. Find out where she lives ...' It was like an advanced battle strategy. One site would get a bit of information and they'd tell another site. Every time I did a site visit, I felt like I was at war with the CIA and the enemy was trying to gain international secrets out of me."

Deborah was looking at him with her mouth hanging open. "What's the big deal about you having met someone? You've been divorced for fifteen years. Surely you've dated other women ..."

He was silent.

"Peter, you said that first day that you had asked other women out ..."

"For *coffee*," he clarified.

Deborah snorted. "What, you never got past the coffee stage?" she said sarcastically.

He was silent again. And he was blushing again.

"Oh, Peter."

They drove in silence for a bit. She tried to make sense of what he was telling her. "You are always so together and capable and self assured when we are together. You're painting a picture of a very shy man who had trouble finding a date. It doesn't fit."

"I *told* you, I'm different with you. I *told* you it took me a good couple of weeks to get up the courage to speak to you."

"You also told me you were tenacious."

Peter nodded. "I am. But up until you, I haven't met a woman I wanted to put my tenacious side to work on."

"Peter, you practically told me that you *loved me* in front of an entire congregation of people. That is *not* a shy man."

He smiled. "I *did* say I loved you in front of an entire congregation of people. You just had to listen very carefully to hear it. How many times do I have to tell you? You make me a different person."

"So, what? This whole thing about you not wanting me to know what you do for a living ..."

Peter sighed. "It was a combination of a lot of things. I needed to find the *perfect* time to let you know exactly what I do. One that would let you see how important it was to me and that it has *nothing* to do with money and prestige. Any wealth I had, was just the means to this end as far as I'm concerned. Up until the Sunday you heard my testimony, hell, you didn't even know my background! You only knew that brief bit I'd told you about my marriage and my failure with it. I knew the right time would come up. I just didn't expect it to happen last Sunday."

"And why couldn't you take me to the site you went to last Sunday?"

He looked at her like she was completely out of her mind. "Are you *crazy*? Jannelle runs the Trenton site."

That meant nothing to her. Deborah frowned. "Yes ..."

"Jannelle is the worst of the bunch. She would have sat you down and pried every personal bit of information out of you right down to your shoe size and your bank balance."

She again looked at him stunned. "Are you telling me that you let me agonize *all week* about this just until you could take me to a site that had a woman that was less of a gossip than another? Am I hearing you correctly?!"

"Being away from me was agony?" He looked absolutely delighted. She glared at him.

Managing to look a bit sheepish, Peter said, "Kalliopi's the tamest one of the bunch … I wasn't even going to take you there, but I couldn't go another day without seeing and talking to you and I really didn't think I could avoid the job topic anymore …"

She was silent. Then she sighed. "So, I'm trying to understand this. You've put me through a week of misery because on one level you didn't want me to think you were bragging …

"Yup."

"On another level you were too shy to handle all the commotion my appearance would cause …"

"Oh yeah."

Deborah looked down at her hands still confused but unsure what else to ask. It was clear Peter wasn't hiding anything from her and yet *she still just didn't get it.*

He sighed. "I'm *so* not doing this right," he muttered to himself in frustration. "Look, I told you that after Janet's death I had some lost years. I was aimless, bitter, angry, guilty, unhappy … depending on the day, depended on which emotion was the worse. In the midst of all that my oldest brother contacted me, still trying to convince me that he deserved a handout. I refused. Again. He was furious. Again. I don't remember exactly what he said, but it was something along the lines of he was glad that he'd lived long enough to see God give me everything I deserved – and he hoped he was around long enough to see me really hit rock bottom."

He chuckled a bitter chuckle. "That added a new one to my list. God. I incorporated all of my emotions with God; I was angry at Him, I was bitter towards Him, I felt my guilt was from Him …" He shook his head sadly. "I was so screwed up …

"Somehow I ended up at church one afternoon. I think the original intention was to show up and have it out with God. Tell Him what I thought. Instead, I encounter some kind old minister who sat with me for *hours* and listened while I ranted and raved. In the end, I was crying like a baby. And I'd made a commitment to God that I was going to be a different person. I was going to give Him a chance to show me what a better man He could make of me."

Peter glanced at her. "I admit that there was a bit of a challenge in that last part. Almost like 'Okay, God, I don't really believe all this crap. Go ahead. I'll give you a chance to fix this train wreck called my life. Go ahead. *I dare you.*' God was patient and loving and faithful to me. And I have tried to not look back." He shrugged. "I have my bad moments, but like I said to you once: I've been sorting some things out. I'm not done, but I'm close." He looked at her then briefly. "It's only taken me about *nine years.*"

They were off the highway now. Driving toward her home. "*Anyway,* my life was different after that. A steady slow progression of goodness crept into the gloom and doom. I was still in California when the idea of the homeless sites came into my head. I'd already done my penance with my brothers and sisters buying them their own places. I thought, 'Hell, I could do so much better with this concept …'

"At church, a man came and gave his testimony. He worked for a company called …" He looked at her.

"CTW."

"Yup. And the rest is history as they say. I chose the east coast because I've always wondered if my mother had had an out, an escape route, that maybe, *just maybe* she would have chosen it and done things differently. The Easton site was the first one. It's near a neighborhood I grew up in. Then the Philly site happened. The Trenton site is the newest."

Peter looked at her fiercely. "And I *don't* own them. The funds that support the sites are in an irrevocable trust, managed by a board of directors in connection with CTW, a worldwide charitable organization known as Care for The World."

"Kalliopi told me that."

That stopped him. "Oh. She did?"

Deborah nodded.

"Oh," he said again.

"I thought that all this was *it,* Deborah. I thought that the enjoyment I got out of doing this work was my reward. I thought that the contentment I felt now in my life was God's way of saying 'Good job,

Peter.' I've been on my own for *fifteen years*. No woman has even registered on my viewing screen. Hell, even Janet proposed to *me*. I married her because I thought it would be expedient -"

Deborah interrupted him. "You married Janet because you thought it would be *expedient*? What does that mean?"

"She was polished, sure of herself, already well thought of in her profession and within the community. I thought we'd make a good example of a power couple."

"So you never loved her?"

Peter looked exasperated, like she hadn't been listening to him. "I've never loved anyone …"

"You've never told a woman that you loved her before?"

"Sure."

"Oh."

"I told you."

They were in the driveway of her house. Deborah had no idea how long they had been there she suddenly realized. "And besides me?"

He was silent, suddenly blushing again.

"Oh, Peter."

"You've been saying that a lot today."

Deborah looked at him with tears in his eyes and he reached over and wiped one that trickled down her cheek.

He tried to explain one more time. "I didn't think there was anymore in store for me. I really felt that the Lord had blessed me enough with the way my life was going. You know, my goodness quota was somehow filled. Deborah, the sites, they're my life. Or I should say they were my life, until you showed up. In bringing my work and you together …" Peter seemed to struggle for words. He looked frustrated. "If I brought you down and introduced you to the people down there and you became a part of that life and then things didn't work out between us … I wouldn't have a place to escape. To go and hide and … get lost. You'd always be there … I wanted to share it all with you. I wanted you to be a part of it. But I was afraid to risk my heart. Hell, I was afraid to risk my sanity."

"So on another level you were afraid."

He sighed. "Yes. I'm sorry this wasn't simpler. I'm sorry I couldn't just be in the mob or something." He looked so defeated. "A life of crime would have been so much easier to explain to you." Peter put his head on the steering wheel.

Deborah started to laugh then. "Oh, do I love you."

He froze. Peter stayed like that for a good few moments. Then he was in a frenzy to get out of the car and to get around to her side and to get her door open and pull her out of the car. He gripped her shoulders and peered at her in the summer moonlight.

"Say it again."

Deborah smiled. "I love you."

He put his arms around her and lifted her clear off the ground. She threw her arms around his neck to steady herself. "*Say it again*," he said fiercely.

She laughed. "I love you," she said softly. "*I love you,*" she said louder.

He kissed her, still with his arms wrapped around her and her feet not touching the ground, smashed up against the car. "Say it again."

"*I love you, Peter.*" Deborah smiled at him, "You're acting as if no one has ever said those words ..." she stopped and just looked at him and he looked at her, silent. "*Oh, Peter.*" She put her head against his shoulder and her feet still weren't touching the ground.

"Say it again," she heard him say and his voice was choked with emotion.

"I love you, Peter Gannon, and I'll keep saying it as many times as you want me to say it, okay?"

Peter sighed and Deborah felt all the tension leave his body. "Okay. It's a deal."

I will go wherever you go and live wherever you live.

Your people will be my people, and your God will be my God.[14]

The Courageous Man's Victory

Sunday Peter picked her up early with an invitation to breakfast at the local diner. Deborah was stunned to walk in and see Todd sitting there looking barely awake. "What are you doing here?" she asked her son.

He looked a little embarrassed. "He bribed me," he said and looked directly at Peter.

She looked at Peter. "What's he talking about?"

Peter smiled at her. "I offered to buy him a steak and egg breakfast if he'd come to church with us afterwards. You know what they say, 'The way to man's soul is through his stomach.'"

Todd frowned. "Is that the way the saying goes? I thought it was different …"

Laughing delightedly, Deborah told Todd, "No, that's the way the saying goes, Todd. I'm certain."

Todd scratched his head, still uncertain.

"I'll treat anyone to breakfast you bring along with you as long as they go to church with us afterwards. It's a standing offer," Peter said as he and Deborah settled into their chairs.

"For how long?" Todd asked practically licking his lips in anticipation.

Peter looked at Deborah but answered Todd. "For as many times as you take me up on it."

"You'll regret that," Todd, chuckled picking up the menu.

"Never," Peter said winking at her.

"How many of you had a childhood fear of monsters? Giants?" Pastor Duncan was standing in the center of the altar, and behind him on the screen flashed various cartoon and old movie depictions of monsters and giants.

"Do you know that in the early Bible times, there were a race of giant men? They were called The Anakim, after their first ancestor named Anak. Anak had three sons who were also giants and from there a race of giants was bred. Goliath, in David's time was a descendant of theirs but by then the race was just about extinct.

"But during the early times, when Moses and then Joshua were leading the Israelites into the Promised Land, this fierce race of giants was supremely powerful. And in case you are wondering if the term 'giant' is an exaggeration, height estimates of these men were between nine and a half to eleven feet tall." Deborah heard surprised murmurs throughout the church. "That would be as tall as," Pastor Duncan pointed, "from the floor up to the top rung of the balcony. Give or take a couple inches." People chuckled. "I don't know about you, but that qualifies as a giant to me …"

"When Moses sent spies into the Promised Land, he sent one man from each of the twelve tribes of Israel – descendants of Jacob. Each man was the tribal head. Caleb represented the tribe of Judah." He grinned. "*Yes*, this is the same Judah we talked about a few weeks ago, the foolish man who triumphed in the end. His descendants at this point in Biblical history are now so numerous they are no longer called sons, or relatives, but a whole *tribe*. And Caleb was their tribal leader."

Pastor Duncan walked back behind the pulpit. "These twelve chosen men are gone for forty days exploring the land that they had been promised when they were just one small family so very, very long ago. Now they number – including the old, the women and the children – probably over a million strong." He shook his head. "I cannot imagine the impatience among the people as they waited for those spies to return with their report. These people had endured a lifetime of brutal slavery by the Egyptians."

Looking out at the congregation, Pastor Duncan said, "I don't know. Can you imagine what it must have been like walking from Egypt with whatever possessions they managed to take all the way to the edge of The Promised Land – hundreds and hundreds of miles. Do you think kids back then asked, 'Are we there yet?' too?" Everyone laughed.

"*At last*, the spies returned. Their initial reports were the stuff dreams were made of - a magnificent country flowing with milk and honey. Why the twelve spies had brought back samples of some of the fruits they had found growing there: pomegranates, figs and a cluster of grapes so large that it had taken two of them to carry it back on a pole between them! Can you imagine what the people must have thought having just walked across a desert?

"But then, the spies gave the bad news. Here, I'll read what they said," Pastor Duncan looked down at his Bible and read, "'But the people living there are powerful, and their cities and towns are fortified and very large. We also saw the descendants of Anak who are living there. We can't go up against them! They are stronger then we are. We felt like grasshoppers next to them, and that's what we looked like to them!'"

Pastor Duncan looked up at the congregation. "Guess what the people of Israel said? But first think: what would you have said? You've grown up *and for your entire life* you've been told of The Promised Land. You've been encouraged because of it, you've dreamed about it, you've staked all of your hopes and dreams in it. What would you do?"

He waited a few moments giving everyone time to think. "This is what the people said," and he began to read again, "'Then all the people began weeping aloud and they cried all night. Their voices rose in a great chorus of complaint against Moses and his brother, Aaron. 'We wish we had died in Egypt, or even here in the wilderness! Why is the Lord taking us to this country only to have us die in battle? Our wives and little ones will be carried off as slaves! Let's get out of here and return to Egypt! Let's choose a new leader and go back to Egypt.'"

Pastor Duncan looked up. "Egypt meant the return to slavery, so take it from me, *they were mighty upset.*"

Pastor Duncan walked out, Bible in hand and stood in front of the congregation. "Remember Caleb? He'd partnered with another man named Hoshea, head of the tribe of Ephraim. In the face of all this weeping and wailing and plotting to overthrow Moses and run back to Egypt, Caleb stepped forward and he spoke to the people." Pastor Duncan looked down and read, "'But Caleb tried to encourage the people as they stood before Moses. 'Let's go at once to take the land,' he said, 'We can certainly conquer it! The land we explored is a wonderful land! And if the Lord is pleased with us, He will bring us safely into the land and give it to us. Do not rebel against the Lord, and don't be afraid of the people of the land. They are only helpless prey to us! They have no protection, but the Lord is with us! Don't be afraid of them!'"[15]

Pastor Duncan looked up. "*One* man, standing up before hundreds of thousands of angry, hysterical people trying to encourage them to attack a land of well fortified cities inhabited by *giants.* They had no skill, no weaponry. They had only one weapon that in Caleb's opinion was so powerful it rendered the giants defenseless. What was the weapon he tried to remind them they had? What was the weapon he tried to remind them they had lived with and witnessed too many times to count?"

Pastor Duncan waited. "Go ahead. Say it. What was the weapon?"

Someone up in the balcony said, "The Lord."

Pastor Duncan looked up into the balcony and nodded. "Right." He looked out at the congregation and asked, "What was the weapon?"

"The Lord," many in the congregation repeated.

"What was the weapon?"

"THE LORD," almost everyone said.

"Ahh, good. Now I know everyone's awake." Many chuckled while he walked back behind the pulpit.

"Hoshea stood with Caleb. He was Moses' right hand man, and was also known as Joshua." Pastor Duncan grinned, "Yeah, the famous one that will eventually fight the battle of Jericho and save Rahab."

"Do you think that Caleb was able to sway the crowd?" Pastor Duncan shook his head sadly. "Nope. The crowd began to talk about not only overthrowing Moses, but *stoning* Caleb and Joshua as well. It was a bad scene …

"Always remember this: *Truth is not always measured by majority opinion.* In fact, in my opinion, it often goes against it."

He shrugged. "God stepped in. He had to. The ten spies that had discouraged the people and incited the rebellion died of a mysterious plague. And God decreed that anyone who was twenty years or older would *never* set foot in The Promised Land. The people were sentenced to forty years of wandering – one year for each day the spies had explored - while those who had wailed and doubted and shouted that they wanted to go back to Egypt got old and died.

"Of the original group of people who Moses brought out of Egypt, only *two* men would step foot on that Promised Land: Caleb and Joshua. Joshua, took over as leader after Moses' death, with Caleb in the position as one of his top military leaders. And when the Promised Land was conquered enough to begin dividing it up amongst the tribes, God specifically told Joshua to give Caleb his very own choice piece of land."

Pastor Duncan walked out from the pulpit and down the stairs. "Now the land was *in no way* conquered when the Israelite tribes began to parcel it out amongst themselves. There had been many stunning victories, but there was still a lot of work to do. God told Joshua to specifically tell the people that they must continue to work towards the eradication of all pagan peoples."

Standing with his hands clasped behind his back, Pastor Duncan said, "So Caleb, comes before his friend Joshua, the leader of the all the hosts of Israel. He was *eighty-five years old!* He was forty when he was the spy, he's wandered with the punished Israelites for forty years, and he's been involved with the conquering of the land these past five years. It is his turn to choose the land he wished to claim as his own and continue in the battle to settle. Other tribes have gone before him and chosen. I'm sure some of the choicest pieces have been already taken." Pastor Duncan grinned and asked quietly. "Guess what land he asked for?"

"Caleb said, 'Give me that hill country. You know the one I mean. It's the same hill country that when we were spies we saw the Anakim living in their great walled cities. The Lord has kept me alive and well and if the Lord is with me, I will drive them out of the land, just as He said.'"[16]

Pastor Duncan grinned and shook his head. "If I had only one small piece of the courage he had. Can you appreciate the magnitude of his courage? Of his faith?" He leaned forward and whispered, "*What was Caleb's greatest weapon?*"

In unison, the congregation said, "The Lord."

"And what should your greatest weapon be in times of despair?"

"The Lord."

"In times of fear?"

"The Lord."

"In times of doubt?"

"The Lord."

Pastor Duncan put his hands on his hips. "Is He? Have you made that personal choice to put the Lord first in your life? For that's what it is. It is a *personal choice.* No one can make that choice but you. You can either be as strong as Caleb or as weak as Achan. You can be as generous as the Woman with Two Mites, as forgiven as Rahab, as decisive as the Wise Woman of Able, as fiery as Deborah, as faithful as Leah, or as redeemed as Judah. You can be as spectacularly honorable as Boaz or as sadly regrettable as Solomon. It is a *personal choice* that you yourself make." He wagged his finger at everyone. "And let me tell you something, choosing to make *no* choice *is* a choice.

"I pray that each and every one of you will be just like Caleb. When everyone else saw giants, he saw *only The Lord.*"

Todd refused lunch saying he couldn't in good conscience mooch more than one meal a day from any one person and they all laughed. On the way home Peter said to her, "If I tell you I can't spend the day with you today are we going to have a fight?"

"Are you being purposely evasive?" Deborah was teasing.

Peter was silent.

"Oh great," she muttered.

"It has nothing to do with my job, if that makes any difference."

She smiled. "I'm a big girl. I can amuse myself."

He looked concerned.

"Peter, less than three months ago I didn't even know you existed."

He rolled his eyes. "Oh, that makes me feel so much better."

She giggled.

"*That* makes me feel better."

Peter looked seriously concerned. "This has the makings of being a fantastically busy week for me."

"Well, you know where I live. You have my number. Try calling and maybe I'll be in." Deborah grinned wickedly at him.

"Are you the same woman that described herself as an embittered widow?"

"You said you loved a challenge."

"I also said I love *you*."

She sighed. "Yes. You did. And that's one of the reasons I'm no longer an embittered widow. Look, Wednesdays seem to have become the group gathering spot at my house. Todd has already asked me if I'd cook my crispy fish."

"How come he always gets to pick the menu?"

She laughed. "I don't know. I'm just happy there's someone who likes my cooking."

"I'll try to make it. Can we make a definite date for Friday night? If the weather's nice we can take the bike."

She nodded.

Deborah was busy. She decided Sunday when she got home that she'd empty out Jonathan's office. It was time. She realized that it was the only remaining piece of him in the house and she all of a sudden desperately wanted it gone. She'd make it into a … Well, she didn't know but she wanted it empty of any memories of Jonathan. In her earliest memories it had been her mother and father's room. The only bedroom on the main floor with the other bedrooms upstairs. After her parents moved out, Jonathan had claimed it as his private study, his home office.

She stood in the doorway for a few minutes, breathing the musty air. That made her cross the room and open each of the three windows. That took some effort! She went and got her trusty box of garbage bags and started on the bookshelves. There were lots of loose papers, file folders, and old trade magazines. She bundled them up for recycling. Next, were rows and rows of hard covered trade texts which she also tied up for recycling. In the end, there wasn't one book she thought was worth saving.

Sitting at Jonathan's desk, Deborah called Good Will. Did they want the furniture? They were more than willing to come and get it when she told them what was here and assured them of its quality. They made arrangements to pick it up Monday afternoon. That forced her to work through the desk drawers and when she'd emptied the last one she realized that she'd gotten progressively more tense, worried about what she might find. Laughing, she finally realized what could she possibly find that would be worse then The Truth she already knew about?

By Sunday evening she had thirteen bags of recycling and seven bags of out right garbage. Deborah had set aside Jonathan's desk set, his collection of fancy pens, and his desk clock for the kids. She was just walking out of the room when she noticed the briefcase behind the door. She stood looking at it for the longest time, trying to figure out how it had gotten there. Then she remembered. John had brought Jonathan's personal affects back after he died and had driven home from the airport in Jonathan's car. Obviously, when the car was sold, Todd had brought the briefcase in here.

Deborah carried the briefcase into the kitchen and sat it on the counter while she fixed herself some dinner. It was a looming, threatening presence. Finally, she got impatient with herself. What was she afraid of? Why was she being so ridiculous?

With a cup of tea in one hand and the briefcase in the other, Deborah went and sat down on the couch. It was filled with more contracts and periodicals, pens and official name tags Jonathan needed to wear when he traveled to different company locations. Would one of the boys want the briefcase? She didn't know. Maybe she'd give it to Neil … She sighed. Just as Deborah was about to close the briefcase she noticed one more pocket with the edge of a paper sticking out. Pulling out the piece of paper, Deborah took a deep shuddering breath. It was a Father's Day card that she and the kids had hand made a long, long time ago. She remembered sitting at the kitchen counter with them. John had carefully written "Happy Father's Day" on the front. Grace had done colorful artwork on every available space. There was a heavy preponderance of red hearts. Todd had been allowed to scribble in a few select corners.

On the back she had carefully traced each one of the children's hands and in each of the tracings she'd written a message from each of the children. John's said, "I hope you are home next Father's Day, Dad. I want to take you out for dinner at Max's." Grace's said, "I love you, Daddy. Here's my heart." Todd's had said, "Mom says we can't come see you. Tell her we can." Carefully written along the bottom was a note from her. It said, "I hope you are having a happy Father's Day in California."

She sat there on the couch. "You have no idea what you missed, Jonathan Lawson," she said out loud. But then Deborah thought about how he'd carried that card with him all those years. "Maybe you did," she finally said out loud. At that moment, she forgave him. She had no anger, no hatred, and no need for revenge. Deborah felt a sorrow for Jonathan, because she was certain that he had been unhappy his entire life. She would never understand what made him make the choices he had made, but that was okay. She heard Grace's strident questions the day she had found out about Jonathan. "Who is this woman? What is going on with her children? Was she an innocent?" And for the first time, Deborah felt a sorrow and concern for her. Deborah prayed for this woman to find peace, for her to be surrounded like she was by wonderful people and things that God had anticipated that she needed, and that she would find happiness in her future.

Peter called her at 1:00 a.m. Tuesday morning. "Are you asleep?"

"No, I'm having a party."

"You always seem a little grumpy when you first wake up, you know. Are you always like that?"

"You'll have to find out for yourself," Deborah heard herself saying in a flip, flirty tone.

"*I can't wait.*"

"Why are you calling me so late?"

"I've lost track of the time, but I needed to hear your voice."

"What do you mean you lost track of the time? Where are you?"

"Can I be evasive?"

"No."

"California."

She sat bolt upright. "What? What are you doing in California?"

"Stuff. Sorry that sounds evasive and it is but that's the most you're going to get out of me right now. Talk to me. I need to hear your voice. What have you been doing with yourself?"

She laid back down and told him about Jonathan's office and how she was busy redoing it.

"What are you going to use it for?"

"An empty room right now."

"Why don't you make it into your office."

"What do I need an office for?"

"I don't know. It was just a thought. Everyone needs a place to do bills, write correspondence, … stuff like that."

"It's an idea …"

"My flight won't get me back in time for dinner on Wednesday. Can I come by for dessert?"

"Yes."

"It might be late, like 10:30."

"I'll wait up."

"Okay. I'll let you get back to sleep."

"Okay …"

"Deborah?"

"Yes?"

"Say it."

Deborah smiled in her bed all by herself curled up with a phone. "I love you, Peter Gannon. Do you know something?"

"No, what?"

"Aside from John, I've never told anyone in California that I loved him."

Peter was quiet for a long time. "Never?"

"No, never."

"Wednesday night is too far away."

"Keep busy. That's what I do. It makes the time go faster."

"Not fast enough."

Her crispy fish was a big hit on Wednesday night. Deborah made homemade French fries, her own special tartar sauce, and baked brownies, too. Everyone was happy. One of Todd's friends (he'd brought two) joked that word was getting around that the best time to hang out with her son was Wednesdays. That made her smile.

10:00 p.m. the doorbell rang. She had just gotten out of the shower and was puzzled, who could it be? Peter had said 10:30 hadn't he? When were planes ever early? Deborah slipped on her bathrobe, came downstairs and peered out the front window. She saw absolutely no one. Just as she was at the top of the stairs walking into her bedroom the doorbell rang again. This time, she opened the door to peer outside.

On the front steps was an enormous bunch of tulips. There had to be three dozen; white ones, red ones, and yellow ones. They were tied up with a big blue ribbon that then trailed off down the stairs and around the corner into the summer darkness. She smiled and stepped out the door to pick up the bouquet.

When she tried to pull the ribbon, it didn't budge. She was forced to follow it down the steps and around the corner. Peter was sitting on the steps by the driveway in the soft glow of the front lights she'd left on for him with the blue ribbon clutched tightly in his hand.

Deborah sat down next to him on the steps, tulips and all, and rested her wet hair on his shoulder.

"God, you smell good," he said and took a deep breath.

"Thank you for the flowers."

"Your welcome." Deborah gave him a kiss, long and sweet. When she went to end it and pull away he reached up, grabbed the back of her head and pulled her back in for more. She smiled against his mouth.

"How was your flight?"

"Not fast enough."

She giggled. "You said you'd be here at 10:30. It's only 10. It seems like you're early."

"It still wasn't fast enough."

"Come on in, I'll put coffee on. I saved you some brownies."

"Do you have anything on under that thing?" Peter asked suddenly.

Deborah looked down at her bathrobe. She blushed. She started to say something and he held up his hand. "Don't bother. I have my answer already."

"You're *early*. I made crispy fish. I smelled strongly of frying oil and flounder. I decided to take a quick shower before you got here. I can't help it if you're early."

"Do you always answer the door in just a bathrobe?"

"If someone stops by at 10:00 at night with three dozen tulips, yes I do."

Peter shook his head in frustration. "Damn. I had no idea it was that easy. If I'd only known earlier …"

She giggled and touched Peter's arm. "Come inside …"

He shook his head emphatically. "No."

"Because of the way I'm dressed?"

He nodded. "Absolutely."

Deborah studied him in the lamplight. "You're serious …"

He blushed. "If you could read my mind right now, lady, you'd be running for safety, let me tell you."

She laughed out loud, delighted.

"It's really not funny."

Deborah nodded. "Yes it is." She purposely let her bathrobe fall open slightly to show her bare legs, never taking her eyes off his face. He closed his eyes as if in physical pain while at the same time reaching over, feeling for the edge of her bathrobe, and pulling it back in place.

Peter sighed. He didn't take his hand away though. Deborah felt his warm hand through her bathrobe resting on her leg just above her knee. He let his fingers work down between her legs and the opening of the bathrobe to touch her bare skin. He sighed again.

It had been so long since Deborah had desired anyone, let alone have someone desire her. That alone was a delicious feeling. She rested her head on Peter's shoulder again and they sat for long moments in silence.

"Did you get done what you needed to get done in California?" she finally asked.

"Yup. The trip was a rip, roaring success."

"Will you have to go again, soon?"

"No. But I'll tell you one thing."

"What's that?"

"If I go again, you're coming with me."

Deborah lifted her head so that she gazed into Peter's serious eyes and smiled. "Really?"

"Absolutely."

Peter's hand was now caressing the inside of her bare thigh and slowly moving upward. He looked at her and then down at his hand. "See why I can't come in? If I don't leave within the next five minutes I'm going to have you on your back right here in the driveway." He said it with such annoyance Deborah laughed out loud again.

"Peter, we're both adults. We've been married …"

He stood up then, carefully took the flowers from her and set them on the step, looked down at the opening of her bathrobe, groaned loudly, and pulled her to her feet. She was standing one step up so she was almost eye-to-eye with him. He kissed her with an intensity that just about took her breath away. His hands ran down the back of her, starting at her neck and across her shoulders, working their way slowly down until they were cupping her backside and pulling her firmly against him. He stopped kissing her and looked at her. "No," he said decisively through gritted teeth.

"No?"

"No."

"When?"

"Soon," he said, his teeth still clenched, "or I'll have to be institutionalized."

She put her arms around him his neck and rubbed her nose with his and grinned at him. "You're enjoying this, aren't you?" he growled.

Deborah nodded, absolutely delighted. "Yup."

"Are we still on for Friday?"

"Yes."

"Kiss me and say good night."

She said good night and went to kiss him, but Peter turned the tables on her. Kissing *her* and holding her tight against him with one hand while he slid his other hand up to touch the side of her breast. Deborah gasped with the jolt of delight. He stopped kissing her mouth and moved to bite her earlobe. She shivered and drew a shaky breath. "Teasing can get you in *a lot* of trouble, Deborah" he breathed in her ear. "Watch yourself ..."

Deborah went shopping on Thursday, spending a long time trying on clothes and enjoyed herself immensely. She bought a few pairs of pants, a few tops, and even two pairs of shoes, staying away from traditional, practical clothes and buying ones that Deborah thought Grace would have picked out for her. As a last impulse, she stopped at the jewelry counter and bought some wild earrings.

As Deborah exited through the men's department, she remembered how Jonathan had never let her buy him clothes. He had said she didn't understand his tastes. After two attempts that had ended with her in tears, Deborah sworn she'd *never* buy him clothes again. And she never had again. Not even socks.

She stood staring at a leather vest for the longest time. Insecurity came and stood next to her and wrapped an arm around her. She walked away. Then walked back. Then walked away again. Then went back. When she touched it, it was soft and supple. Like butter. She could picture Peter wearing it so clearly. *Trust your gut*, she heard her head say. That made her smile. God seemed to like both of them wearing leather and giggled when she thought of telling Pastor Duncan about that.

Friday Deborah wrapped up Peter's vest with some paper she found in the closet and dressed carefully. He'd called briefly in the morning to say that the weather looked perfect to go by bike so she should dress accordingly. She wore her new black jeans, new black boots with lots of funny buckles and a new bright pink top. Putting on the wild earrings she shook her head at the image that stared back at her in the mirror. Nope. Tiny little diamond studs were much more her style. Better. And why bother much with her hair? Helmet hair was inevitable no matter what.

When she opened up the door, Peter just stood there staring at her. She became more and more uncomfortable as the moments ticked by. "Is something wrong?" she finally asked him.

"No," he said quietly, seeming to shake himself out of a fog. "Everything's *just fine*."

Deborah pulled him in the house. "I have a gift for you," she said. She made him sit down on the chair in the living room and brought him the package. "When I thought to buy you the gift, it never occurred to me to buy wrapping paper." She smiled as Peter looked down at the gift wrapped in a red and green Christmas theme.

He opened it and smiled with delight; immediately put it on.

"Oh, thank goodness it fits."

Peter nodded in agreement. "Perfectly."

She smiled, tremendously pleased with herself. It looked very good on him. "It was a gut decision," she said.

"God must like us in leather."

Deborah laughed. "That's exactly what I thought."

Like her, he was wearing black jeans and a bright white long sleeved shirt. The vest looked great with it. Peter smiled at her, "I'm going to wear it tonight."

"You don't have to. You can keep it here and pick it up when you drop me off."

"I'm going to wear it tonight."

Deborah smiled and nodded, suddenly overcome and wanting to cry. How stupid was that? Then she remembered her newest decorating attempt. "Come, see what I did." Grabbing his hand, she pulled him through the living room, the dining room and into Jonathan's old office. She turned and smiled and then swung her arm out to her side. "Welcome to my new study ..."

Peter walked around the room, studying it from various angles. "I never knew this room was here."

"No, I always kept the door closed."

"Explain what you've done. It looks ... nice and spacious."

Deborah laughed. "It's completely empty! I know, but that's great, really." She told him how she'd pulled up the carpet, painted the walls, and bought and hung new curtains. Then she described the new book shelves, desk, wingchair, and lamps she'd bought and which were on order. She looked at him. "I took your advice. I'm going to make it my own personal office. Will you help me set up a computer and get email? The kids have been bugging me *forever* to get it."

He nodded, "Yes, I'll help you do that."

"There's no rush."

Peter looked like he was going to say something and then stopped himself.

She got nervous. Maybe the top was too much. It *was* bright pink. She didn't usually wear such bright colors. Maybe he was uncomfortable. "Peter, do I look all right? The top's new and kind of bright. Maybe I should go change ..."

"You look ... amazing."

Deborah put her hands on her hips. "Well *something's* wrong. Is it the vest? Do you not like it?" She glared at him. "Come on Mr. Non-Evasive, Honest Man, let's have it."

Peter arched his eyebrow at her. "*Mr. Non-Evasive, Honest Man? Where the hell did that come from?*"

Deborah gave him a smart look, opened her mouth like she was going to say something and then shut it.

"What were you going to say?"

She arched her eyebrow at him.

Peter started to open his mouth again and at Deborah's look shut it again. He shook his head. "Get your coat and let's go."

She'd bought a little purse that crossed over her chest and fit securely to her side. It was small enough that it fit comfortably under her leather jacket. She grabbed the purse, pulled on the jacket and looked at him. "Ready."

They ended up at another lovely restaurant that was quiet and secluded. The food was spectacular and the atmosphere was very romantic. But although the conversation went well, she felt distinctly like things were not right. As the evening wore on, Peter seemed to become more and more preoccupied and distant.

"What made this week so busy for you?"

"Why do you ask that?" Peter said.

Had he sounded defensive? Deborah frowned. "I remember you saying on Sunday that this week had the makings of being a fantastically busy week. I just was wondering what made it so busy."

He sighed. "Well, the trip to California, kind of crunched everything together. I lost three days there and then had to catch up with other things."

"Did you get down to see Kalliopi and Niesha?"

"No."

"Did you get to any of the other sites?"

"No."

She frowned. "Peter, is everything okay?"

"Yes, everything's -"

Deborah interrupted him, saying through gritted teeth, "If you tell me everything's 'just fine' one more time, so help me I'll scream. I don't think you've heard me scream but I've got one that's been stored up for well over two years and I think I could probably shatter a few windows."

"Can we go?"

Out in the parking lot, leaning against the motorcycle seat with her pulled between his legs, Peter helped her do up her jacket, lingering over the zipper and the buckles. Before he helped Deborah put her helmet on, he kissed her. For a very long time. "Can I be honest with you?" she finally said after he'd stopped kissing her.

"Absolutely."

"You're scaring me."

Peter sighed and leaned his head down until it touched her head. He sighed again. "I'm screwing this all up. I should have said something Wednesday night but you came out in that damned bathrobe."

"Wednesday night!? Something's been bothering you since Wednesday night? Now I am upset." Peter tried to pull her back into his embrace and when she wouldn't let him he rubbed his hands up and down her arms instead. Deborah just stood there stiff and tense.

"Peter, tell me, *what's wrong?*"

"Everything's fi- "

Deborah opened her mouth wide to scream and Peter clamped his hand over it. "Okay, *okay,* so everything's not fine. But everything's okay. Look, can we just go? I shouldn't have tried to go out and do dinner tonight. I've got too much on my mind. I've never been a very good conversationalist when I've got too much on my mind."

He took his hand away from her mouth. "Sure," she said in a tight voice. "Let's go."

Every time Peter had to stop the motorcycle he would reach to her to touch her and either smooth her hand or her leg. Once he shouted back, "Are you okay?"

Deborah wasn't going to play his game. She yelled back, "No!" Peter shook his head and she swore that he chuckled. How could it be that the longer she knew him the harder he was getting to understand? Wasn't it supposed to be the other way around? What could be bothering him? She already knew about his job, his past, his ex-wife, the old person he was, the new one he wished to be ... Riding home on the back of the bike Deborah racked her brain trying to come up with something that they hadn't already discussed that would be a potential problem.

Suddenly, she thought she hit on something. It had something to do with the trip to California. Peter been tense the Sunday before, there had been that odd 1 a.m. phone call, and he hadn't been the same since he got back. *And* she remembered with a start, he'd specifically said that whatever he had to do on Sunday it *wasn't* anything to do with his job. Something personal. Related to his life in California. Something he'd struggled with saying on Wednesday but had decided not to. By the time the bike came to a stop Deborah was in a real state. She decided then and there that the unknown was much worse than the known. Whatever he had to tell her, she could handle, but this worrying and stewing over stuff just sucked. And she'd tell him that, too. As soon as she got her helmet off.

But they weren't home. They were at the park where they had gone on their first real date and they'd eaten ice cream cones and sat at the picnic table laughing at the geese. Deborah got off the bike and unhooked her helmet. She looked at him ready to give him a piece of her mind and tell him to stop this unknown worry stuff.

But Peter spoke before her. "Don't say anything, okay? I've got stuff to tell you and I need to get my thoughts just right so it comes out right, okay?"

She looked at him and then nodded stiffly. *Okay, you can go first,* her head said, *but I'm going to have the last word.*

Peter hung their helmets on the bike and then went to one of the side compartments and took out a beautifully carved wooden box. Huh? He tucked it under his arm, grabbed Deborah's hand and walked her over to the picnic bench.

He straddled the bench and she did the same looking at him. He cleared his throat, took a deep breath and opened the box.

"This is the key to the Philly site." Peter put a shiny key on the table and it glowed in the moonlight.

"This is the key to the Easton site.

"This is the key to the Trenton site.

"This is the key to my townhouse."

Deborah looked at Peter like he was absolutely insane.

"These keys, Deborah, are my life.

"This key is the key to John's place."

Deborah couldn't help but interrupt. "John who?"

He was definitely annoyed with her interruption, frowning and saying, "Your son, John. You're not supposed to interrupt. Remember? I'll loose my train of thought."

Tough, Deborah's head said.   "What are you doing with John's house key?"

"He gave it to me.'"

"When?"

Peter sighed in frustration.   "When I went and saw him in California on Tuesday."

If she'd been upset and tense before, everything ratcheted up by a significant degree. *"You saw John in California on Tuesday?"* Deborah managed to gasp out.

Peter nodded. "Yes. Now will you let me finish?"

She nodded reluctantly, sitting still and looking at Peter, her mouth drawn into a tight line.

"This is Todd's house key," he said, picking up where he'd left off.

She started to open her mouth but Peter arched his eyebrow at her and she stayed quiet. She did try to peer into the box, though, and he quickly shut the lid, frowned at her and shook his head 'no'.

"This is Grace's house key.

"This is your house key."

She started to open her mouth but Peter stopped her. "Grace gave it to me," he said in anticipation of her question and with a little bit of frustration.

Peter gestured toward all the keys carefully lined up on the table. "These keys represent your life."

He took a deep breath. "I'd very much like to put all these keys together on one key ring." He took something out of the box and laid it on the table. It was a beautiful shiny key ring with a large gold medallion. Deborah looked at the engraving and saw it said, 'Peter and Deborah Gannon.'

She looked up at him, now stunned into speechlessness and Peter looked very, very serious. He pulled one more thing out of the box. It was a beautiful ring, the band twisted with gold and silver with two large dark stones mounted in an elaborate setting. The stones flashed briefly in the moonlight. "Deborah, will you marry me?"

She just looked at him, for what seemed like forever, and he sat there before her, patiently watching her, holding out the ring. Swallowing, Deborah managed, "You went to California to see John?"

"Oh course, I had to speak with him and tell him my intentions."

"So you talked with Todd, too?"

He nodded.

"And Grace?"

He nodded again.

"And what did they say?"

Peter thought carefully. "John was impressed I'd made the effort to go out and speak with him. He's a good man. He asked me some very pointed questions about my past and I think, in the end, that my honesty was what impressed him the most.

"Grace, cried. A lot. At first I thought she was crying because of everything that's gone on so recently about Jonathan, but when she was able to get herself together enough to talk she said that she'd been praying for so long that you would find happiness that this was just what she had wanted.

"Todd wanted to know if we got married were you still going to cook dinners for him and his friends on Wednesday nights and if I was still going to spring for breakfast on Sunday mornings."

Deborah gasped out a laugh that got caught up in a sob. Her hand flew to her mouth. Peter reached up, took her hand and kissed it. He didn't let it go.

"You know he likes to play the buffoon sometimes but he's the sharpest one of the three, I think." Deborah nodded. She knew. She could hear him saying, *I'm not worried about you, Mom.*

"And you were going to ask me all this on Wednesday?"

Shrugging, Peter explained, "Well, I had the ring and John's key, but I hadn't been to see Grace and Todd yet. It wasn't the right time, but the waiting was killing me. Then you came out practically stark naked."

"I wasn't stark naked!"

He looked at her pointedly. "I could have had you stark naked in about five seconds flat." He hesitated. "No, probably two."

Deborah chose to ignore the topic. "If you talked with my kids, did you talk with Kalliopi and the others?" She grinned because she knew the answer.

He said with absolute certainty. "I'm not telling them until we're on the honeymoon."

"Aren't you jumping to conclusions?"

"What?"

"I haven't answered you yet."

"It's a long walk home ..." Peter said in a threatening tone.

"Let me see the ring."

He handed it to her. It was heavy. "I have a jeweler friend in California. We talked about it together over the phone and he made it up for me. That's a ruby – my birthstone and that's a sapphire – your birthstone."

She looked at the ring. Inside was engraved, '*Luke12:34*'

Peter whispered in her ear, "Wherever your treasure is, there your heart and thoughts will also be."

Then she started to cry. He brushed his big hand across her cheeks to wipe away the tears. "I knew I had to propose, when you promised you'd tell me you loved me as many times as I wanted you to. We made a deal, remember?"

Nodding through her tears, Deborah murmured, "Yes I remember."

"We've been hooked since we made that deal, you know."

With shining eyes, Deborah looked at Peter and said, "Yes, I knew."

"So, you'll marry me?"

"Yes, I'll marry you."

"Next Saturday?"

"Next Saturday!" she exploded.

"Well, Pastor Duncan said that tomorrow would be rushing it."

Deborah looked at Peter. "You've talked with Pastor Duncan already?!"

"Oh yeah," he shook his head and rolled his eyes, "and *man* is that guy smug about it all."

She laughed and threw her arms around him. "Really next Saturday?!"

"Really next Saturday."

Peter took the ring and carefully slipped it on her finger. It felt wonderfully heavy and solid on her hand. He grinned. "I feel like Caleb must have felt when he told Joshua, 'I'll take that mountain' … fearless, excited, full of breathless anticipation."

He looked at her then and his face was full of love, and tenderness, and absolute joy. "We'll conquer any giants we find together, okay?"

"Oh, yes," Deborah said smiling through her tears, "together."

And if you find a love that's tender, if you find someone who's true,

Then thank the Lord -- He's been doubly good to you.[17]

The Great Love Story

Deborah wouldn't let Peter, of course. She not only made him tell Kalliopi, Jannelle, and Pilar (the supervisor of the Easton site) but she told him if they couldn't all make it next Saturday they'd have to postpone things until they could make it. Peter looked incredulous and she looked absolutely serious. She jangled the key ring in front of him as he sat on the couch with her the next day. *"They're your life, Peter.* Those are your words. They will be here next Saturday or we'll wait." She handed him the phone and curled up next to him to listen.

Sighing in resignation, Peter picked up the phone and dialed. "Kalliopi? It's Peter. Are you free next Saturday? No, I'm not coming down there, I want you to come up here."

He listened for a moment, she could hear Kalliopi's voice, but couldn't make out the words.

He sighed. "No, no problem. Deborah and I just wanted you to come up for the wedding." He took a deep breath. "Ours."

Deborah could hear the shouts on the other end and covered her mouth to stifle her giggles. She felt Peter start.

"What do you mean *'you won the bet'?!*" She heard more muffled, excited talk, and Peter's horrified voice say, "And you all had a pool going? About when we'd get married?!" Deborah snuck a peek at him and he was blushing scarlet. She scooted up and kissed him and then rested her head on his shoulder. Peter sighed and leaned his head into her, still listening to Kalliopi's excited talk.

"Yes, bring Niesha … No, I haven't called the others … *Yes*, I want to do it …" He sounded exasperated. "Will you at least give me ten minutes to call Jannelle and Pilar before you all start phoning each other? … Yes, okay, I'll tell her. *Now?* … Okay, wait a minute."

Peter took the phone away from his ear, Deborah sat up and he looked at her. "I'm to tell you from Kalliopi, 'Welcome to the family…'" They could both hear Kalliopi's voice shouting in the phone. He put the receiver to his ear.

"What?" he sounded impatient.

Peter rolled his eyes. "No, I didn't tell her … *No*, I haven't discussed it with her …" He nodded his head. "Yes, I will talk with her about it … We've got a few *other, more important,* things to talk about right now, like a *wedding* …" He sighed, closed his eyes, and pinched the area under his glasses. She could hear Kalliopi talking a mile a minute. "I'll leave that up to Deborah, okay? … Yes, I'll tell her … Hell, I'll let you talk to her about it … *No, not now* … Yes, YES, I promise I'll tell her."

When he hung up Peter looked at her fiercely. "Remember, *I warned you.*" He then dialed Jannelle and finally Pilar and had almost identical conversations with them. When he hung up he put his head against the back of the couch seemingly exhausted.

Deborah leaned over and kissed his nose. He grabbed her and pulled her into his lap and kissed her for a long while. "Tell me what?" she said when they came up for air.

He sighed. "Can't this wait? We've got a wedding to plan."

"You don't seem in too much of hurry right now to plan a wedding. You seem more interested in kissing. Besides, I didn't choose a date that's only six days away, *you* did."

"*First off,* I will *always* be more interested in kissing you than anything else. Above and beyond all of the basic necessities of life including food, water, shelter, air ..." He leaned over and bit her ear. "Mmmmm," he mumbled contentedly. She shivered and then giggled. Peter continued. "Second, you better get it in your head that Kalliopi, Jannelle, and Pilar *all* think that each one of them is the most important in the hierarchy of my business life. So this upcoming problem – should it be handled incorrectly – could be monumental."

"What upcoming problem?" She asked him, suddenly very concerned. Peter sounded serious.

"Just before I met you, it was decided between the board of directors and myself and the supervisors that we'd try to add a teaching component to each one of the sites. We no longer wanted it to be a full time volunteer position, which tends to be too casual and haphazard for serious results. We talked about hiring professional teachers or tutors. People that would be capable with the children as well as the women and would be diverse enough to be able to handle anything that might crop up." He sighed and looked at her. "They're already battling with each other over who gets you."

"Who gets me? You mean they know I used to be a teacher?"

Peter looked completely exasperated. "Haven't you been listening to anything I've been telling you?! These three women could be head of the CIA." Deborah laughed at him and Peter shook his head at her obvious failure to appreciate what she was getting herself into. "*Of course*, they all know you have teaching credentials. Couple that with how well you did on your brief visit with Niesha and it's just possible there could be blood letting over this."

"I could be a teacher at one of the sites?" Deborah felt like another beautiful carved wooden box had just opened filled with another wonderful collection of bright shiny things.

"If you wanted to ... I don't want you to feel forced or pressured or anything. Hell, I'm happy to let you handle the whole mess. See if *you* can control the three of them any better then me. I have to be completely honest with you though ..."

"What?"

His eyes twinkled, "It's really the only reason I'm marrying you."

"To get a teacher?"

Peter nodded and shrugged. "I figured it was a very easy way to get cheap help."

"Oh no," Deborah said shaking her head, "I'm going to be *fantastically* expensive."

"And worth every penny, I imagine," he said as Peter pulled Deborah back into his arms and started kissing her again.

Saturday at 1:00 p.m. they stood side by side in front of Pastor Duncan at church surrounded by their collective "family". Zoe stood next to her in her Tinkerbell dress and matching plastic high heels ("I'm *so sorry*, Mother, it was either let her wear that or be nude ..." Grace had said to her) and Niesha standing silently by Peter with her thumb in her mouth and bunny clutched in her other hand.

Looking at Pastor Duncan, Deborah thought he did look rather smug. And rightly so she supposed.

"We gather here on this joyous day to celebrate the union of Peter Alexander Gannon and Deborah Ellen Lawson," he began. Deborah could hear Grace sniffling behind her. Pastor Duncan spoke for a few brief moments about the sanctity of marriage, the faithfulness of God, and the delight of watching the lives of Peter and Deborah meet and join. She tried her best to pay attention, but she felt the very opposite of numbness – too stimulated by the sights and sounds and feelings inside her and outside her to be able to deal with it all. She had one brief wave of panic – could this all be a wonderful dream? Was there a chance she would wake up and still be Bee?

Then Peter was looking at her. He took both of her hands in his at Pastor Duncan's direction. Pastor Duncan said to Peter, "Please, Peter, repeat these words after me ..."

Peter looked directly at Deborah, but spoke to Pastor Duncan. "Actually Pastor, if it's okay with you I have a few things I'd rather say on my own instead."

Deborah glanced at Pastor Duncan who looked somewhat befuddled. Peter looked at him then, too. "I've done this before, Pastor. I know what's involved. I've just got my own speech I'd like to say if it's okay with you."

Pastor Duncan recovered his composure and nodded.

Peter looked at Deborah and smiled. He took a deep breath and squeezed her hand. He looked absolutely calm. Where was the shy man he'd told her about? *You make me a different person,* she heard him tell her.

"I make these promises to you, Deborah before God and our friends and family. I promise to treat you like an equal, to value your thoughts, opinions, and perceptions - whether we agree or not - to show you things you want me to show you and learn things you want to teach me. I will encourage you in your weak times and cheer you on in your strong times, I will trust you, love you, cherish you, and will spend the rest of my life wanting to be nowhere else than right beside you."

Deborah felt her heart swell as he spoke for *they were her words.* The words she had shouted at Peter in the car. The words that had poured out of her mouth that she had never consciously thought of but had always unconsciously treasured *and dreamed of.* He'd remembered them and in front of all of these people he had given them right back to her in a pledge before God. Deborah looked at him and Peter looked back at her. He arched one eyebrow. She smiled.

Pastor Duncan was uncertain what to do. He hesitated for a brief moment, obviously unsure whether she had something to say as well. Deborah gave Peter a look. He could have told her he had planned to say something so that she could have had some time to prepare something too ... Peter grinned at her. He knew he'd caught her off guard and he was enjoying it, too.

She glanced at Pastor Duncan. "I've got something to say, too."

"You go girl," someone said from the audience. Deborah thought it was Jannelle.

She took a moment to gather her thoughts. "I, Deborah, promise before God and our family and friends, that I will support you, encourage you, delight in you, laugh with you, cry with you, and will love you with all my heart every moment for the rest of my life." Peter smiled at her and *she* arched her eyebrow at *him*. "I also promise to speak my mind when I think it needs to be heard, to always be honest and forthright, to listen to all viable arguments before I make final decisions, and to continue to grow and change into the woman God intends for me to be. I delight in the fact that doing these things will be hand in hand with you, Peter Alexander Gannon, for you make me a better person with your love."

"I want you to promise me that you *will not* always be so perfectly well behaved, obedient, and cooperative," Peter said to her.

Deborah blushed. "Do you know what you're getting yourself into?"

"I do."

She sighed. "I promise."

He winked at her.

Deborah said, "I want you to promise me that you will always be tenacious about things that you feel strongly about no matter how great a challenge it seems to be."

Peter grinned. "Do *you* know what *you're* getting yourself into?"

"I do."

Peter leaned down, pulled Deborah to him and kissed her. *Was that allowed?* her head thought briefly. "I promise," he breathed against her mouth.

"I'm not exactly sure if I'm even needed here anymore," Pastor Duncan said and everyone laughed.

Alita had a gift for them. It was a song. After Deborah and Peter had finished their vows, but before Pastor Duncan officially declared them husband and wife, she came up to the altar. She sang in a clear, pure voice without any musical accompaniment.

If you see the moon, rising gently on your fields.
If the wind blows softly on your face.

If the sunset lingers, while cathedral bells peal,

And the moon has risen to her place,

You can thank the Father for the things that He has done.

And thank Him for the things He's yet to do.

And if you find a love that's tender, if you find someone who's true,

Then thank the Lord -- He's been doubly good to you.

If you look in the mirror, at the end of a hard day,

And you know in your heart you have not lied.

And if you gave love freely, if you earned an honest wage,

And if you've got Jesus by your side,

You can thank the Father for the things that He has done.

And thank Him for the things He's yet to do.

And if you find a love that's tender, if you find someone who's true,

Thank the Lord -- He's been doubly good to you.[18].

When Pastor Duncan pronounced them husband and wife there was such a loud collective cheer that Deborah turned around expecting to find the church full of people. But it was just the small group they had invited, each of them beaming from ear to ear and all rushing forward to hug them, kiss them, and wish them well.

They all went to a local Spanish restaurant that Peter explained was his favorite place to eat. "How come you never took me here?" Deborah asked him puzzled.

He laughed. "We never had time. We've only been together for about three months you know."

"Is that all? I feel like I've known you all my life."

Peter smiled at her. "No," he said and kissed her, "we've been *waiting* our whole lives to meet each other. The perfect moment has just arrived. *Now* we're going to have fun making up for lost time."

She sighed and leaned her head against his shoulder. "I'm ready for my great love story. Alita told me I still had time …"

"Ahhh," he said with a twinkle in his eyes as he took her hand, pulled her to her feet and started making the motions to leave with her. "Let's go then, *Mrs. Deborah Gannon.* It's time we get this story started then."

Acknowledgements

A *Well Behaved Woman's Life* is a work of fiction, however, the lives of real women built the story. Deborah, in essence, is me although I have experienced little of the pain and heartache she has. More accurately, Deborah behaved as I believe I would have had I been in her place.

The Bible study group I lead out of my house was born out of the desire to study Ann Spangler and Jean E. Syswerda's fantastic book *Women of the Bible: A One-Year Devotional Study of Women in Scripture.* We accomplished our goal to finish the book, although it took us close to three years! There was a profound lesson in studying those Biblical women. From my little Baptist girl perspective, they had always been these distant, lifeless icons of either faith or failure. In reality, they were *exactly* (and I mean exactly) like we women of today. They had the same struggles, the same heartaches, and the same joys. Our dedicated Bible study group became sisters with each other as we talked and prayed, learned and grew in the Lord. But even more wonderful, we became sisters with those Biblical women who walked this same life path so much sooner than we did.

I wrote *A Well Behaved Woman's Life* over an intense two and a half week period during the summer of 2004. By then, I was leading the group through Ann Spangler's book *Men of the Bible!* All of a sudden all of the stories we had read about in the Bible and all of the stories we had shared sitting on my living room couch melded together in one glorious collection of words. I literally couldn't type fast enough. The book's dedication speaks to those women, past and present, who have made this wonderful story possible. *I am so proud to be called your sister ...*

There are a few more people whom I'd wish to thank that didn't make it to the dedication page, however. So here goes:

To Pastor Todd Buurstra, minister of North Branch Reformed Church here in good 'ole Bridgewater, New Jersey who, although he doesn't like donuts as much as Pastor Duncan, is very similar in other more important ways. Ways such as the how he cares about his church family, how he puts such heart and soul into his sermons, and how he projects both a strong spiritual example while at the same time convincing you that he's just a regular guy.

To Pam Frueh, proofreader extraordinaire, who made over *two thousand* corrections and changes in my original manuscript. She offered excellent insight and suggestions and gave me rock solid advice. (To give you an idea how terrific she is, when she proofread Pastor Todd's doctoral thesis he called me in awe and said, "Sue, she even corrected *God!*" having punctuated properly a Biblical reference.)

To my babies, Ian, Grace and Luke who, although they are not as old as John, Grace, and Todd are in the story, are nevertheless miniature versions of them. I have every expectation that they will grow up to be the loving, capable, unique individuals that I portrayed them as in the book.

And lastly, to my husband, David, who taught me the phrase 'breathless anticipation of things to come' and continues to encourage me in all I do. I could go on and on about his good points - for he is the antithesis of Jonathan and all that is good in Peter. But rather than write anymore, let's just say, *thanks for those tulips ...*

Sue McGeown

About The Author

Susan McGeown is a wife, mother, daughter, sister, friend, aunt, uncle (don't ask), teacher, author ... but, most importantly, a "woman after God's own heart." Living in Bridgewater, New Jersey, with her husband of over fifteen years and their three children, writing stories is just about the best way she can imagine spending her free time. Each of Sue's stories champions those emotions nearest and dearest to her: faith, joy, hope and love.

Philippians 1:20-21

For I fully expect and hope that I will never be ashamed, but that I will continue to be bold for Christ, as I have been in the past. And I trust that my life will bring honor to Christ, whether I live or die. For to me, living means living for Christ, and dying is even better.